SIXTEEN CANDLES
An *it* CHICKS Novel

by
Tia Williams

JUMP AT THE SUN

HYPERION PAPERBACKS FOR CHILDREN · NEW YORK

AN IMPRINT OF DISNEY BOOK GROUP

2013

2/16

SEP

HU
(9)

ALSO BY TIA WILLIAMS

The Accidental Diva

It Chicks

COAUTHORED (WITH IMAN)

The Beauty of Color

Text copyright © 2008 by Tia Williams

All rights reserved. Published by Hyperion Paperbacks for Children, an imprint of Disney Book Group. No part of this book may be reproduced or transmitted in any form or by any means, electronic or mechanical, including photocopying, recording, or by any information storage and retrieval system, without written permission from the publisher. For information address Hyperion Books for Children, 114 Fifth Avenue, New York, New York 10011-5690.

Printed in the United States of America
First Edition
1 3 5 7 9 10 8 6 4 2

Library of Congress Cataloging-in-Data on file
ISBN 978-1-4231-1032-3
Visit www.jumpatthesun.com

ACKNOWLEDGMENTS

I'm so grateful to my crew of family and friends, who helped me whip this book into shape! I dedicate this book to my brilliant sisters, Devon and Lauren, who tell me I'm good even when I'm not, and provide me with more plot points than I can count ("seriously, why not have Skye perform a really atrocious monologue at her party?"). Huge thanks to my whip-smart friends Charlotte and Margeaux, who came up with the title when I was stumped, stumped, stumped. A big kiss to my profoundly clever literary agent, Mary Ann Naples, for (A) always reading my mind and (B) having a surprising amount of insight into the lives of urban teens (I've long suspected she must live a double life as a black woman). Huge props to Ari, my editor, for always, always getting it! I'm endlessly grateful to my parents, Andi and Aldred, for their unflagging support, patience, and the use of their summer mountain home when I needed to bang out the final edit. I love you! Big *gracias* to my SYB Babes for their unflagging encouragement, and to my terror-dog, Chappie, for his snuggles. And, honestly, I'd be nowhere without It Chicks's fans and their wonderful, hilarious, passionate e-mails—thank you for believing wholeheartedly in Tangie, C.J., Skye, and the Armstrong crew! And finally, I thank my husband, Adam, *la luz de mi vida*, my insides, the reason I do it all.

Name: Tangela Marcia Adams
Class: Sophomore
Major: Dance
Self-Awareness Session #: 5

Well, hello, Miss Adams. I see you've missed your last two sessions.

I know, I know, I can explain. . . .

As you know, *all* Armstrong students are required to report to their guidance counselors for weekly Self-Awareness Sessions. As performers and artists, it's important to be in touch with your emotions.

You know what? I think I'm too in touch.

Meaning?

Meaning, I'm an emotional wreck! Look, all I wanted was to get into Armstrong so I could be with Skye and C.J. and get good enough to dance backup for Ciara one day. And now my life is a hot mess. Skye's turned into this crazy diva nightmare, and C.J. . . . . well, I think this time we're finally a wrap. I mean, technically he was never even my boyfriend, but we always had this thing, since we were kids. But he's such a slut! Seriously, why do guys have to be such slaves to their damn PENISES?!

Yes, it's true—as boys in their pubescent years find their bodies changing, they become, um, quite alert, you know, *sexually*, and . . .

Okay, eww. Anyway, you know what makes it worse? The girl he's talking to, Izzy, is one of the coolest girls I've met this year. We've gotten really tight, except I haven't told her about me and C.J. What would I even say? You can't mess with C.J. 'cause we're on-the-low soul mates? So wack. No, what's really wack is that I felt so rejected I started kinda talking to my senior dance tutor, and he played me completely. I mean, who picks THE Trey Stevens to be their rebound jump-off? God, I'm so stupid! Waaaaaah!

Let it out, Miss Adams. Sometimes you just need a good cry. One question, though—what's a jump-off? Is it a noun?

1.

GROWN AND SEXY AT THE COFFEE SHOP

"UM, CAN I *HELP* YOU GIRLS?" The skinny blond hostess with the skyscraper-high legs and the nose bling was clearly a model. *All* the hostesses and waitresses at the Coffee Shop were models. The fancy diner, located on Sixteenth Street in Manhattan's Union Square neighborhood, was a people-watching paradise, where fashionistas, random starlets, and members of the hip-hop industry elite loved to mingle.

No one really ate the food, which was a shame, since the herbed french fries were *insane.*

A group of fifteen-year-old girls was not usually welcome at the Coffee Shop, especially not ones from Louis Armstrong Academy of Performing and Creative Arts. The prestigious high school for budding superstars was right in the neighborhood, and the students were always hanging out outside the restaurant. The Coffee Shop didn't like to waste a table on a bunch of loud, obnoxious teens. It just wasn't a sexy look.

Knowing this, Tangie and her two new friends from

Armstrong, Kamillah and Regina, had tried to look as grown-and-sexy as possible. Kamillah, a Harlem-born gossipista who studied drama with Skye, was rocking skinny Seven jeans and cherry-red patent-leather Steve Madden stilettos. Regina, a pretty biracial aspiring filmmaker (her mom was Filipino, her dad black) had let out her signature Pocahontas braids, so her hair was cutely crimped. Meanwhile, Tangie had pulled her out-of-control curls back in a wide black headband (her hair was always about five minutes away from major frizz) and was wearing her favorite H&M sundress over leggings and platform wedges; her toned dancer's legs were her favorite feature, and the high shoes made them look *sick*. She even dusted bronzer over her milk chocolate–brown skin and applied mascara. The girls looked fierce!

Too bad they had no idea what they were doing there. All they knew was that they'd each received a mysterious text message a couple of hours ago.

It was Saturday afternoon in the last week of September, and almost a month since Tangie's first day at the school she'd been dying to go to since birth. Since she'd enrolled at Armstrong as a sophomore, most of the dancers in her classes had a whole year of training on her—so she had tons of catching up to do. This morning, Tangie had been obsessively marking her Advanced Beginners Hip-hop routine in her bedroom mirror when she got the text message from her best friend since kindergarten, Skye Carmichael. It said: GIRLZ! MT ME AT CFEE SHP 4 BRUNCH, 12:30. V. IMP! THA RES IZ UNDER ALEXA'S NAME.

And that was it! What made it really weird was that this

was the first time anyone had heard from Skye in almost three weeks. Since Friday, September 9, 2005, to be exact. That had been the night of Skye's drama-filled Back to School party, when she'd had a huge falling-out with Tangie—among other things. The party had been such a disaster, Skye had practically disappeared, sneaking home for lunch and ignoring her friends in the hallway.

At least Skye had seen to it that they got seated. She'd made a reservation under the name of her mom, Alexa Carmichael, the famous TV actress. She'd played a backstabbing black super-model on *Shoulder Pads*, the long-running '80s nighttime soap about a glamorous modeling agency. Her name was able to get Skye into any restaurant, club, or party in Manhattan.

Must be nice being showbiz royalty, thought Tangie.

"Um, yes, you can help us," said Tangie, a little nervous to be dealing with one of the infamously bitchy Coffee Shop hostesses. "We actually have a reservation?"

"Oh, really?" The hostess stifled a giggle, her diamond nose ring twinkling.

"She didn't stutter," snapped Kamillah, narrowing her eyes at the hostess. She was not the type to take any kind of attitude.

Regina elbowed her discreetly in the ribs, hoping she'd shut up before they were politely thrown out on their asses.

"We have a reservation under Alexa Carmichael? You know, from . . ."

"From *Shoulder Pads? The* Alexa Carmichael?" Nose Bling's

entire attitude did a one-eighty. "Holy ish, I, like, grew up watching her! I was Alexa for one Halloween, like, when I was in third grade! Omigod, follow me, I'll take you guys to the star table—you know, the big booth in the corner, over there? It's dope, 'cause you can see everything that's going on. . . ." She lowered her voice. ". . . And everyone can see *you*."

Tangie, Kamillah, and Regina glanced at each other, beyond excited but trying to look blasé, as if they were used to getting star-table treatment.

"Why, thank you, *dahhling*, I suppose that table will do," Kamillah said, putting on the voice she had used the previous year in the freshman production of *The Women*, when she'd played a billionaire socialite.

Stifling giggles, they followed Nose Bling to the booth, taking in the scene as they went. At a table to the far left, they saw Ne-Yo surrounded by three video-vixen-looking girls. And was that Vanessa Minnillo sitting at the bar? Everywhere they looked, there were beautiful people, true VIPs, and *they* were going to the star table!

"Have a seat, girls, and your waitress'll be back to take your order!"

"Oh, we're expecting one more person," blurted out Regina. Where was Skye, anyway?

"Well, obviously," said Nose Bling. "Alexa! I'll be on the lookout for her. Ciao!"

With that, she spun on her heel and sashayed back to the hostess stand as if she were working a catwalk. Her twig legs looked like they might snap in two.

"This is crazy, y'all!" Kamillah was beside herself. *"Crazy!* Thank God I wore my Steve Madden heels. They're knockoffs of the Christian Louboutins Nicole Richie's rocking in last week's *Us Weekly*."

"I cannot believe we're sitting at this table. It's like we're on display or something." Tangie fiddled with her hair, always worried that her ringlets were getting too, well, poufy. She hoped Skye would hurry up and get there before everyone realized they were total frauds. How dumb was Nose Bling? Why would a bunch of kids be meeting Alexa Carmichael at the Coffee Shop?

Meanwhile, Regina pulled a pen and a tiny, battered spiral notebook out of her Dooney & Bourke bag, and began furiously scribbling.

"Oh, hell, no, Reggie-Reg," hissed Kamillah. "You're *so* not taking notes in here. We're supposed to be looking grown and sexy, not like we're in AP History." She tried to grab the journal, but Regina snatched it away.

"I can't help it if I'm devoted to my art." Regina was constantly taking notes. By senior year, she hoped to have filmed a documentary about the performing-arts schoolkids, so it was very important for her to remember every detail of their lives. Plus, she'd promised Skye that she'd ghostwrite her memoirs once she became a famous actress—and her exhaustive notes would come in handy for that.

"Where *is* Skye?" Tangie was getting impatient. "I'm dying to know why she brought us here. It'd better be to apologize for how she treated me at her party."

"How about how she dissed all of us, after her party?" Kamillah rolled her eyes. "Yeah, I get that she was embarassed that it bombed, but that ain't my fault."

"Well, I hope she gets here soon," said Tangie, looking toward the door.

"You know Skye's always gotta make an entrance." Regina looked up from her notebook and smiled dreamily, thinking about her. Her girl-crush on Skye was a well-known thing.

Feeling antsy, Tangie scanned the restaurant, thinking maybe Skye hadn't seen them come in and was waiting over by the wavy, groovy-looking bar. There was no sign of Skye, but Tangie did see someone she recognized. A spiky-haired, honey-skinned waitress was behind the bar at the register, typing up someone's bill. Shocked, Tangie grabbed Kamillah's arm.

"Omigod, don't be obvious, but look over at the bar. Isn't that Naima? Is she *waitressing*?"

"Naima who?" Kamillah craned her neck to stare at the girl. "Wait, what's her major?"

"What? No, Naima, from *America's Next Top Model*! Look, she's right over there, bringing a check to that table. See her?"

"Oh, *Naima* Naima! Hold up, an *America's Next Top Model* winner should not be waitressing, that's just wrong."

"It's not Naima, it's her twin sister," said Regina, without looking up from her notebook; she was an encyclopedia of random information. "I read in Page Six that she worked here. Her name's Nia."

"I really hope it ain't Naima, 'cause that'd be too embarass-ing." Kamillah shook her head in disgust. "I don't care how slow my career is going; once I become famous you will not catch me working at a restaurant. If you're a star and your career's floundering, you're supposed to just disappear for a minute. Then, when you come back, you say you were taking time off to 'find your center' and 'grow spiritually.'"

Tangie nodded slowly, thinking. "You know what? Maybe that's why Skye's been so incognito these past three weeks."

"She's been finding her center?" Regina looked confused.

"No, she's been on the low, regrouping, 'cause her Back to School party was such a mess," Tangie said.

". . . On so many levels," murmured Kamillah.

"Right," Tangie said, "and I guess she wanted to lie low until everybody stopped talking about it."

"I know she's been mad shady, but I actually kinda feel bad for Skye," said Regina, shrugging sheepishly.

"Shocker," said Kamillah, adjusting her heart-shaped door-knocker earrings.

"For real, though. You know how dead serious she takes her parties," Tangie said.

Regina was right. Skye'd been *so* amped about her Back to School Jump Off. Right up until Kamillah got into that very unsexy knock-down, drag-out girl-fight with Izzy, the mysterious new freshman with the shady past that nobody could stop gossiping about. On top of that, Skye was convinced that her crush, Nick, the sexy new white boy in her Southern Playwrights class, had spent the whole party flirting with Regina (which couldn't have been further from the truth). And the worst part? Tangie and Skye ended up in the worst fight the worst fight they'd had since they were five, and Skye insisted that Ginuwine could dance better than Tangie's crush, Sisqó. And now, neither one was going to be the first to speak.

". . . Still, I don't see why *Skye's* been so damn D.L," said Kamillah, fiddling with one of her supercute Afro-puffs. "After that crazy bitch Izzy jumped me, *I'm* the one that should be hiding out. I've gone through two tubes of Mederma trying to fade that scratch by my nose! Seriously, Tangie, I don't know what you see in her."

"I still can't believe I missed that," said Tangie, shaking her head. She felt kind of bad that she hadn't been there to defend Izzy. If she'd been in the kitchen when it all went down, she would've stopped it. After all, Tangie and the controversial freshman had been insta-friends ever since they met a month earlier at Orientation. Which was crazy, because they were so different—Tangie was a good girl who never drank or smoked and who lived to dance, while Izzy was a dangerously sexy Ethiopian-born artist with a faux hawk, a notebook full of rhymes, and a shady past.

Well, they did have one thing in common.

When they met on the first day of school, Tangie had quickly realized that Izzy was dating her lifelong BFF and undercover soul mate, C.J. (the two had met over the summer, while Tangie was away at dance camp and during one of her infamous spats with C.J.). Despite feeling she could tell Izzy anything— even stuff about her mom, like how Tangie hadn't seen or heard from her since her mother had taken off to join a German ballet company seven years earlier—Tangie couldn't bring herself to be open about C.J. How they *weren't* just friends. How he had painted a beautiful mural on the wall of his project building and dedicated it to her. How he'd cried in her arms the night his grandma almost died. How he was her first kiss. How she got all tingly if he so much as brushed up against her arm. . . .

Oh, the drama.

"All I'm saying is, your girl Izzy's lucky I was twisted, or I would've knocked that cubic zirconia stud out her nose. You think I'm playin'." Kamillah pounded the table for emphasis, the silverware clanking together. At the next table, an important-looking man in an expensive suit looked at her and made a face.

"Okay, yeah, she was out of line," said Tangie, snapping out of her daze. "But can you imagine? Izzy's brand-new at Armstrong, and there you were, telling everyone she used to be homeless! Seriously, it's humiliating."

"Please, girl. Don't cry for Izzy. Ever since I outed her shady-ass past, the whole damned school's been obsessed with her. I don't know what's so fascinating about a girl who wears gold liquid liner and ran away from home to join a rap group and used to live in a filthy commune under a bridge."

"That's not fascinating?" Regina rolled her eyes.

Kamilla ignored her. "Y'all heard about that weird Indian kid, right? The one that started a stalkerazzi blog called Izzy Breezy Beautiful?"

Regina nodded, her eyes wide. "Oh, yeah, I know! He

writes crazy, psycho stuff, like *At ten forty-five, I saw Izzy eating Cheetos in the art hall*. Or *Today, Izzy wore striped leggings and red feather earrings*."

"She finally caught him spying on her yesterday." Tangie shook her head, her spirals bouncing. "Apparently, he's a journalism major, and he wants to submit his blog to *Star* as a clip when he graduates."

The guy was clearly nuts, but Tangie understood why he was so into Izzy. She was an original. She stood out without even trying, and that was a big deal at a school where folks were working their asses off to be famous.

She almost couldn't blame C.J. for going with her. *Almost*.

"Okay, now I'm starting to get worried," said Regina, her almond-shaped eyes widening. "We've been here for twenty minutes. What if something happened to Skye?"

"Stop buggin', she's fine." Kamillah waved her away. "Besides, I don't know why you're all concerned. Out of all of us, she's the most mad at you."

"Please, Kammie. Her neighbors called the police after your girl-fight!"

"So? You stole Nick from her, and you know how much she likes that boy."

"I didn't steal Nick. We're just friends."

"For years Beyoncé insisted that she and Jay were only friends." Kamillah shrugged. "I'm just saying."

"Look, Nick's faithful to his girl back in DC, *that's* why he and Skye aren't happening. It's got nothing to do with her—or me. If he didn't have a girl, he'd be all over her." Regina gulped

They went back to arguing about who Skye was most mad at, until Tangie finally interrupted them. "She's the most mad at me," she said glumly, staring into her water glass.

"Oh, yeah," said Regina, nodding in agreement. "'Cause you messed with her sister's ex-boyfriend, the first week of school."

"We hardly even 'messed,'" said Tangie, her cheeks flushing maroon. "Trey was my hip-hop dance tutor, and we just kissed, like, three times. We didn't even go out out anywhere."

"I never understood Skye getting mad at that," said Kamillah. "I mean, yeah, Trey dated Skye's sister, Eden, for, like, four years, and yeah, they were like the black, high school version of Brangelina, but whatever. They're so done."

"Skye worships Eden, though," said Regina, always quick to defend her idol.

"So? It's not like Tangie was trying to take Eden's place or anything. The boy was her *tutor*."

But that's exactly what Skye had said to her during their terrible fight at her party. *"You can't just sweep in and be the new Eden! Wake up, Tangie—Trey will never make you his girlfriend."* So harsh, right? The funny thing was, Tangie never really believed that a boy on Trey's level would take her seriously, either. She knew she was cute—well, if you minused the badonkadonk and the frizz—but she was just a sophomore. And a virgin. And definitely not enough woman for a gorgeous senior—a b-boy and hip-hop dancing *god*—like Trey Stevens.

Besides, wasn't the whole point to make C.J. jealous, anyway?

Tangie didn't say any of this to Regina or Kamillah. It was weird, but after a whole month at school, she still felt as if they were Skye's friends, not hers. Skye'd had a whole year to bond with them before Tangie got to Armstrong. Tangie was still the new girl, trying to find her place in the It chicks clique. Or, as Skye called them, the . . .

"*Superbad bee-yatches!* I *see* you!"

The three girls whipped their heads around to the front of the restaurant, and there was Skye. Decked out in an Chloe eyelet minidress and gold Sigerson Morrison flats, she pushed past Naima/Nia and rushed toward their table. She looked fantastic. Everyone in the Coffee Shop was staring at her, even Ne-Yo. Her cheeks were rosy, her eyes were shining, and she was grinning as if she hadn't seen her friends in thirty years.

Squealing, she slid into the booth on Tangie's side and threw her arms around her best friend's neck, kissing her on the cheek. Before Tangie could open her mouth to speak, Skye lunged across the table and planted a loud, dramatic kiss first on Kamillah's cheek and then Regina's. Once she'd left smears of bronzy lip gloss on everyone's faces, she sat back in the booth, downed Regina's water, then spoke.

"What's good, y'all?"

Tangie, Kamillah, and Regina looked at one another, totally confused.

"What do you mean, *what's good?*" Tangie couldn't believe her nerve. "Skye, where have you been? You haven't talked to any of us in, like . . ."

"I know, I know. Since my party. I've been a hot mess, girls, believe it. And I want to apologize for how I acted. You three are my best friends—especially you, Tangie; you're like a sister to me, you know that." Skye put her hand over her heart and bit her bottom lip, trying to look sincere. It was working, actually.

Not for nothing, the girl *was* a damned good actress.

"Don't worry about it, sweetie," said Regina, practically hopping up and down in her seat with happiness. She was just glad Skye was talking to her again. "You were under a lot of stress. I mean, throwing a party can take a lot out of you."

Yeah, right, thought Tangie. *It's right up there with running the New York Marathon, or taking the SATs.*

"Right? I mean, I really took the whole thing way too seriously. Listen, I don't want any more beef in the streets. I need you guys. Are we cool?" She flagged down a waitress from across the restaurant.

"Of course! You know we love you to death." Regina reached out and squeezed her hand.

"Please, I was just worried about you, girl, 'cause you were so MIA," said Kamillah, relieved that things were back to normal. She was all for drama in other people's lives, just not hers.

They all glanced expectantly at Tangie, waiting for her to respond. She was just sitting there, twirling a straw wrapper around her finger and frowning. *Something feels really off*, she thought. Regina and Kamillah had known Skye for only a year, but she'd known that girl her whole life—and it was obvious that there was something behind this apology. Her change of heart was a little too out of nowhere. And hello? Were they supposed to gloss over how terribly Skye had acted at her Back to School party?

But for now, she'd fake it.

"Yeah, I guess we're cool," Tangie said reluctantly, with a weak smile.

"I'm so-o-o glad! 'Cause my world's about to get mad crazy, and I need to know my girls have my back. You know, to keep me humble."

"Wait, why's your world about to get crazy?" Kamillah's emerald-lined eyes were sparkling with anticipation.

"Well, I have huge news."

Here it is, thought Tangie. *The reason she wanted to see us today. What's the point of having good news if your friends aren't there to gloat to?*

"I just found out I'm going to star in an episode of *Sixteen Candles*! On MVN! *My very own episode!* The party's two weeks from Monday!"

As if on cue, Skye's three friends simultaneously screamed, "What?" *Sixteen Candles* was one of Music Video Network's hottest reality shows! Each episode followed a very rich, very spoiled girl—usually the daughter of famous parents—as she planned an over-the-top, extravagant, Sweet Sixteen party. Each episode tried to top the last, but they all shared a few basic elements: the nail-bitingly intense invitation ceremony (those excluded usually ended up in tears); the birthday girl's "grand entrance" (the most memorable was a girl who parachuted down to her party, the wind blowing her extensions clean off her head); a surprise performance by a famous singer or group; and, at the end of the party, the presentation to the star by her parents of a gorgeous car (usually a BMW, and always wrapped in a red ribbon).

But most importantly, the show had single-handedly turned all of its girls into bona fide reality stars. And Skye would be one of them!

Tangie was totally in shock. "Hold up, your birthday isn't until the end of October!"

"Yeah, I know, but Alexa knows the VP of programming at MVN—they take a tap dancing class together, or something!" Skye was talking a mile a minute; she could barely catch her breath. "Anyway, she said they really needed an episode about a black girl, like, as soon as possible, 'cause they need some diversity. So, here I am!"

"Stop playin'! You're kidding me, right?" Kamillah looked as if she had won the lottery.

Regina immediately began scribbling in her notebook, grinning madly. "Skye, this is huge! I can't believe . . . I mean, this is so huge!"

"I know, I know! I'm gonna have the most bomb-ass, *sickest* party ever. A total extravaganza! And I want you three to be in on it with me. Bee-yatches, we're gonna be famous, famous, *famous*!"

"Congratulations, Skye," said Tangie, hugging her. She was happy for Skye, but there was an uncomfortable, fluttery feeling in the pit of her stomach. It wasn't easy all of a sudden to forget how Skye had hated on her for seeing Trey. Or how, during the weeks Skye wasn't speaking to her, she'd felt alone and horrible and had to socially fend for herself at a brand-new, hypercompetitive, stressful-beyond-belief school—and as a result, she felt closer to Izzy, a girl she'd known for a month, than to Skye, who was basically her *sister*. But whatever. For the sake of not being petty, she'd forgive her.

But forget? That was a different story.

Name: Kamillah Decker
Class: Sophomore
Major: Drama
Self-Awareness Session #: 43

So, that's huge news, your friend starring in her own *Sixteen Candles* episode.

Yeah, I guess.

You don't seem too excited.

I'm, like, a very superstitious person, you know? My Haitian grandma always taught me that what you put out in the world comes back to you. You know, karma and all that shi—stuff. Anyway, Skye's been mad shady lately. She didn't speak to any of us for three weeks—just dropped us cold. Even Tangie. And now, all of a sudden, she wants to be all chummy just 'cause she's gonna be on TV? I mean, her angle on the show is that she's this big, popular chick, and it would look kinda funny if she didn't have any friends, right? So, now we have to pretend like nothing ever happened. I don't know, it's kinda suspect.

Look, I'm not the one to start drama, so I'm gonna go along with it. But I can't help but think something's really gonna go wrong with this party. I can feel it.

What do you think will happen?

I guess we'll see, right? But my hunches are never wrong. There's bad karma all over this thing.

2.

KILL IT

MS. CARMEN, ARMSTRONG'S MOST powerful and feared dance instructor, was not pleased. She paced back and forth in front of her Advanced Beginners Street Funk class, hitting the floor with her cane at every step. Her students, mostly sophomores and a few superadvanced freshmen, sat sprawled out on the dusty studio floor, their backs to the wall-to-wall mirrors. Their regulation practice uniforms—leotards, tights and tiny, retro, terry cloth shorts for girls, warm-up pants and wife-beaters for boys—were soaked with sweat. After forty minutes of high-energy, music video–level choreography, everyone was totally exhausted—but still alert enough to be afraid of their teacher.

"Pookies, we've been rehearsing this piece since the first day you set foot in my studio, am I right?"

"Mm-hmm, you right, Ms. Cah-men." Zenobia, a tough Bronx native with the most gorgeous arabesque anyone had ever seen, did not realize this was a rhetorical question.

"I know I'm right!" Abruptly, Ms. Carmen stopped pacing and faced the class, one hand planted on her hip. With her massive black waves, signature bloodred lipstick, and low-cut leotard, she was sexy, and she knew it. She caught her reflection in the mirror and broke into a smooth hip swivel and triple pirouette. *"That's* what the final combination should look like, Pumpkins. By the time you make it here," she said, punctuating the word *here* by thumping her cane on the floor, "I expect all of you to have pirouette control. Hip-hop does not mean choppy and ungraceful. You do realize, don't you, that the dancers you look up to in videos all have extensive ballet, jazz, and contemporary training? It's not enough to pop and tick and look hard. You have to *serve*, you have to *pull up*, you have to *slay*!"

Tangie nodded vigorously, hanging on Ms. Carmen's every word. She knew she had a lot to learn before she reached the same level as the second-year dancers. Not only were they all pin-thin, but they'd also all had extensive training, practically since birth. Growing up, Tangie hadn't been allowed to dance during the school year, so all she had on them was four years of summer camp at Debbie Allen's Dance Academy—and teaching herself choreography from old Aaliyah and Usher videos and movies like *Rize*, *West Side Story*, *Center Stage*, *Flashdance*, and *You Got Served*.

Despite her inexperience, Ms. Carmen singled her out on the first day of school, telling her she had "extraordinary raw talent" and that she'd be watching her! In her no-effing-around, vaguely Nuyorican accent, Ms. Carmen also made

Tangie promise three things—that she'd work on losing weight in her hips and butt (mortifying), find a senior tutor to help develop her technique (easy enough), and avoid Trey Stevens at all costs (um, *what?*).

Tangie'd had success with the first two. The last one, not so much.

"Okay, Pumpkins, moving on," announced Ms. Carmen, running a hand distractedly through her rippling, raven black waves. "Whose turn is it to perform their Spotlight Student choreography?"

Departmentwide Spotlight Student tryouts were in two and a half weeks. At auditions, each department (art, dance, creative writing, drama, music, and voice) picked three Spotlight Students per grade to perform a solo at Fall Fling, the first big recital of the year. But not just anyone could audition. First, you had to be elected by your teachers based on your overall performance during the first week of school—and Tangie, to her surprise and delight, was picked!

Ms. Carmen assigned some extra credit to the lucky kids in her class who had been chosen to audition—they each had to choreograph a one-minute routine to Usher's "Yeah!" She'd pick one of them randomly to perform at the end of class.

"Gigi, we already saw your routine last week, and Damon went three days ago. . . . So, Tangie, it's all you, Cupcake."

Tangie had been holding her breath, and now she exhaled all of her pent-up excitement. She had a feeling she'd be up next, and she couldn't wait to show off her skills! It was like practice for the real audition. The thought that she could possibly be performing a solo at Fall Fling was almost too much for her to bear.

Ms. Carmen cued her senior helper, Casey, to hit the music. A white guy rocking blond dreadlocks and a T reading *Future of the Funk*, Casey lazily shuffled over to the windowsill and turned on the stereo. As the unmistakable bass line of Usher's hit song thumped through the studio, Tangie took a spot in front of her classmates. Almost instantly, she felt a weird coldness aimed at her by some of the girls. Amy Steiner, a bulimic redhead whose mom had once played Belle in the Macy's Thanksgiving Day Parade, was actually sneering.

Instantly self-conscious, Tangie tugged her gym shorts over her ample booty (whenever she got nervous, she swore she could actually feel her butt growing bigger and bigger, till it was *Big Momma's House*–size). But then she overheard Amy mutter to a lanky brunette, "You know she only got picked to audition 'cause Trey stepped up her game. Maybe if I tutored with him every damned night and did God knows what else, I'd get Spotlight love, too." And then a couple of girls tittered nastily.

Tangie froze, missing her starting count. *Is that what everyone thinks?* she silently wondered, feeling her legs go weak. *That I'm only good because of him?* And what was "God knows what else" supposed to mean? Tangie was a good girl! Not only was Trey just the second boy she'd ever even *sort of* hooked up with, but she wasn't even sure she'd done it right. Sweating, she glanced over at Trey, who was sprawled out in a corner, leaning back on his elbows. He grinned at her, obviously loving the fact that the girls were talking about it. Tangie fought the urge to give him the finger.

"Ahem?" Ms. Carmen hollered over the music. "Are you having some sort of epileptic fit, or would you like to perform? You pull this at Spotlight auditions and it's a wrap, Sugarplum."

"No, no, I'm fine," sputtered Tangie. "Casey, c—can you start the music again?"

Rolling his half-closed eyes, the bored music major restarted the disc. The fact that he'd rather be smoking a bowl or playing the drums, or both, was written all over his face.

Come on, Tangie, she said to herself, holding her starting position until she heard her cue. *You know they're just hating 'cause the new girl got picked to audition over them. Shake it off like Mariah.* But she couldn't. In that second, she wished she could have been more like Izzy, who probably would've knocked that bitchy expression off Amy's face. Or Skye, who would've shot back an even snarkier remark. But no, she was mild-mannered Tangie, the girl who just wanted everyone to like her.

She hated feeling jitters before a performance—especially when she was so ready to kill it! Tangie knew her choreography like the back of her hand. Over the past three socially challenged weeks, she'd practiced for two hours a night. In fact, practicing had become her entire life. In Ms. Carmen's class, she'd turned into Little Miss Overachiever: always pushing herself a step beyond everyone else (she had actually landed in the infirmary the week before, after passing out during cool-down). Tangie knew her classmates thought she was an overambitious suck-up, but that wasn't it at all.

The reason she was working her ass off in Advanced Beginners Street Funk was so that she'd be too busy to face Trey, even for a second. The few times he'd tried to speak to her, she'd pretended she couldn't hear him over the music. Once, when he tried to dance in her line, she had discreetly pas de bourrée'd away from him (and tripped over her own feet in the process). Basically, Tangie wanted to forget that Trey Stevens, that irresistibly delicious break-dancing beast, even existed.

Which was kind of hard, because he was always there. The notoriously cocky senior was taking a sophomore class, as punishment for blatantly ignoring Armstrong's biggest rule—no professional performing—when he danced backup in a Missy video over the summer.

Having Trey in her class had been a good thing for Tangie at first. Not only had she landed Armstrong's hottest dancer as a tutor, but she got to date him, too! Well, maybe *date* was too strong a word. For Tangie, who'd never had a real boyfriend, the daily hip-hop-and-hooking-up tutorials had *felt* like dating.

At least, until he became the ass that Skye and C.J. and Ms. Carmen had warned her about.

"Any time now, Pookie!" shouted Ms. Carmen.

Suddenly, Tangie jerked herself out of her trance. Why was she letting herself get so distracted over a couple of idiots like Amy Steiner and Trey? It wasn't like her to get all shook when it was time to dance. Dancing was her safe place, something that made her feel special, powerful, alive. When she danced, she was invincible—no one could touch her, not Trey, not the skinny bitches brigade, not anybody. As she heard her cue coming up again, she closed her eyes and focused.

Okay, T., imagine you're about to compete for the final spot on *So You Think You Can Dance*, she thought, hyping herself up. The crowd's going nuts and Blake McGrath is a guest judge and he just yelled, "Kill it! Kill it!"

And kill it she did. Despite their obvious hating, Tangie's classmates couldn't take their eyes off her. By now, they were familiar with her unique dance style (a heart-stopping combination of ballet, African, gymnastics, Britney-esque pop, and Ciara-style hip-hop), but this was on a whole different level. Today, Tangie tore through her choreography as if she were on fire, commanding the attention of every person in the studio.

At the fourth eight-count, Tangie hit two backflips and a back handspring, landing in her signature jazz split. She held her final count, waiting for a signal from Ms. Carmen to break out. But the studio was dead quiet, except for Tangie's own ragged, exhausted breathing. After what felt like hours, the class slowly began to clap (except for Amy, who looked as if she had irritable bowel syndrome). It was sporadic at first and then changed to thunderous applause.

Beaming, Tangie glanced over at Ms. Carmen, who nodded and smiled proudly. The bell sounded, and everyone scrambled to grab their dance bags and rush off to the next class. On their way out, a bunch of her classmates stopped to big her up, patting her on the back and complimenting her on her inventive choreography. As Tangie headed for the door, Ms. Carmen grabbed her arm.

"Very nice, Tangela."

Tangie smiled, her dimples dancing. It was always surprising when Ms. Carmen called students by their real names, instead of the usual Pookie, Pumpkin, Sugar, or Cupcake. "Thanks," Tangie said, still out of breath. "I was so nervous. I don't know why; it wasn't the first time I did a solo in class."

"Yeah, but it was the first time it was *your* material, Pumpkin."

"Well, I have to be honest," Tangie began, sheepishly half smiling, "a lot of it was you. I've been watching a lot of your old videos, and . . ."

"Obviously," said Ms. Carmen, cutting her off. As if she wouldn't recognize her own work. Back in the late '80s and '90s, she'd been one of the top video and tour choreographers, working with superstars like Madonna, Janet Jackson, and Paula Abdul. "So, how's the tutoring going? I haven't seen you talking to Trey in weeks."

"Oh. Oh, well . . . yeah, he's not my tutor anymore."

"Hallelujah," said Ms. Carmen, only half joking. She had meant it when she warned Tangie about Trey. She tried not to get too involved in her student's lives, but Tangie wasn't an ordinary student. A long time ago, Ms. Carmen had promised an old friend that she'd look out for Tangie. She had seen too many young dancers get distracted after Trey Adams broke their hearts. She would never have forgiven herself if it happened to Tangie. "You finally took my advice and traded him in for someone else?"

"Actually, no, I don't have a tutor now." Tangie noticed Ms. Carmen raise her right eyebrow, and she began to babble. "I— I just, well, I sort of thought . . ."

"Well don't," the teacher snapped, in the "don't fuck with me" tone that turned her students' knees to mush. "Do you think I told you to get a tutor for my *health*? Your technique is improving, but you're still too raw. If you are going to have a prayer of making Spotlight, you'd better step it up."

"You're right, Ms. Carmen. I . . ."

"Spotlight is about more than just bragging rights, Tangie. Every chance you get to perform alone, separate from your competition, is an opportunity to dazzle. The Spotlight Students are the ones we remember come twelfth grade, when we're picking out leads in the Senior Showcase." This was the final performance for Armstrong students: the one that had major casting agents, talent scouts, and show producers in the audience.

"You're right. Of course, I'll find another tutor," said Tangie, feeling like a naughty five-year-old put in a Time Out.

"Good, now, go on, or you'll be late for your Broadway Jazz class."

Trey Stevens was leaning up against the whitewashed brick wall outside Ms. Carmen's studio. Practically every girl walking out of Advanced Beginners Street Funk (and one swishy boy wearing lavender leg warmers) stopped to shoot him flirtatious, hopeful smiles, or to say something inane like, "I'm *super* into your dreads today—Pantene?" Usually quick with sexy comebacks, Trey was coming up short today. He could barely think. He couldn't believe it—Trey Stevens, junior prom prince and true playa, was shook.

In almost four years of dancing at Armstrong, he'd never been so impressed. Tangie was a hot dancer, if kinda amateur-ish, but today she was downright amazing. She was so power-ful, so, so . . . fuck it, so sexy. Like, crazy, out of control, *King* magazine sexy. He'd always thought she was cute, with those corkscrew curls, and that perfect chocolate skin, and that *ass* (and the sweet, gullible way she believed everything he told her), but today, she looked like a woman.

Tangie hadn't said a word to Trey since the time he'd basi-cally pretended he didn't know her in front of his friends. Clearly, she had started to catch feelings, so Trey had felt the need to show her that they were definitely not official. He kind of regretted it now, though. And since then, he'd been half-heartedly trying to flirt with her again (though she wasn't having it at all). It had been more of a "let's see if I can get her back" game than anything else. But now, playtime was over.

Trey was suddenly feeling all kinds of things he didn't nor-mally feel. He wanted Tangie more than ever. Luckily for him, he always got what he wanted.

Tangie bounded out of the studio into the crowded hallway, too preoccupied even to notice Trey.

"Hey," he said, reaching out to grab her arm.

Tangie looked down at his hand, one eyebrow raised, and he removed it. "What do you want, Trey?"

"Whoa, shorty, why you comin' at me with all this animonsity?"

"*Animosity*, you mean?" Tangie rolled her eyes and sighed. She'd forgotten how silly his thuggish, dumb-on-purpose lingo was. Trey was a brilliant hip-hop dancer and B-boy, but the fact was, he'd taken ballet for ten years and wore a G-string and tights in his contemporary classes. So he always acted extra gangsta to overcompensate.

"Whatever, yo. I just wanted to tell you, you murdered that Usher choreo today, kid. Like, where'd that shit come from?"

Tangie shrugged, flattered but playing it off. "I don't know. I mean, thanks. Um, I gotta go."

"What you been ignoring me for, ma? I'm sayin', I thought we was cool and shit."

She looked at him as if he were insane. "You thought we were cool? Trey, you totally tried to play me in front of your boys. Do you think I'm stupid?"

She tried to walk away, but Trey stepped in front of her, blocking her path. As much as she wanted to kick him in the balls and run for her life, she didn't. He was a jackass, but he was a beautiful jackass. With his creamy dark skin, high cheekbones, and lush dreadlocks tied up in a big, bulky knot—not to mention that insanely cut, athletic body—the boy looked like a Sean John model.

"Listen, I'm sorry I ignored you that day, okay?" He scratched the back of his head and let out a tortured sigh.

Frowning and pacing in front of her, he let it all out. "Real talk? I just got scared."

"Scared?"

"Yeah. True playas like me can get scared, too." It was a weak stab at a joke, but Tangie didn't crack a smile. So Trey cleared his throat and continued. "Look, me and Eden had just had that ill breakup—and I guess I was scared to get all deep again. So I acted shady to protect my feelings, you understand? It was fucked up, but I hope you forgive me."

Tangie's mouth opened a bit, in utter surprise. That was the most emotion she'd ever seen come out of Trey. And she had to admit, he'd just kind of made sense. He and Eden had had a tumultuous relationship, and she could see how he'd have been scared to start up something new. Then again, there were all those rumors. She'd heard that Trey had been cheating on Eden the whole time they went out, and that every year he picked an underclassman dancer to hook up with (preferably a virgin, as the gossip went).

What was Tangie supposed to believe?

"Trey, I know all about you." She brought her voice down to a whisper. "I know you cheated on Eden, and I know all about your track record with dance department newbies."

"Oh, word?" Trey raised an eyebrow. "Then, why'd you start shit up with me in the first place?"

Good point, she thought. "I didn't want to believe the rumors, because, well, because you were such a good tutor." Inwardly she groaned, knowing how ridiculous that sounded.

He frowned, biting his lower lip. "Honestly, it kills me that

that's my rep. It really ain't even like that. A), me and Eden broke up 'cause she was bonkers. And secondly, I ain't got time to fuck around with 'dance department newbies,'" he said, making air quotes with his fingers. "I'm steady on the grind, ya heard? I'm hollerin' at agents, hitting castings on the low— I really ain't got the time."

Tangie sighed. "Whatever, Trey. Can I go now?"

"You got a new tutor?"

"No."

Trey didn't say anything, so Tangie stormed off into the crowd, totally fed up.

"Tangie," he said, forcefully.

She whipped her head around, shocked that he had spoken her name so loud. A group of girls holding tap shoes looked up from where they were stretching, fascinated. Trey made it a point never to be seen speaking in public to the same girl for more than a couple of seconds, especially in the dance wing (not only were dancers the biggest gossips of all, but you never knew who was secretly filming stuff on their camera phones— all he needed was for his extracurricular activities with females to show up on YouTube or somebody's MySpace page). And Tangie could count on one hand the number of times he had even walked with her down the crowded hallway. Now he was calling her out loud?

"I miss you."

The tap girls gasped. A tall Latina girl walking by almost dropped her dance bag. Tangie felt her cheeks grow hot.

"Why you so surprised for?" Trey called out, grinning. He

pushed through the crowd until he stood in front of Tangie. To her great surprise, he backed her up against somebody's locker, leaned in close to her ear and said, "You blow my fuckin' mind, Dimples. *And that's wassup.*"

He winked, pointed at her, then disappeared down the hallway. Tangie's mouth hung open, as if she'd just seen a leprechaun or a solar eclipse, right there in the dance department wing.

She was both flattered beyond belief and tragically late to Broadway Jazz class.

3.
OWN YOUR DIRTY

AFTER BROADWAY JAZZ, Tangie met Izzy at the freshman lockers for their daily walk to lunch. Since Izzy obviously didn't get along with Skye and Co., it was really the only time they hung out at school.

"Skye's gonna have her own *Sixteen Candles* episode," Tangie repeated for the third time, feeling weird about the news. "I mean, that's nuts, right?"

"Nuts ain't the word for it, baby," cracked Izzy, grabbing her thrift-store Smurfs lunch box out of her locker. Together, the girls made an odd-looking couple. Tangie was the quintessential Bunhead in her denim mini and off-the-shoulder H&M T-shirt over a leotard, tights, and ballet flats. Meanwhile, Izzy's style screamed *funky-eclectic artist*: her delicate features were at odds with her blue-tipped faux hawk, nose ring, and ripped camouflage knee-shorts.

By now, Tangie was used to the crowds of people who stared, pointed, and whispered about Izzy as they walked

through the halls. If Armstrong was a school full of freaks (i.e.,
kids who loved Stephen Sondheim show tunes and obscure
German cinema classics instead of Fergie and the *Scary Movie*
films), then Izzy was their queen. By now, her Lifetime-movie-
of-the-week-worthy life story was legendary: two years before,
her sadistic dad had kicked her out of the house for having too
many tattoos, and she had run off and joined her boyfriend's
successful underground hip-hop band, pretending to be eighteen. When the boyfriend (or, as Izzy called him, the "totally
fucked-up love of her life") dumped her, she ended up living
with a bunch of street kids in some weird commune under a
bridge in Newark—at which point she met a sociologist writing a book about homeless runaway teens, and he basically
adopted her. Now she lived with this thirty-year-old sociologist
in his Upper West Side apartment, a fact that most people
found both shocking and deeply glamorous.

"I'm sayin', I think she'll fit right in," Izzy said, chewing on
a toothpick. For the past twelve hours, Izzy had been trying to
quit smoking. "I generally hate all the spoiled, bratty bitches
on *Sixteen Candles*, and I hate Skye, so it all makes sense."

"She really isn't that bad, Izzy. I mean, yeah, she's spoiled
and stuff, but once you get to know her, she's cool." Tangie
smiled sweetly, hooking her arm through Izzy's. "Why don't
you eat lunch with us today?"

"Sure. And then I'll set myself on fire."

"I'm serious."

"Well, then, *seriously*, why would I eat lunch with your
girls, T.?"

"How about so everybody'll get over what happened at Skye's party, for once and for all? Don't get me wrong, Kamillah was dead wrong telling everybody about your past. But it's kinda good that everything came out, don't you think? You're not hiding anything anymore."

I love you, Tangie, Izzy thought, *but you're crazy naive if you think I ain't hiding anything.* "Yeah, whatever. You know what's funny? Everybody made such a big deal about me and Kamillah fighting, but I really been in much worse scraps. Look." She lifted up her red-and-white-striped tube top and showed Tangie a zigzag scar traveling up her rib cage. "Butter knife, okay? Some crazy albino bitch tried to kill me in my sleep when I was on the streets."

Tangie gasped in horror, clapping her hand over her mouth. "Damn, Izzy! That's awful. Why'd she try to kill you?"

"'Cause I stole her friggin' deodorant."

"You stole her deodorant," Tangie repeated, stunned. "Why?"

"Um, to sell it?" Izzy looked at her as if to say, *duh.* "The point is, Kamillah and Skye and them are wack, but I really ain't trippin' off them. It could be a lot worse." She smiled at Tangie, and they pushed through the heavy metal doors to the underclassman cafeteria. They were immediately swept up in the loud, bustling crowd that was rushing outside to the courtyard.

"While we're on the subject," said Izzy, "I could be asking you the same thing."

"What same thing?"

"Why you never sit with me. You know, with C.J. and Black and them."

"Ha! You know I'm *so* not a tomboy like you. My mind goes totally blank around a bunch of boys. Plus, they're always freestyling and stuff, and I just feel wack." It was true. The only boy Tangie had ever felt truly comfortable with was C.J. With anyone else, she got all jittery and self-conscious, and her personality seemed to vaporize instantly. She wished she could hold up a sign saying, NO, REALLY, I'M NOT THIS STUTTERING IDIOT—I'M ACTUALLY FUNNY AND SEXY AND COOL! whenever she spoke to a boy.

"I just don't get how you always know what to say to them," said Tangie.

"I just trust dudes more than girls," answered Izzy with a shrug. "They say what they mean. And they don't get upset over random shit that doesn't matter. Take Kamillah. I know it fucks with her that I chill with her man, Black." Kamillah's boyfriend and C.J.'s best friend, Raj Jamison, had changed his name to Blackadocious after reading *Roots* over the summer. "But whatever, he's just part of the crew." She shook her head in frustration. "I don't know, man, I never felt possessive like that over a boy. It's better to act like you don't care—that's when they go nuts for you."

Tangie never ceased to be amazed at how wise Izzy was for a fourteen-year-old. *I guess having to sell Soft & Dri for survival makes you grow up fast,* she thought.

"That's how you should be with Trey," Izzy continued. Earlier, Tangie had recapped the whole scene with Trey for her.

"He's clearly a playa, so why don't you be one, too? Life's short, and he *is* fine. Have fun, just don't expect anything."

Tangie sighed, speechless. That was *so* not her. *Be a playa.* Yeah, right. Izzy might just as well have said, "Be an elephant." It just wasn't in Tangie to take dating lightly, or to hook up with a boy just because it was "fun." To her, that stuff was serious.

"Anyway, back to the point. I know why you don't chill with us, and it's C.J." Izzy folded her arms in front of her tiny chest. "When you gonna tell me what happened with y'all two? You're the coolest people I know at this school, it makes no sense that we don't hang out."

"I told you, nothing really happened," insisted Tangie, hoping she sounded convincing. "He's Skye's cousin, so we'd been friends since we were little. We just grew apart, that's all."

"Blah, blah, and blah," said Izzy, pushing open the double doors that led into the packed courtyard. "I'm gonna dead your beef, if it's the last thing I do."

It was seventy-three degrees, an unseasonably warm day for the end of September. Everyone was so amped off the warm weather that food was an afterthought. Actually, lunchtime at Armstrong was never really about food. Instead, it was when the showbiz-obsessed divas and divos showed off their many talents. Artists and writers sketched away in their notebooks, actors practiced impromptu weeping, singers *tra-la-la-laaa*'d through vocal warm-ups, MCs battled, and musicians honked away on every instrument under the sun. It was loud, chaotic, and, at first, totally intimidating—but now, Tangie loved every minute of it. After spending ninth grade at her local public high school, where she was endlessly teased about her duck walk (so unfair—what dancer didn't walk with her toes pointed out?), it was cool to finally be around kids who got her.

Tangie's gaze immediately focused on the cipher of boys under the last tree on the left. It was C.J. and his crew: Vineet Naveen, a drummer-slash-deejay (and the most keeping-it-'hood Indian anyone knew); and Kyle Clarke, a Japanime-addicted metrosexual. Beyond being fanatics for old-school hip-hop, underground mix tapes, and sneakers, they were all ridiculously talented and generally regarded as the cutest boys in the sophomore class.

Tangie was pretending not to stare, but of course she saw C.J. freestyling in the middle of the group, and saw his boys fall out laughing when he was done. Always the artist, he had his sketch pad sticking out of the back of his jeans. Oh, he was so cute, so effortlessly adorable in his grown-and-sexy jeans, Ice Cream T-shirt, and signature Yankees cap. Tangie wondered if he missed her at all.

Izzy gave her a kiss on the cheek, then ran over to the group.

Tangie turned away after watching her and C.J. give each other pounds. She was over being jealous of their relationship; now she was just sad. *I wonder when I'll be able to look at him without feeling like I just got hit by a truck,* she thought.

As Tangie made her way over to her friends (nudging past two girls dressed in full eighteenth-century garb belting out a Pavarotti classic), she wondered if maybe she should give Trey another chance. After all, there was no sense in pining over a relationship that was totally dead.

And besides, things could be worse than Trey Stevens announcing to the entire dance wing that he missed her!

"Wassup, sexy?" hollered Skye as Tangie approached their usual bench, which was situated between a group of open-mike-loving, spoken-word-obsessed drama girls (all rocking colorful head wraps) and the Young Liberal Filmmakers of America crowd (with filthy hair and hipster horn-rimmed glasses). She motioned for Regina to move over so Tangie could sit down. "Eww, I hate that you fraternize with that slutty homeless liar. When are you gonna be over her?"

"This is not *Mean Girls*, Skye," Tangie responded, pulling a package of cinnamon-apple rice cakes out of her dance bag. Tangie loved Skye to death, but had zero patience for her bitchiness. "I told you, she's been a really good friend to me, and I'm not gonna drop her just 'cause you guys don't like her."

"I don't think Skye meant to say that you should *drop* her, per se," said Regina, jumping to her idol's defense, as usual. She was constantly shocked at how quick Tangie was to put Skye in her place. No matter how badly Skye treated Regina, she'd never have spoken to her that way.

"Whatever; let's change the subject." Skye waved Regina away, already bored with the Izzy talk. She poured an Emergen-C packet into her bottle of Poland Spring water.

"Where's Kamillah?" asked Tangie.

"She and Black snuck out to Forever 21." The store was

conveniently located three buildings over from Armstrong in Union Square. "Black saw some dashikilike caftans in the window that he wanted her to try on. His Afrocentric shit is getting played out real fast. Okay, on to the really important stuff. Look what I have for my ladies!"

Skye pulled a stack of xeroxed papers out of her Louis Vuitton City bag and slapped it down on the picnic table. "These are your release forms from MVN! They wanna start filming tomorrow, so we need your parents to sign them tonight. Oh, I'm so excited, I've been constipated for *days*."

Tangie and Regina each picked up a release and read it over. The forms were like minicontracts, saying that their parents approved of their being on camera.

"Also, I really want you guys to start quietly breaking the news to people," Skye continued, lowering her voice. "That's what celebrities do when they want stuff about their personal lives leaked to tabloids. On the low, they have their publicists whisper the right thing in the right ears, and then it can never be traced back to them."

"Interesting," said Regina, jotting down notes in her pad.

"I can't believe filming starts tomorrow; that's so soon," said Tangie. "What's the plan?"

"I want us all to meet at my house tomorrow night so we can brainstorm about the party," said Skye. "You know, who's doing what, the theme, stuff like that. Come a couple hours earlier, because Alexa is hiring her makeup-and-hair guru, Penny, to fix us all up. Are you dying?"

"Dying!" squealed Regina, on cue.

"Yeah, dying," said Tangie, absentmindedly. She was thinking about who was going to sign her permission slip. Her
father was never around, and her twenty-one-year-old step-
mother didn't speak a word of English. "Um, Skye, do you
think your mom can sign for me?"

Skye looked at Tangie, her eyes softening. She knew what
she was worrying about. "I *dare* your deadbeat dad not to come
out of his black hole for, like, two seconds to help you out.
You're a dream daughter to that man; this is the least he can do
for you." Skye kissed Tangie on the cheek and gave her a quick
squeeze. "Oooh, my episode is gonna be the best *ever*!"

"This is the calm before the storm," said Regina. "Our lives
will never be the same."

"I know," said Tangie, forcing a smile.

"Listen, I gotta go holla at Principal Fischer and make sure
this doesn't break the whole 'no professional gigs' rule," said
Skye. "Get those slips signed!"

As she ran off, waving cutely at a couple of boys from her
Dramatic Breathing class, Kamillah and Black entered the
courtyard, each carrying a Forever 21 bag. They kissed each
other, and then Black went off to join C.J., Vineet, Kyle, and
Izzy. Watching Izzy give her boyfriend a pound, Kamillah
rolled her eyes, spun on her wedge heel, and marched over to
the It chicks bench.

"Tangela Adams," Kamillah hollered, slamming her shopping bag down on the table, "how the hell can you fraternize
with that slutty homeless liar?"

Tangie couldn't believe she'd heard the phrase *slutty*

homeless liar twice in one day. She sighed, suddenly very tired. When had her life become such a soap opera?

On the way to meet with Principal Fischer, Skye stopped by her locker to primp a little. As far back as she could remember, Skye's way of dealing with stress had been to find the nearest mirror, apply a little lip gloss, and fluff up her long, honey-streaked weave (actually, the weave was a new thing—and it was only to add a little body, as she was quick to point out to anyone who asked). And this definitely qualified as a stressful situation.

Armstrong's rule banning students from performing professionally was taken very seriously, and if Principal Fischer felt that Skye's appearing with her friends on a reality show counted as "professional" and forbade it, then Skye would absolutely die of disappointment. *Sixteen Candles* was the best thing that had ever happened to her. This would make her famous! Everyone she knew would be jealous. And even better, she'd finally emerge from her big sister's shadow. Not only was Eden the darling of Armstrong's drama department, she was also a former child star on the hit '90s sitcom *Family Chatter*.

And then there was that whole Smoove Killah thing. For the past couple of weeks, the movie-star-beautiful senior had been "quietly" seeing Smoove, the outrageously sexy platinum-selling rapper and sometime actor. Even though it was supposed to be on the low (Smoove was engaged to the Grammy-award-winning R & B singer Pearl), the glamorous relationship had raised Eden's profile to legendary status at Armstrong.

As if Eden needed one more reason to for folks to kiss her ass.

In a hurry, Skye opened her locker door and reached for a pink vinyl makeup kit (gift-with-purchase from Chanel). Peering into the mirror hanging on the inside of the locker door, she pursed her lips and very carefully began applying Lip Venom, a tingly plumping gloss that made her lips look irresistibly luscious. *I dare Principal Fischer to say no to me,* she thought, blowing herself a kiss.

Feeling confident, she packed up her makeup kit and slammed the locker door closed. And there was Trey, leaning against the next locker.

"What it do, Li'l Sis?" Trey smiled and swept Skye up in a huge, overaffectionate bear hug.

Skye was shocked speechless. A hug? True, she'd known Trey since she was twelve years old, back when he and Eden had first started dating. He'd spent the past four New Year's holidays with her family in St. Barths; he'd toasted her parents at their anniversary gala the previous year; he'd even come to her great-grandma's funeral—but Skye couldn't remember his ever saying more than two words to her. And he'd *never* called her Li'l Sis.

Despite her confusion, Skye couldn't help feeling flattered. Trey was a conceited, overflossing jerk, but he also practically *ran* Armstrong. And everyone was watching him sweat her. Nice.

"Wassup, Trey?" She softened her voice to a Paris Hilton purr. "How you been?" From watching Eden over the years, she'd learned how to transform herself quickly into a love goddess when talking to a boy. She tossed her head, flipping her long, swooping bangs out of her face, and threw back her shoulders to make her size-A boobs look fuller.

"Chillin', chillin'," said Trey, shuddering a bit. All of a sudden, Skye looked exactly like Eden, and the resemblance made him kind of nauseous. "Yo, uh, you got a minute?"

Skye cocked her head prettily. "For you, of course. What's the deal?"

Trey folded his arms across his chest, making his biceps bulge under his crisp white T. He gave her his most devastating smile. "You ain't still got beef with me about, like, what went down with Edie, right?"

"Whatever. I mean, it's really none of my business, you know? She's clearly moved on, so I guess it's all good. Why?" She raised her eyebrows. "Tell me you're not trying to get back with her?"

Trey burst out laughing, shaking his head. "Naw, naw, naw, not Eden. Tangie."

"*Tangie?*" So that was why he was talking to her. Skye felt like her social stock had plummeted from A-list to D-list in just seconds.

"Yeah, no doubt. What's her story, man? She dealin' with anybody?"

Suddenly, Skye was in a bad mood. *I can't believe I'm back here again*, she thought, groaning inwardly. When Tangie and Trey were talking the first week of school, she'd hated it—and not just because her best friend was being disloyal to Eden and was definitely going to get hurt in the process. No, she had been irritated because Tangie was brand-new to the school and was already getting more shine than she was! She'd landed a Spotlight audition when Skye hadn't, and she had a hot guy while Skye was alone. It wasn't fair.

She planted a hand on her hip. "You're bold as hell, you know that?"

"Whatchu mean, bold?" Trey looked both ways, then lowered his voice. "I'm sayin', I'm really feelin' her. Seriously." He smiled and knocked his shoulder against hers. "Come on, Li'l Sis, I thought we went way back. You ain't tryin' to help me out?"

"Stop calling me Li'l Sis." She pushed him away. "Are you forgetting I'm Eden's sister? I saw what you did to her; do you honestly think I'm gonna cosign you ruining my best friend's life, too?"

"Come on, man, I ain't ruined nobody's life."

"Omigod, Trey, *own your dirty*!" Skye threw her hands up in the air, totally exasperated. "Eden caught you going down on Courtney Van der Maal at the junior prom!"

"Whatever, man, it was all a miscommunication." Trey cleared his throat, changing the subject. "Look, I'm sweatin' your girl. What's her story?"

"You really wanna know her story? I'll tell you." Skye took a deep breath and let it all out. "Tangie is hopelessly, desperately in love with C. J. Parker. And he loves her, too, since we were in the sixth grade. It's the real thing, okay?"

Trey shrugged, unfazed. "Why they ain't together, then?"

"Because they're hardheaded and stupid and fight over dumb shit. But they're soul mates, Trey. *They're* supposed to be together, not you two. The only reason Tangie hooked up with you was to make C.J. jealous. Get it? So back the fuck up."

"Hold up, hold up, hold up; C. J. Parker? The kid from Marcy? You and Eden's ghetto-ass cousin, right?"

"Yes, but don't call him ghetto. He's a brilliant artist, you asshole." Yeah, Skye and C.J. fought a lot, but she'd be damned if she'd let anyone else talk shit about him.

"Yeah, I think I bought a dime bag off him once." Trey smirked, looking smug. "Please, I ain't trippin' off that pretty boy."

"You really don't have a chance," Skye said with a cold smile.

"Yeah, we'll see."

Annoyed, Skye smoothed her empire-waisted BCBG tunic over her leggings and flounced away. Over her shoulder, just for good measure, she added, "Stay away from her." She turned around to see if Trey'd heard her, but he was long gone.

C.J. and Izzy were crouching behind the trash bins outside Armstrong's auditorium, discreetly smoking a bowl before the bell rang for their next class, intermediate charcoal sketching. Smoking at the end of lunch had become a sort of ritual—they were convinced that weed, somehow, enhanced their artistic abilities.

"So, listen," C.J. began, taking two puffs from Izzy's bowl. "Promise me you'll keep the whole OutKast thing on the low."

"Make me," said Izzy, her gorgeous eyes flashing.

"Oh, really?"

She nodded.

With a shrug, C.J. took a deep drag from the bowl. He put his lips over Izzy's and blew practically a lungful of smoke into her mouth. Overwhelmed, she started half choking, half giggling and pushed him away.

"Okay, okay!" she sputtered, playfully knocking him in the head and snatching the bowl from him. "I promise!"

"Yeah, I thought so," he said, suddenly getting serious. "On the real, though, I only told you and Black. I don't want nobody else to know."

"No doubt, no doubt," she said. "I mean, there's that 'no professional' rule. You could get expelled. It ain't worth it, love."

Wasn't it, though? C.J. thought about that. A couple of weeks earlier, his entire life had changed. He'd drawn a nude portrait of Izzy for a charcoal sketch project on the human body, and he'd accidentally left it on the counter at Tower Records, where he worked part time. It was just his luck that Big Boi and Andre 3000 had a promotions meeting there that day—because they saw his sketch and wanted it for the cover of OutKast's upcoming greatest-hits CD! Since then, C.J. and the art director for the album cover had been going back and forth trying to set up a meeting. But something in C.J.'s gut was holding him back.

On the one hand, this could be the biggest break of his life. He lived and breathed art of all kinds—sculpture, sketching, painting, but especially graffiti—and this cover would put him on the map. But what if he did get caught? Everything he had worked for would be lost if he got expelled.

And then there was Tangie. They'd always had a passionate, deep, on-and-off relationship, but now things were definitely "off." She hadn't spoken to him since she found out he had sketched Izzy naked (the fact that C.J. and Tangie had exchanged their first "I love you's" the night before didn't help—yeah, his timing had always sucked). In the back of his mind, though, it was never really over. He was just giving her a minute to cool off.

But if Tangie ever found out that the whole world was gonna see that portrait, she'd probably cut him back for good. And that would be tragic, he thought, rubbing his eyes.

He didn't say any of that to Izzy, though. She was cool and ridiculously sexy—in fact, C.J. had never met such a chill, down-for-whatever girl in his life—but they sort of had an understanding. Their relationship was about good sex, good weed, and good times, nothing more. The truth was, C.J. suspected she was still hung up on her mysterious ex, and Izzy got the feeling he was sick over some other girl—but they never really got superdeep with each other. It was easier that way.

"Why you lookin' all serious, though? I thought you'd be geeked." Izzy studied C.J., who was leaning up against the brick wall of the building, staring into the bowl as if it were a magic crystal ball. Her gaze traveled from his irresistibly sexy, moody, amber brown eyes down to his strong hands, the ones that created award-winning graffiti art and made her melt a thousand times. This boy has the tortured artist thing down to a science, she thought, and he knows it.

"I am, I am. I was just thinking, though. I wanna keep it low 'cause of the Armstrong rule, obviously, but also 'cause I really ain't tryin' to hype this up and then have it not happen."

"It's gonna happen, Ceej."

"You don't know that."

"Yeah, I do, I got a feeling," she said, biting her bottom lip excitedly.

"Yeah, I know all about your feelings," he teased, passing her the bowl.

She smiled, pushing her shoulder against his.

"Seriously, though," he continued. "The CD could not drop for some reason, or they might do me greasy and pick some other artist. You and I both know shit can go very wrong."

Izzy nodded. She knew what he was saying. Just like her, he'd been familiar with tragedy from a young age. C.J.'s mom had died of a drug overdose when he was little, so he'd been raised by his sickly grandma in Brooklyn's notoriously tough Marcy projects. He'd been hustling since he was nine years old to pay her medical bills. Both C.J. and Izzy were street-smart, used to taking care of themselves, and knew they couldn't count on much of anything. But their brains and talent had taken them to Armstrong, and they weren't trying to mess it up.

"I mean, yeah, anything can happen, Ceej. We could, like, die tomorrow," she pointed out, feeling philosophical. "The point is, OutKast's cover could make you a damned *legend*, do you realize that?"

A slow, stoned smile crept across C.J.'s face. "I mean, yeah, it could. And I guess I could kick it underground style and use an alias. Armstrong don't have to know it was me."

"That's all I'm sayin', kid!"

They heard a tentative knock on one of the trash cans in front of them.

"'Sup?" called out C.J.

"It's Phoung. Phoung Tran. I, uh, need to borrow your World Civ notes."

"Aiight." C.J. motioned for Izzy to hide the bowl, and then a lanky Asian kid in a backward Giants cap and Air Force Ones stepped out from behind the trash cans.

"Wassup? Uh, I'm here to buy some . . ."

"I know what you here for, homie. Lemme see your pockets. You got any camera phones on you?" C.J. didn't want to show up on YouTube selling drugs at school. They quickly made the transaction, and Phoung stuffed the tiny plastic bag into his jeans pocket. C.J. nodded his head, peacing him out, but the slouchy boy didn't move an inch.

"Cool. Uh, thanks, man. So, uh, this your girlfriend?"

"Man, go 'head with all that."

"No, it's just that I've heard a lot about . . . it's Izzy, right?"

She nodded, looking suddenly very bored.

Phoung's cheeks flushed rosy pink, and he started talking superfast, as if he were in the presence of a true celebrity. "Yeah, I've been reading that Indian dude's blog about you, man, and it's mad entertaining! Yo, I heard Fiddy actually came to one of your hip-hop band's shows. Wait, or was it Lil Wayne? Is that real talk, or . . ."

"I no longer comment on my past life," interrupted Izzy, putting on a prissy, upper-class accent. She pulled a pair of knockoff Dior shades out of her messenger bag and put them on, perfectly playing the part of the harassed superstar. C.J. had to bite his lip to keep from laughing. "No offense, I just really need to keep my private life private. I'm sure you understand."

"No, of course," Phuoung said, nodding briskly. "I think you're the shit, though. So many sucka MCs here pretend to be hood, but you really lived that gutter life, and your art tells the tale, man. You're just so real!"

"Aww! Thanks so much, doll, that really means a lot," Izzy squealed in her snooty accent. "You're so sweet—Ceej, isn't he the *sweetest*?"

"Yeah; I'm getting a toothache," answered C.J., totally impressed and amused by Izzy's little act. She should've majored in drama, not art. "Yo, enjoy the smokes, Phoung."

The boy smiled broadly and broke out. As soon as he was gone, C.J. and Izzy collapsed in smoked-out giggles. Good weed, good sex, good times—and no questions.

Name: Aziza "Izzy" Abdelrashid
Class: Freshman
Major: Visual Arts
Self-Awareness Session #: 5

It's not like me to even bring this up, but we're supposed to get real deep sessions, right? Or else what's the point?

Exactly, Miss Abdulrayjid.

Abdelrashid.

A . . . del . . .

Fuck it. Just call me Jane Smith. Can I get to my problem?

Please, go right ahead.

There's the guy in my life—from my past life, back when I was a lot, um, wilder. And I thought I'd gotten him totally out of my system, but now he's back. Well, he's trying to come back, and I'm not really hearing him.

But you want to.

Sort of. I know he's not good for me, but it's hard. We've been through so much together—serious stuff, life-and-death stuff—I can't just turn my back on him.

You've started over at a new school; you've made new friends—why move backward?

Some of the people I met here are real cool, but none of them know me like he does. He saw me at my worst and loved me anyway. He saved me from a messed-up situation, but then . . . I guess, then he became another terrible situation.

Can I ask you something? Where did you get the bruise on your shoulder?

I think our time's up.

4.

THE FOUR LONG-LOST PUSSYCAT DOLLS

". . . AND WHEN THE MVN people get here, don't let the cameras make you nervous. We don't have time for stage fright, bee-yatches. It's Tuesday, and the party's on Saturday! And this is MVN, y'all! This shit is not a game! I mean, who knows what could come out of this episode! If America thinks we're fabulous enough, we might get a spin-off or something. . . ."

Skye was pacing back and forth in her sprawling, plush bedroom, delivering a passionate motivational speech to her best friends, who were barely listening. Tangie was on the floor, doing her seventh set of crunches (she'd been obsessed with getting stick-thin ever since she found out cameras would be following them around for a week). Regina was sitting on a beanbag chair pretending to take notes on Skye's speech; but the future filmmaker was actually jotting down questions she intended to ask the *Sixteen Candles* head camerawoman. And Kamillah had just disappeared into Skye's walk-in closet to fight with her boyfriend on her cell.

"Skye," started Tangie, "how much Red Bull have you had today?"

Regina burst into giggles, then stopped when she saw Skye's eyes narrowing.

"Y'all two can really kiss my narrow yellow ass."

Tangie blew her a kiss.

Skye rolled her eyes and got back down to business. "Anyway, we have tons to go over before they get here. Regina, you taking notes, babe?"

If Skye—who looked like a Mischa Barton rip-off, in a BCBG baby doll dress, cropped leggings, and a tangle of ropy necklaces—was a little too hyper, she had every reason to be. It was the first day of her *Sixteen Candles* shoot, and in less than twenty minutes the producer and head camerawoman would be stopping by to tape the girls discussing party plans.

Oh, the pressure!

Skye had had Tangie, Kamillah, and Regina come over for a complete makeover the millisecond that school ended. Well, not *complete*—Skye was lucky to have very fly friends. Tangie was all about a perky-girlie, Forever 21 moment; Kamillah was Harlem World fly, with her door-knocker earrings and label fetish; and Regina was the hot tomboy, with her signature Pocahontas braids and wifey airs. But even the cutest It chicks could use a little sexing up—so Skye'd surprised them with her mom's personal hairstylist and makeup artist, Penny McPayne (after Penny worked her magic, she stood back from the girls, gasped and exclaimed, "Behold, the four long-lost members of the Pussycat Dolls!")

But the real reason Skye had made them meet her three hours before the taping? She wanted to coach them. Growing up with a mom and a sister who were TV stars, the girl knew a thing or two about the industry. And reality production could be really tricky—producers cornered you, basically forcing you to say hideous, revealing things about people for the sake of drama. And Skye wasn't trying to look crazy just because her girls weren't media-trained enough to know when to shut the hell up.

Meanwhile, Skye had done her homework, too. After spending the entire weekend glued to a *Sixteen Candles* marathon, she'd learned that the most memorable *SC* girls shared the same characteristics—they were spoiled-rotten, rich-girl divas who pimped their friends for the sake of a hot party and demanded the best of everything (and who would've happily screamed till they were blue in the face to get what they wanted). Temper tantrums and day-of-party meltdowns were a must. In less than two minutes, the birthday girls often went from sweet-as-pie angels to cussing, crying, screaming lunatics. And guess what! If that was what the producers wanted, then Skye would give it to them. *Times fifty.*

After all, she was Skye Carmichael, future movie star who'd one day win a Golden Globe for playing Beyoncé in *Jay Z: The Life of Young Hova* (this was the fantasy she held on to when she felt blue—or had cramps).

"Do you realize that we're gonna be household names?"

"God, I can't imagine that," said Tangie. Thoroughly exhausted after a zillion crunches, she lay spread-eagled on the floor, waving her hand over her sweaty face in an effort to save her flawless makeup job.

"No it's true," insisted Skye, still pacing. "The producers told me their girls are recognized all over the damn world! Europe, South America . . . um, New Jersey . . ."

Kamillah burst out of Skye's closet and threw her electric-pink Sidekick across the room. "Blackadocious is officially dead to me, y'all!"

"What happened?" asked Regina, blinking weirdly. She wasn't used to false eyelashes.

"He doesn't want me to do *Sixteen Candles*! Like it's even up to his ashy, back-to-Africa ass," Kamillah said, swiveling her neck.

"Ex-*cuse* me?" Skye put her hands on her hips and waited for an explanation.

"You know how he's all about 'the struggle' and dashikis— which I find hilarious, since last year he wore throwback jerseys every day." Stepping over Tangie, Kamillah flung herself down on Skye's bed. "Anyway, he says that MVN is like the 'big house,' and if I do this I'm just a slave to some corporate white agenda."

"God, that's *so* seventies," Skye rolled her eyes. "Remind me why you love him again?"

"I can't; I'm a lady," Kamillah said, with a naughty grin.

Tangie pulled herself off the floor and sat on the bed, putting her arm around Kamillah. "You know Black's just being his crazy, militant self. Don't listen to him."

"Girl, I'm way too much of a ham to listen to that boy."

Kamillah's "whatever" act was almost convincing.

"Maybe he's jealous, K. He tries to act like Malcolm X, but Black is a damned MC, okay? He wants to be just as famous as all of us." A delighted grin slowly spread over Skye's face. "Seriously, y'all, do you realize how jealous everybody's gonna be? How jealous *Tabby Montgomery*'s gonna be? She thinks she's the shit because some third grader asked for her autograph in Macy's."

Tabby was probably the best actress in Armstrong's junior class. She'd gotten her family on *Extreme Makeover: Home Edition* the previous summer, to upgrade their run-down Long Island home. After delivering a deeply moving speech when her fancy new bedroom was unveiled, she'd become a breakout reality TV star.

Kamillah snorted. "You know the house they made over wasn't even her family's."

"Stop playin'!'"

"Please, Tabby's dad's is a judge. They live on Central Park West! The house they used was her cousin's shack, up in Rochester." Spreading gossip usually gave Kamillah a surge of adrenaline, but right now it wasn't happening. Despite Black's crazy ideas and ridiculous outfits, she loved him to death, and his lack of support had hurt her feelings.

Skye cocked her head and nodded, visibly impressed. Game recognizes game, and she had to admit that Tabby's getting cast on the show was a brilliant move.

But Skye had heard enough about Tabby.

"Whatever, let's get back to my episode. The camerawoman

and producer are gonna be here in, like, twenty minutes, so let's make sure we're all on the same page." Skye glanced over at Regina. "You taking notes, babe?"

Regina held up her pad.

"Now, Kamillah's an actress, so she knows this stuff, but Regina and T., it's time for some media training," said Skye. "The most important thing to remember? Don't ever eat on camera, suck in your stomach at all times, and smile when you talk so you don't look evil. Especially you, Kammie. Your face can look really bitchy sometimes."

"STFU," answered Kamillah, flipping up her middle finger.

"So, what exactly will we talk about in front of the producer?" Regina chewed her pencil, ready to take some notes. "We don't even know your party theme."

Tangie nodded. "Yeah, shouldn't we practice or something?"

"No practicing!" Skye shook her head vigorously. "No, we have to save all our material for the camera. It has to sound spontaneous."

"Wait, you really haven't even thought about your theme?" Regina looked concerned.

"Not at all. Not even a little bit. The whole point of a reality show is to catch people being spontaneous. If we practice, we'll lose the unpredictability factor. It's very important in reality TV. We learned all about it in Modern Television Performance class. Remember, Kamillah?"

Kamillah didn't reply. She was busy typing into her Sidekick, changing her MySpace relationship status.

"Oh, my God, I just got really nervous all of a sudden," said Tangie, grimacing.

"There's no reason to be nervous, babe. No offense, but really, you guys are just background. *I'm* the one that has all the pressure," said Skye, touching up her blush in the mirror. "Honestly, the most famous reality stars bring mad drama. I have so much to live up to!"

"Poor you," muttered Kamillah, thumbs flying on her Sidekick.

"Oh, and don't be alarmed when Simone comes out. Just go with it, okay?" Simone was Skye's onstage alter ego. Skye had gotten the idea when she found out that Beyoncé called her performance personality Sasha. While Beyoncé was a mild-mannered Southern girl, Sasha was a hair-flipping, body-rolling, butt-popping diva. The same went for Simone, minus the intricate choreography.

They heard a buzz; then the doorman's voice blared through the penthouse. "Skye, I have a Jenna Aliabadi and Kiki Jackson here to see you from MVN? Should I send them up to you?"

Skye sprinted over to the intercom on her wall and said, "Yes, yes, yes! Thanks, Dmitri!" Immediately, the girls burst into squeals, falling over one another to get to the mirror for last-minute touch-ups. What felt like two seconds later, the doorbell rang. Suddenly feeling unsure of herself, Skye looked anxiously at her lifelong best friend, the one person in the world who knew her inside and out—and then Tangie gave her a big hug and whispered, "You got this, girl. Just give 'em Skye, and they'll fall in love with you."

"You're so right!" Skye squealed. That was all she needed to hear. Fluffing up her hair, she sprinted out of the room. The girls heard her open the door and greet her guests. She returned to the room with two visitors.

"Hey, girls!" Skye beamed at Tangie, Kamillah and Regina like she hadn't seen them in twelve years. "Please meet Jenna Aliabadi, our producer, and Kiki Jackson, our camerawoman. Jenna and Kiki, these are my girls! Aren't they sexy? You know, my mom, Alexa Carmichael, the legendary star of *Shoulder Pads*, always says, 'You're only as fly as your friends!' So true, right? Anyway, don't worry, I prepped them on how to just be their natural, fabulous selves. We're gonna have so much fun, *woo-hoo*!"

Simone is definitely in the building, Tangie thought.

"Lovely to meet you all," said Jenna, a tall, lanky, Middle Eastern woman wearing skinny cords and a T-shirt that read: I LIKE MY SMALL TATAS. She strode right up to each of the girls and shook their hands. "It's a pleasure. Now, I don't want you to be nervous. This process really is so much fun! Kiki and I are gonna follow you around this week, except when you're at school or in the bathroom—those times are off limits. Kiki's in charge of all the up-close-and-personal camera work, but we also have a very experienced crew who'll film more environmental, wide-angle shots; you know, when we shoot bigger scenes. Also, I'll be interviewing some of you individually, during the week. We call these confessionals. They're a big part of the episode, so try to be as honest as possible, okay?"

"I have no problem being honest, girl," said Kamillah.

"Awesome! We're going to start taping now, so just relax, be yourselves and pretend we're not even here. Oh, and whatever you do, don't look into the camera. Right, Kiki?"

Jenna looked at the camerawoman, who wasn't really paying attention. Kiki, a petite, tomboyish hipster rocking pink Chuck Taylors and an adorable pixie cut, had locked eyes with Regina.

"Do you two know each other?" Jenna asked, looking back and forth between the two.

Regina shook her head, her heartbeat quickening. Suddenly, she felt as if all the air had been sucked out of the room.

"Not to be weird or whatever," Kiki began, "but do you have any Filipina in you? You look exactly like my cousin. Really, the resemblance is nuts."

"Actually, I do," Regina replied, feeling her palms start to sweat. "I mean, I'm *half* Filipina. . . . My mom is black."

"So's mine!" Kiki smiled broadly, revealing dimples. "I mean, I'm the other way around—my dad's black, and my mom's Filipina. That some crazy stuff, right?"

"The craziest," muttered Skye, annoyed that she wasn't the subject of their small talk. "So, how about we get this thing started, girls? Jenna, where do you want us?"

Five minutes later, Kiki had unpacked her camera equipment, set up the lighting, and attached tiny microphones to the front of the girls' shirts. After accepting all of their permission slips, Jenna gave them some pointers on what to talk about, then positioned the girls so that they were sitting in a semicircle on Skye's fluffy, king-size bed. She had Skye pull out the previous year's Armstrong yearbook so that they could skim through it while coming up with the guest list.

"Okay, ladies; you ready?"

No one would've believed that the answer was yes. Tangie had the toothiest, most artificial ear-to-ear grin imaginable plastered on her face (this was always her immediate reaction to being in front of a camera), Skye was overdoing a pinup-girl sexy pout, Regina was pretending not to stare at Kiki, and Kamillah—well, Kamillah looked like a girl who was furious with her bossy, fake-Afrocentric boyfriend.

"Just relax, okay?" Jenna smiled at them, hoping they'd loosen up. "Think natural!"

"Here we go," said Kiki, peering into her compact handheld video camera. "Five, four, three, two, one . . . *action.*"

"So-o-o," began Skye, batting her eyelashes and speaking in a breathy, Paris-meets-Eden voice that was totally artificial-sounding, "should we first talk about a theme for the party? Any suggestions?"

"I have a suggestion!" Missing "natural" by about a mile, Tangie sounded like she'd just downed twelve espresso shots. And the great big cartoon smile showed no signs of diminishing. "How about an eighties party, where everyone dresses like Madonna or something? The eighties are kind of in style right now."

"Meh," Skye said, shrugging. She flipped her hair and stuck out her chest. She was wearing two bras—one strapless, and a padded one over that—to make her look bustier. "The eighties are over."

"I think we should do an *America's Next Top Model* party. Then I can wear a big fuschia lace-front wig and do my Tyra-at-panel impression," Kamillah said drily, knowing her idea was ridiculous and not caring. The beef with Black had destroyed the experience for her. She cleared her throat and launched into her very best Tyra Banks voice. "Girls, I want you to note the difference between *this*," she said, flashing an intense look with her eyes, "and *this*." She did, not change a thing about her expression on the second "this."

Skye shot her a "shut the eff up" look and then remembered the cameras. Smiling prettily, she shrugged and said, "I don't think so. Next?"

Regina realized this was her cue to suggest a theme. Of course she had no idea—she'd been preoccupied with stealing glances at Kiki. Not only did they have an obvious connection, but she was obsessed with the camerawoman's technique. She couldn't wait to talk shop with her. "Um, we could . . . how about a *Sex and the City* party?"

"Okay, no. No, no, no! Your ideas are all *strictly wack*," blurted out Skye, brattily slamming her hand down on the bed. The girls jumped, stunned by her personality switch-up (meanwhile, Skye was thrilled with her cleverness, knowing she was giving Jenna and Kiki tons of great material).

"I don't think you guys get how important this moment is for me! I'm a *princess*, okay? I deserve the hottest, craziest, most off-the-chain party of the century! Enough already with the generic McBeamers and the embarrassing dance routines—my *Sixteen Candles* party is gonna be the best the series has ever seen! We're gonna make P. Diddy's White Party look like an Episcopalian church social!" She paused for dramatic effect, her tiny chest heaving. "And guess what? I already have a theme. One that'll blow all the other *Sixteen Candles* joints out of the water. For my Sweet Sixteen, I want a Gangsters and Glamour Girls party."

The girls looked at each other, surprised and confused. Hadn't Skye just insisted that she'd never even *thought* about a theme?

She totally played us, thought Tangie. *I should've known.*

"My dad's a Broadway producer, but he's also a drama coach for singers, dancers, and models who want to get into acting. He coached Andre 3000 for his new movie, *Idlewild*, and I saw a trailer and thought, *That's so me!*" Skye had been practicing this speech for the past three days. "It's set in the thirties, kinda like a black *Chicago* . . . and the girls are in slinky gowns with feather boas and fishnet stockings, and the guys are rocking, like, pin-striped three-piece suits and fedoras. It's so dope! And I was thinking, we could do it at Club Tropicana, which kinda looks like an old-school cabaret nightclub, and it has this fly VIP balcony, where all of us and the boys could chill above the crowd and get our sexy on! Me and Alexa already checked it out, and they're way into it."

Jenna motioned for Kiki to cut. "Skye, you didn't tell us that! We're going to have to go back there soon and reshoot that conversation, if you don't mind. Do you think you can pretend that you're going there and talking to management for the first time?"

Skye looked worried. "Well, isn't that gonna look un-natural?"

"Please, reality shows do it all the time—especially ones like *The Hills* and *Laguna Beach*, where they don't have cameras on them twenty-four seven. If the producer finds out that a juicy conversation happened off camera, they just ask the stars to reproduce it." Jenna was pleased to reveal the behind-the-scenes tricks of MVN's biggest competitor, MTV.

"But, but that's not reality—is it?" To Tangie, learning this information was like finding out that the tooth fairy was a sham.

"Of course it is! All of it really happened. It just happened twice."

The girls were silent, taking in this shocking backstage secret. Jenna signaled Kiki, and the taping began again. "Skye," started Jenna, "please pick off where you left off. You were talking about the party venue."

Skye cleared her throat, threw back her shoulders, and transformed back into Simone. "So, I was thinking we could have casino stations, but with fake money? And I want confetti everywhere, and a celebrity deejay to emcee the whole thing, and he'll be all dressed up in a tux and tails . . . and, oh, that's the other thing: all my guest have to totally be in character—all the boys have to dress like old-school nineteen-thirties gangsters, and the girls will wear gorgeous gowns, red lipstick, and wavy, Old Hollywood hair. . . ."

"Not to interrupt," interjected Kamillah, "but where are we supposed to get the outfits?"

Skye grinned excitedly. "My dad has a hookup with this famous Broadway costume store, and they're loaning all my guests whatever they want, at a seventy-five percent discount."

"That's so cool!" Tangie's enormous cartoon smile was back in full effect.

"What about a performer?" wondered Regina. "Who do you want?"

"Smoove Killah, *obvi*," said Skye. "I mean, that's such a no-brainer, with my sister dating him and everything." What she didn't say was how nervous she would be asking Eden to talk to Smoove for her. Her sister was not really the kind of girl to do a favor for free—especially not for Skye, her least favorite person on earth.

"Oh, and guess what? Since you're my girls, I want you all to be, like, mad involved. So, I gave you all jobs!"

"Yay!" Regina was the only one who was thrilled.

"Right before my grand entrance, I want a really fabulous, show-stopping performance to introduce me. Maybe some supersexy showgirls doing, like, a burlesque-type, Pussycat Dolls number?" Skye put her arm around Tangie. "This is all you, girl! I want you, Kamillah, and Regina to do the routine—and you can choreograph it however you want. Don't you love that?"

Tangie felt like her heart had stopped. Was Skye serious? She was giving her a chance not only to *choreograph* a dance, but to *perform* it on national—no, international—TV? Who knew what doors that could open? She felt hysterical, as if she were two seconds from either bursting into giggles or having a panic attack. Instead of falling apart, though, she just nodded and kept flashing that huge, comical grin.

"Skye, I don't know what to say! I . . . thank you, I'm so excited!"

Kamillah was not excited. "Hold up, Skye; you *know* I'm not the best dancer. I mean, Black always says that when I dance it looks like I'm putting out a fire!"

"Sweetie, you'll be fine," said Tangie. "I'm a really good choreographer; I know how to make easy steps look complicated."

Kamillah didn't look convinced, so Skye quickly announced her job. "Kamillah, you know gossip about literally everyone in the school, so you're in charge of the invite list. I only want the hottest people there—no dorks, no Goths, no fat or ugly people . . ."

Regina raised her hand as if she were in school. "I'd like to, um, shadow Kiki for the week, if that's cool. I just really want to learn more about camerawork. Maybe I could sort of be her assistant."

"Sure, yeah. That's cool." Skye didn't understand Regina's fascination with the camera girl, but whatever. "Speaking of skills, I thought maybe C.J. could paint some amazing mural of my court—you know, all of us and the boys—looking all pimped-out and fierce in our costumes. And we could hang it on the wall across from the dance floor. It's a good idea, right, Tangie?" Skye smiled pointedly at her.

Skye had to be very careful about what she said next. Ever since her talk with Trey, she'd been trying to think of ingenious ways to bring Tangie and C.J. back together, once and for all. The possibility of Tangie and Trey as a couple was too wrong to imagine. She had to put a stop to it before the madness began.

"Tangie, I know you and C.J. aren't, like, buddy-buddy or anything . . . but you're still speaking, right? You should ask him to do the mural. He'd do anything for you."

Tangie froze, mortified that Skye was bringing up her and C.J.'s torturous relationship on national TV. For the first time, her smile disappeared (she could have sworn she heard Jenna utter a sigh of relief). "He's *your* cousin," she said, coldly.

"You don't have to sound so bitchy." Skye shot Kiki a pained look. "I'm sorry, can we cut?"

Jenna hopped up from her chair. "Actually, Skye, you don't have to cut. We're taking continuous footage, and then we'll end up editing most of this out, anyway. It's a half-hour show, so we can only use so much."

Kiki nodded. "And actually, conflict between you and your friends isn't necessarily a bad thing. It adds drama! We've even had girls make up fights, just to make thing interesting."

Tangie was glaring at Skye. "I'll ask C.J., under one condition."

"What?"

Regina noticed that Kiki had quietly started filming again.

"You have to ask Izzy to the party. Seriously, Skye, I'm so over all the beef. You don't have to kiss her ass, just be nice."

"No, no, no!" Skye screamed, thrashing around on the bed. She took it over the top, knowing that the crazier you acted the more screen time you got. "I will not have some gross street urchin *ruin the sexy* at my party! No way in hell!"

"It's okay, Skye, just calm down," said Regina, fighting the urge to break the rules and sneak a glance at Kiki. There was something about her—those dimples, those pitch black waves, that adorable, skater-tomboy style.

As Skye continued her tantrum, Jenna gave her a subtle thumbs-up sign behind Kiki's back. This was the stuff of a reality producer's dreams.

But then everyone's attention turned from Skye to her mom, Alexa, who had just appeared in the doorway. The former TV star looked spectacular, as usual—she was wearing a Diane von Furstenberg wrap dress that showed off her supermodel figure, and her swingy, shoulder-length haircut perfectly accented the face that, in the eighties, had sold more than four million posters to horny frat boys.

Immediately, Skye stopped her hysterical yelling. *What the hell is Alexa doing here?* she thought. *She promised not to make this all about her!*

"Well, hello, darlings! Jenna, lovely to meet you, finally. And, oh, look at this adorable, exotic-looking girl. You must be Kiki!" Alexa walked over to her and shook her hand. "My goodness, so much has changed from when I was a TV star. . . . Look at this darling little camera! Sweetheart, you're far too short to be a camerawoman. They're usually tall, strapping men. Jenna, could they get no one else?"

"Alexa! You promised!" Skye was distraught. "Will you just get out, please?"

"But this is so much fun, Skye. Girls, isn't this fun? It's just like a televised slumber party." Shockingly, Alexa crawled onto the bed, squeezing in between Tangie and Kamillah. Everyone smelled the liquor on her breath, but no one said anything.

"Honey, we have so much to do for your party, and no time. There's the catering, the decorator . . . and we have to get you some cortisone injections for that huge pimple coming up on your chin, darling." Alexa tsked, tipping Skye's chin up with her index finger. Skye slapped her hand away. "The next few days are gonna be *madness*. By the way, you'll miss your morning classes tomorrow, because I scheduled your photo shoot and stationery appointment for the invites. Jenna, you'll be there, yes?"

"Please stop addressing me, Mrs. Carmichael," said Jenna, annoyed that the take was ruined. "But, yes, we'll be filming Skye everywhere but at school. Also—"

Jenna stopped abruptly, noticing Eden poking her head into the room. She whispered something to Kiki, who stopped filming.

"Hi, there, are you . . . did you play Kendra on *Family Chatter*, like, years ago?"

Eden beamed a perfect smile, her eyes glassy from her daily Valium. "Yep, that's me."

"Well, we have to get you in the shot."

"No, no, no, I just wanted to see what was going on. Really, it's not about me."

"Don't listen to her," muttered Skye. "It's always about Eden."

"Seriously, the editors will love having footage of you and Alexa," gushed Jenna. "The more famous people in the episode, the better. I'm already seeing the edit, here—Skye, you're the narcissistic glamour girl who has to have everything her way. Eden, why don't you be sugary-sweet to play off that energy? Meanwhile, Skye, you could really resent your sister for being so perfect. What do you think?" Jenna bit her bottom lip, her eyes shining. She *lived* for this. "Eden, maybe you have some suggestions?"

"Of course I do," Eden purred, joining the others on the bed. "I'm an actress."

Within seconds, Eden had completely commanded everyone's attention. She seemed to come alive in front of the camera, completely overshadowing "Simone." Skye wanted to kill her, but at the same time, she noticed a perfect opportunity to ask her sister about Smoove. Eden had the MVN crew totally believing her perfect, golden-girl image, and she'd look like a real bitch if she refused to help her own sister.

"Hey, Eden? I wanted to ask you something."

"Anything, sweetie."

"Obviously, I need a really hot performer for my party, and I was wondering if—well, you know Smoove Killah really well, so I thought you could ask him to perform." Skye shot her sister a look that said, *I got you now, sucka*, and Eden narrowed her eyes.

She quickly remembered she was on camera, though, and

rearranged her face. Smiling coyly, she said, "Of course I can ask my *good friend* Smoove. I think he'd love performing at your Sweet Sixteen."

And that, my friends, is how you make lemonade out of lemons.

5.

A KYNDRA MOMENT

"WHAT THE HELL YOU GOT ON, PLAYA?"

"Me? What about you? You look fifteen."

"I *am* fifteen, stupid."

C.J. and Black stood in the lobby of the enormous midtown high-rise building, sizing each other up. C.J. was wearing a typical outfit for him—a fitted Yankees cap turned to the side, dark-wash jeans, a print hoodie, and a white T that said: FAKE SNEAKERS AREN'T FRESH. Black, on the other hand, was wearing an ill-fitting wool suit (the shoulders were about three sizes too big), a navy tie, and wire-rimmed glasses. And he was clearly pissed.

"The fuck, man! This is a *business meeting*. I'm coming grown with mine. Ain't we tryin'-a get this paper?"

"I mean, clearly, but, but . . . you don't even wear glasses, man." C.J. looked Black up and down and frowned. "Yo, I'm sorry. You look nuts."

"I'm here to help *you* out, you ungrateful motherfucker.

You told me to look professional, right? How're OutKast's people gonna believe I'm your agent if I'm rocking some young shit?"

C.J. squinted, noticing that the elbows and knees of Black's suit were faded and worn-out-looking. "Whose suit is that?"

Black straightened his tie and grinned. "My grandaddy's."

"Jesus Christ," C.J. exhaled. Yanking his hood over his head, he started pacing back and forth. For the first time in forever, C.J. Parker was nervous. Crazy nervous. And Black's showing up looking like Fonzworth Bentley was not helping.

Two days before, a woman from OutKast's management had called him about using his nude sketch of Izzy for the greatest hits CD cover. The woman, Melanie O'Donnell, had asked to meet with C.J. and his agent today. C.J. was completely cool on the phone—after all, he was basically *born* hustling. It wasn't until after he hung up that reality had set in. And the reality was, there were a thousand things to worry about (and for now, the fact that he was risking expulsion from the school was the least of them). Melanie mentioned the fact that she didn't work with artists who didn't have representation, which meant that C.J. would have to come up with an agent, and fast. At the time, he had thought it was a good idea to ask Blackadocious to pose as his agent, but now he was seriously reconsidering.

With Black in on the OutKast situation, C.J. worried about things spiraling out of control. Especially since the poet and wannabe MC loved to politick. C.J. had briefed him before school, telling him exactly what to say and what not to say ("please, please, *please* keep that power-to-the-people talk to a minimum"), but Black was known for going off on random tangents.

This would either turn out to be the best idea C.J. had ever had, or the worst mistake he'd ever made.

The funny thing was that, until now, C.J. had been pretty blasé about the whole OutKast thing. He had refused to get all excited about it until he saw his sketch on the album cover with his own two eyes. Or even better, until he had the check in his hands. But now that C.J. was in the building, about to negotiate a deal with the biggest hip-hop duo in history, he realized how much he wanted everything to work out. If he got a huge chunk of money from this, he wouldn't have to hustle anymore. Maybe he could get his grandma a better apartment. And as an artist, he could write his own ticket.

But for now, C.J. had to pull it together for this meeting.

"I can't believe *you're* the one trippin' right now." Black was offended by the fact that C.J. had dissed his outfit. "I'm in the middle of a major beef with my girl—and I could be at her house right now, begging her to take my ass back."

"Why're you and Kamillah beefin'?" Clearly, C.J. was stalling. He didn't really care what they were fighting about. Kamillah wasn't his favorite person—he'd never understood why Black wanted to deal with such a gossipy, bossy busybody.

"This *Sixteen Candles* bullshit. I just think it's retarded. I'm sayin', you see what happens to reality stars? I really ain't trying to see some sex tape we did floating around YouTube."

"Y'all got a sex tape?"

"No. I'm just saying." Black was silent for a minute. "You okay with Tangie doing it, too? Kammie told me they're all gonna get, like, serious screen time or whatever. Your sweet little Tangie might never be the same again. Next thing you know, she's gonna be a MySpace celebrity and end up posing for *King* magazine. . . ."

"Man, go 'head with that." C.J. flinched just hearing her name. "Your girl, maybe, but not Tangie. She won't get caught up—she ain't all rah-rah like that."

Black looked at C.J.'s face, which had gotten suddenly serious at the mention of Tangie. "You gonna cry now?"

"Fuck you," he said, checking his watch. If he thought too much about Tangie, he couldn't focus. "Yo, you ready to do this, or what? It's six fifty-five."

"Yep, let's do the damn thing, baby," said Black, amped to play the part of a twentysomething artist's agent.

C.J. didn't like it one bit. "Just please keep it tight, okay?"

Black slapped him on the back as they headed for the front desk. "Who you gonna trust if you can't trust me?"

Minutes later, after showing every piece of ID they owned to security, C.J. and "Will Gates, agent extraordinaire" (it was the most official name Black could think of) were upstairs on the forty-ninth floor, sitting in the huge, beige office of Melanie O'Donnell. She didn't look anything like what C.J. had pictured. She was youngish, maybe around twenty-nine, with pin-straight blond hair, puffy lips, and ginormous breasts that seemed to be silicon-enhanced.

Whatever they were, he couldn't keep his eyes off them.

"I have to tell you, this portrait is *outstanding*." Melanie had a slight lisp, which C.J. thought was sexy. His eyes went from her breasts to her lisping mouth, unable to focus.

Black kneed him, and he jumped a little. "Yeah. Um, thanks. Thank you."

"If you don't mind, who's the model? She's so exotic-looking . . . you know, not the usual video girl or *Maxim* model. Is she a friend?"

"Um, she's just a girl I know."

Black cleared his throat. "Actually, yes," he said, in the corporate voice he'd practiced all the previous night. "She is. That's where the expression 'in his strokes' comes from. He really knows this girl, inside and out. And it shows, wouldn't you say?"

"Oh, yes, it does, Mr. Gates."

C.J. glared at Black, but he wasn't even paying attention. He grabbed the portrait from Melanie's desk and pointed to Izzy's legs. "Do you see the slight muscular definition here, the gorgeous lines? This is pure C.J. This is what you get from him when he's in the zone. He's got stacks of portraits at home, hundreds."

"Well, I have to tell you, Big Boi and André were truly impressed by the work. . . ."

"C.J. is a true renaissance man. He's a writer, too. And he beat-boxes. C.J., hit a beat."

"Nah, man, I'm good," C.J. said, kicking Black hard under the table.

Melanie's eyes sparkled with excitement. "Oh, let me hear it! I love beat-boxing. Like Justin Timberlake?"

Like *Justin Timberlake*? C.J. fought the urge to groan.

"Yeah, he's the beat, and I'm the lyrics," said Black. "Wanna hear us flow?"

"Um, I'm almost positive she doesn't want to hear us flow." C.J. was mortified. "Maybe we should talk about the cover. We don't wanna waste Ms. O'Donnell's . . ."

"Melanie."

"Right. *Melanie's* time."

"Right," said Black, nodding professionally. "So, what were you planning on offering my client for his brilliant artwork?"

Melanie rested her chin on her fist, looking Black directly in the eye. "Well, what were *you* thinking?"

"You know, the other two times he's done covers, he's charged about fifty thousand dollars each." Black was a very talented liar. "Since this is Outkast, I'd love to aim higher, but fifty grand is my starting point."

Melanie sat back in her chair. "That's actually not bad."

C.J.'s stomach lurched. *This can't really be happening*, he thought.

"And you're in high school, yes? I'm not sure what our policy is in terms of hiring people under eighteen. I think we need parental permission, and there are all kinds of child labor laws. . . ."

"I'm eighteen," C.J. piped up.

"Yeah, he's eighteen," said Black quickly. "A senior. He'll be out by the end of the year."

"That's still awfully young. I don't know. . . ."

C.J. leaned forward. "I might be young, Ms. O'Donnell, but you ain't gonna find another cat can do what I do."

She smirked a little, obviously impressed by his forwardness. "Is that right?"

C.J. looked her in the eye and held up his notepad. The whole time Black and Melanie were talking, he'd been silently drawing away. When she saw the sketch, her jaw dropped and her hand went over her heart, as if she were about to say the Pledge of Allegiance. The picture was a slightly abstract portrait of Melanie sitting at her desk—and she'd never seen herself look so beautiful. C.J.'s sketch was a reflection of her very best self, the woman she was on her hottest, sexiest day. She couldn't believe that some kid had managed to see all that in her!

Awestruck, she reached across the table and took the notepad from C.J. (was that a tear glistening in the corner of her eye?) And at that moment, he knew he had her. It was almost too easy.

"You like it?"

"*Ohhh, Seee Jaaay.* It's . . . it's remarkable. I've never . . . I mean, how did you . . ."

Black sat back and smiled, watching C.J. in action. Clearly he didn't need him anymore.

C.J. shrugged. "I had an inspiring subject. What, you never had your portrait done?"

"No. I . . . well, I never had a reason to."

"A damned shame," he said, his gaze traveling slowly from

her eyes to her chest and back up again. "What a waste."

Melanie blushed and giggled. "You're a piece of work, aren't you?"

"You have no idea," said Black, rolling his eyes.

"So, we got a deal?"

Still gazing at her portrait, she said, "Yeah, yeah, of course."

"One thing, though," said C.J. "I don't like to use my real name on my work. I'm, uh, just a private-type person, I guess."

"What name would you like me to use?"

"Donatello." It was the name the older boys in his building had called him when he was little and used to draw chalkboard masterpieces on the sidewalk.

"Donatello it is," Melanie said with a slow smile. In seconds, her entire body language had changed from businessey to flirty. She settled back in her chair and slipped a foot out of her stiletto, rubbing it up and down her leg. "You're really cute, you know. Did anyone ever tell you you look like that 'Run It!' boy? Chris Brown?"

"Did anyone ever tell you you look like Jessica Simpson?"

Her eyes flashed. "Let's stay in touch, okay?"

"Absolutely," C.J. said, shaking her hand.

As Melanie showed them out, he felt her slip a tiny piece of paper into the pocket of his hoodie. Once they were outside, he read the note:

"Call me, C.J. 212-555-7834."

Girls, thought C.J. *Whether they're thirty or thirteen, they're all the same.*

* * *

Tangie was sitting cross-legged on her bedroom floor, jotting down some of the steps she'd already put together for Skye's grand entrance routine. When she got home from Skye's, she raced through her homework and immediately began dancing in front of her bedroom mirror, choreographing the beginning of the piece. It was almost too much excitement to take! *I, boring little Tangie Adams from Fort Greene, am performing my very own routine on MVN*, she thought, *in front of the entire world!* How had she gotten so lucky?

Suddenly, Tangie saw her entire life as a dancer pass before her eyes. She flashed back to being five again, falling in the shower and breaking her arm in an attempt to do the Bankead Bounce from TLC's "Waterfalls" video. And then she was eight, performing the choreography from Aaliyah's "Are You That Somebody?" in the playground with Skye and witnessing with delight, for the first time in the history of their friendship, that *no one* was looking at Skye. Now she was twelve, wearing only a training bra and biker shorts, and *murdering* Britney's sexy "Slave 4 U" routine until her curls frizzed out into a crazy helmet (the next morning, she attended her confirmation looking like Macy Gray). Finally, she saw herself as a fourteen-year-old the previous January, dancing *Sweet Charity*'s "Rich Man's Frug" at her Armstrong audition, and knowing in her bones that she'd be accepted for her sophomore year—because when Tangie danced, no one could touch her.

She was a *dancer*, damn it. It was her destiny, her calling. No matter what craziness was going down in her personal life, she always had that to hold on to.

And, speaking of her personal life . . .

There was only one person who'd understand her excitement. She dropped her notebook and grabbed her cell from her bed. Smiling to herself, she began texting a message to C.J.—and caught herself the second before she hit SEND.

"Shit, shit, shit!" she cried out, quickly erasing the message. What was she thinking? She and C.J. were *so* not like that anymore! *He and his penis have moved on to Izzy*, she reminded herself. *Besides, I'm mad at him.* And that reminded her—how dead wrong was that of Skye, making her ask C.J. about the mural? Deep down, she knew her best friend was just trying to get them talking again, but it wasn't going to work. It was over.

Tangie felt the tears welling up behind her eyes, but she refused to let them fall. God, she missed him so much, but what could she do? C.J. was a distracted, tortured artist, a too-intense-for-his-own-good, natural-born hustler whose itty-bitty attention span prevented him from staying with one girl for more than twelve seconds. C.J. Parker was not about commitment; she *knew* that. How many times over the years had she helped him figure out the nicest way to tell some poor, lovesick slut that she was "cool, but he wasn't trying to get all official?"

The funny thing was, knowing that didn't change the fact that she fantasized about their being a legitimate couple—for real, boyfriend and girlfriend—all damn day. And it really didn't change the fact that the first and only time he had kissed her, she'd felt it in her toenails.

Oh, that kiss! Afterward, Tangie had seriously been two seconds from handing C.J. her virginity on a platter. *He said he loved me that night,* she thought sadly. *Didn't that mean anything?* Apparently not, because the very next day he sketched a beautiful, butt-ass-naked picture of Izzy.

And that was when her ring tone blared, making her jump a foot off her bed in surprise. She had to look twice at the screen before she could believe who was calling her.

"H—hello?"

"What's good witchu, Dimples? It's Trey."

Tangie's mouth went dry. "Trey?"

"What, you can't hear me? It's Trey!" he hollered.

"No—I mean, yeah—I can hear you." God, why did it still feel so awkward talking to him? He certainly wasn't a stranger anymore—she had to get over the whole "oh, my God, it's Trey Adams" thing. "How are you?"

"Just tryin' to live, mama, you know how I do. But I wanted to axe you something. I'm missing my Panamanian-flag do-rag. . . . I was thinking maybe you accidentally took it after one of our tutoring sessions."

"Are you Panamanian?"

"You gotta be Panamanian to rock a Panamanian do-rag?"

"Um, I guess not, but . . ."

"You seen it anywhere?"

"Actually no, I haven't."

"Daaamn." He strung out the word so that it lasted three syllables. "That's extra ill. Well, anyway, what's good witchu?"

"You asked me that already." She realized she'd been holding her breath a little, so she exhaled. "Trey, did you really call to ask about your do-rag?"

A silence followed. "No," he admitted; Tangie could tell he was smiling. *Okay,* she thought, *that's kind of cute.*

"I was calling to tell you . . . Look, I wasn't bullshitting today at school, ya heard? I seriously and officially, like, miss you."

"Seriously and officially, huh?"

"I'm sayin', remember how tight our tutoring sessions were? We used to kill some choreography, Dimples." He paused again, and Tangie could almost hear him smile. "Remember we had that beef about Omarion versus Usher?"

Tangie smiled in spite of herself. "I still kinda think Usher's the best. Just on versatility alone."

"Girl, you trippin'. Omarion's a straight *beast* with the pop-and-lock. You *know* this! Besides, you wanna talk about versatility? I heard this kid's gonna star in *Chicago* on Broadway."

"Oh, really? That's amazing," said Tangie. "Yeah, I guess you're right. Usher's annoying." But that was not what she thought at all. And she knew Trey had his facts wrong—Usher was the one slated to star in *Chicago* in the summer of '06. But for some reason, she didn't correct him.

It was weird. She'd noticed that, around Trey, she pretended not to know anything. Tangie knew it was bad, but she couldn't help it. He made her nervous.

"See, man? See how we talk when we together? Tangie, I don't vibe like this with nobody else. Don't you miss what we had together, girl?"

Tangie was stunned. Number one, the reality was that their little almost-relationship had barely lasted a week. There really wasn't a lot to miss! Number two, Trey Stevens could have had any girl in the school (hell, in the city!) that he wanted—so, really, why Tangie? Why not some other senior, a hottie who had sex and maybe a fake ID to offer? Some fast girl who knew how to hook up with a boy without sending him to the emergency room (sadly, the first and *only* time Tangie had tried to go near a boy's penis, it was Trey's—and she'd practically ripped it off. He was okay, but she was still emotionally black-and-blue).

Tangie would never figure out why this intimidating, drop-dead-gorgeous older boy paid so much attention to her. And the crazy thing was, she'd always had a crush on him, in a far-away, celebrity-worship kind of way (when she and Skye were in middle school, they used to spy on him and Eden making out in the Carmichaels' living room, and she would get all kinds of mysterious tingles in mysterious places). It boggled Tangie's mind that her fantasy crush from seventh grade was now begging her to consider dating him.

But did it really matter why? The truth was, talking to Trey—as dumb as he was—made her feel, well, *A-list*. The fact that a popular senior liked her made her feel like That Girl. You know, the one with the right clothes, the right body, and the right boys hollering at her. Basically, Kyndra on *Laguna Beach*. And right now, drowning in misery over her used-to-be true love C.J., she wouldn't have minded going for a stroll in Kyndra's Charles David stilettos.

But even a girl as boy-clueless as Tangie knew that she had to play hard to get, a little. Especially when she was dealing with a guy who was constantly surrounded by a giggling clique of leotard-clad freshmen whom people referred to as Serving Treys.

Tangie was no Serving Trey.

"Okay, it's true," she said, choosing her words carefully, "we had fun when you were my tutor. But I know all about your reputation. I just don't think I can trust you."

"Yes, you can. And you will." He paused. "Real talk? I can't stop thinking about you. I'm a fucking wreck. Look, just give your boy another chance. I already got a sprained ACL, why you want me to suffer even more?"

"You're crazy, Trey," said Tangie, giggling. (And it was unlike any giggle she'd ever heard come out of her mouth—all dainty and flirty, not the honking blast of a laugh she was known for.) "Look, maybe we'll talk tomorrow after school or something."

"Where you gonna be?"

"I'm practicing in Studio 7 for Skye's *Sixteen Candles* routine, but . . ."

"Cool, I'll meet you after."

"Um . . . okay, cool," said Tangie, but inside she was screaming, *no-o-o-o!* Ugh, she'd be all sweaty and gross from practice, and her hair would be a frizzy mess. But she felt like she had to go along with what he wanted. Trey was older and more popular than her—and when it came down to it, wasn't Tangie lucky that he even liked her? She hated to admit it, but she didn't want to give him a reason to change his mind.

"Oh, and T.?"

"Yeah?"

"Can I be honest for a second?"

"I guess so."

"I ain't been this sick over a shorty since Eden. So don't break a brutha's heart."

Tangie could feel her face flush all the way to her hairline. Eden had been his One True Love. Was Trey really comparing Tangie to *her*? "I don't—I don't really know what to say."

"Don't say anything, Dimples. Just think about it, and I'll get at you tomorrow. One."

And then he hung up, leaving Tangie confused and exhausted. She had no idea whether or not she should take him seriously. Was this the line he used on all the girls?

What if it *wasn't*?

"How ya livin', Grandma P.?" C.J. walked into the kitchen in his grandmother's tiny one-and-a-half-bedroom apartment. He'd lived there since he was seven, after his mom's death. Since he barely remembered his mother and had never known his father, C.J. considered the eighty-year-old, dangerously asthmatic woman his parent.

"*What?*" Besides having breathing problems, Grandma Parker couldn't hear a damned thing.

"I said, how are you?" C.J. shouted. He walked over to the stove, where she was frying steak, and gave the tiny, wheezing woman a kiss on the cheek.

"I'm fine. Jesus, you always mutterin'. This ain't no movie theater, boy, you don't hafta whisper."

He grinned. "Did you get your blood test today?"

"Did I get my butt rest today?"

C.J. had to bite the inside of his cheek to keep from laughing.

"I said, did you get your blood test?"

"Oh. No. I don't need no blood test."

"What? Yes, you do. Remember Dr. Franklin's testing you for that new medicine? Ms. Miller said she was gonna stop by and take you to the hospice. What happened?"

Grandma Parker waved her hand. "Oh, I told her to go on. I ain't felt like going nowhere today. Besides, I need new shoes before I go back to that hospice." She looked down at her scuffed orthopedic flats. "I don't want Dr. Franklin thinkin' we got financial problems."

"I'll get you new shoes, Grandma. But promise me you'll go tomorrow."

"What? You said it's gonna snow tomorrow? Oh, hell."

"I said promise me you'll *go* tomorrow. *To the hospice!*" C.J. yelled. "I'll get you new shoes after school, a-iight?"

"Fine." She flipped the steak, wheezing heavily. "Now stop hoverin'. My steak needs to breathe."

"*You* need to breathe, woman," he muttered, walking out of the kitchen.

"I heard that!"

She hears me when I'm halfway across the room, thought C.J., *but up close she thinks I'm telling her butt to rest.*

His grandmother was out of her mind, but he loved her. The difference between Grandma Parker (his father's mother), and Grandma Mellon, the grandmother he shared with Skye and Eden, was incredible. Grandma Mellon was seventy-nine, looked fifty, and took salsa lessons three times a week. She also lived in a beachside villa in Malibu, and she had thrown a $100,000 wedding for her two Chihuahuas the previous year. It really was crazy how having a little bit of money could change everything.

And if everything went right with OutKast, C.J. and Grandma Parker were about to know exactly what that felt like.

C.J. plopped down on his bed, his hands clasped behind his head, as he mentally reviewed the day. He couldn't believe that the meeting with Melanie O'Donnell had gone so well (her note was still burning a hole in his pocket)—and that Black hadn't ruined the negotiations with his ridiculous freestyling. C.J. would cuss him out for that later, but right now, he was too excited to care. For all he knew, this would be his last day as C.J. Parker, around-the-way boy and drug dealer with a heart of gold.

On his way home, he stopped by Kevvy-Kev's office outside of Not Ray's Pizza to pick up a bag of weed. Kevvy-Kev, Bed-Stuy's premier weed guy, was not only C.J.'s boss, he was also famous for having the best stuff in Brooklyn. As he made his transaction, C.J. promised himself that this would be the last time he'd buy a bunch of weed to sell. The only reason he hustled anyway was that, at fifteen, he was in the bizarre position of having to pay the rent *and* Grandma Parker's medical expenses. And his Tower Records salary would hardly cover Grandma's damn shoes.

But after this last batch, C.J. decided he'd never sell drugs again. When he got that $50,000 check, his life was going to change. First of all, he'd move Grandma Parker out of the projects—he'd rent a huge duplex apartment in a ritzier neighborhood, something with an extra room for his art. Maybe he'd do some Web research and figure out how to invest. Something he would *not* do with his money? Buy a blingy Jesus-piece. C.J. saw what happened to the so-called ballers in the neighborhood when they got a little bit of paper—they'd blow it all on jewelry, clothes, girls, and cars, and then quickly go broke. Yep, it was the definition of "hood rich."

And that *so* wasn't going to be C.J.

Feeling inspired, he dragged his oversize sketch pad out from under his bed, flipped back the top page, and started drawing his foot, which was his charcoal sketching class homework. Every time he started, though, he'd get distracted thinking about his OutKast deal, and his eyes would wander around his tiny bedroom. Actually, it wasn't really a bedroom—it was more like a biggish closet. The only furniture that fit in it was a child-size twin bed and a four-drawer dresser. Despite its tiny size, every available surface of C.J.'s room was plastered with his art. The ceiling, the walls, the floor, the door—the entire room was a cluttered collection of funky, spray-painted graffiti; beautiful charcoal portraits; paintings of elaborate city scenes; scraps of random things he'd drawn; and magazine clippings of stuff that inspired him.

And then there was C.J.'s top secret, ultra-down-low Tangie collage—a messy, slapped-together collection of drawings displayed in the space above his bed. He'd started the collage back in sixth grade and had never been able to bring himself to take it down, not even when they were fighting (which was half the time). The space was cluttered with portrait after portrait of Tangie's face, each one different from the last. Some were in color, some black and white; a few were cartoony, others were more realistic; but together, they were like a timeline of the way Tangie had changed throughout the years.

When she and he were eleven, she had had braces and glasses and hadn't yet learned how to control her head full of curls. But to C.J., Tangie was the prettiest girl he'd ever seen. And about two dozen random hookups later, that was still true. Her face was just inspiring—he could always find something new to focus on. When C.J. was stuck working on a piece, all he had to do was stare at the Tangie wall for a minute, and without fail he would find his muse again.

The funny thing was, Tangie had never seen the collage. Absolutely *no one* had. When people came over, C.J. covered it with an enormous Megan Good poster. He just wasn't really prepared for folks to think he was that whipped over *anyone*. Especially over a chick he'd never even had sex with. How would that look?

Gazing around his room, C.J. realized that art had always brought him good luck. Every positive thing that happened in his life was a result of his artwork. He had learned at a young age that he could get any chick he wanted simply by whipping up some overcomplimentary portrait of her (exhibit A: Melanie O'Donnell). His pieces had gained him entry into some of the

best schools in New York City. And now, a homework assignment for charcoal sketching class had possibly gotten him not
only $50,000, but perhaps also fame, success, and notoriety! If
that wasn't good luck, he didn't know what was. And really,
when he was working, it *did* feel like a higher force was working through him. When he picked up a pencil, a spray-paint
can, or a paintbrush and created beautiful stuff, sometimes it
felt as if he didn't even try. He just *went* with it.

That's why, when C.J. got the call from Melanie O'Donnell,
he didn't think to say no, despite Armstrong's stupid rule
against working professionally while in school. Who *knew*
where art, his good-luck charm, would take him this time? His
work was going to be printed on millions of CD's all over the
world! That kind of exposure was downright life-changing.

C.J. could find a real agent (ahem, not "Will Gates") and
start commissioning his work for more hip-hop covers, movie
posters, advertising stuff, anything. And eventually, he'd bank
enough paper make to show his paintings and graffiti at a fancy
gallery in SoHo and become the darling of the downtown art
world. He'd go from being a street kid obsessed with graffiti to
being a bona fide art world star, beloved by the masses (just like
his idol, '80s street art and graffiti pioneer Basquiat!). So, no,
C.J. didn't think twice about risking getting expelled. It was a
chance he was ready to take.

And besides, C.J. wasn't trying to think about what would
happen if his luck ran out. If, by some crazy accident, Principal
Fischer found out about the OutKast cover and expelled his ass,
what then? All his life had been spent working to get into

Louis Armstrong Academy of Performing and Creative Arts, the school that would give him opportunities he couldn't get anywhere else. He'd have had to start over at PS 431, a high school so abysmal that 25 percent of the sophomore class was pregnant, some for the second time. In spite of the metal detectors and security guards on every floor, the violence at the school was *miserable*. One of his boys had gotten stabbed in the arm at lunch, and he knew a girl who had actually tried to shoot her geography teacher (she had missed and hit the window, which still wasn't fixed a year later. Try memorizing the names of countries in Africa when it's ten degrees out, there's no heat, and snow is coming through a shattered window). Art programs were the last thing PS 431 was concerned with. C.J. would have slipped through the cracks, and everything he was working for would have been lost.

I won't think about that now, C.J. told himself while shading in a sketch of his foot. *I ain't got no reason to believe my winning streak is over.*

Right now, he was going to draw the best foot he could, sell off his last bag of weed, and look forward to moving up in the world—maybe sooner than he thought.

6.

THE NAME ON EVERYBODY'S LIPS

LUNCH HAD STARTED TWENTY minutes earlier, but food was the furthest thing from Skye's mind. It was Wednesday, and the most important event in her life (well, next to her future wedding to T.I.) was popping off in *three days*. She had tons of preparing to do! And the first order of business was perfecting her grand-entrance monologue.

In the best *Sixteen Candles* episodes, the birthday girl did some kind of performance (most of them embarrassing white-girl attempts at doing some hip-hop dance). But none of the girls, so far, had been trained actresses. Skye planned to wipe them all out with her performance of Roxie Hart's crowd-pleasing monologue from the Broadway musical and hit movie *Chicago*. With its story line about a wannabe nightclub performer in the 1930s, surrounded by seedy gangsters and gorgeous glamour girls, *Chicago* fit her theme perfectly. And Roxie Hart's speech about wanting to be the world's biggest star was perfect for Skye! It would truly sound as if she were speaking from the heart.

But even the best actresses needed coaching, so Skye asked her crush, Nick, to help her out. A few things about Nick: not only did he have the most swoonworthy looks (messy black curls, tanned Mediterranean skin, and turquoise eyes—delish!) and kick-ass style (vintage Adidas, concert T-shirts, and blazers—so Justin!), he also happened to be an incredible actor. So, it was only *natural* that she had asked him to coach her, right?

Wrong. This was a sneaky move on Skye's part, and she knew it. After unsuccessfully throwing herself at him during her Back to School party, Skye had promised Nick that she'd respect his long-distance relationship with somebody else (even though she thought that any girl naive enough to believe that her movie-star-beautiful boyfriend would be faithful a zillion miles away *deserved* to get cheated on). Skye had every intention of pursuing Nick, but she had to revise her initial plan. This time, she was going to play the "friend" card. They'd spend quality time together practicing her monologue, and then, when he saw her looking impossibly stunning at her party, he'd obviously have to jump her bones.

Good plan, right?

In the meantime, though, it was all about prepping for her Roxie Hart speech; Skye was onstage in one of the drama department's small rehearsal theaters, as Nick watched her from the first row.

"I *always* wanted to have my name in all the papuhs," began Skye-as-Roxie, in a breathy, bimbo-ish New Yawk accent. "You know, all my life, I wanted to have my own act. Oh, it's *such* a special night! And you're such a great audience. . . ."

Nick cleared his throat, interrupting her. "Hey, Skye? That's really good, but I'd make it just a little bigger, you know what I'm saying? Roxie is a down-on-her-luck chorus girl. This is her one big chance to really make it. She's really gonna go there."

"Oh, my God, *yes*, I totally agree. You're *so* right, Nick." Skye paused, wondering if she was overdoing it. "Should I keep going?"

"Yeah, definitely. From the 'name on everybody's lips' part."

"The name on everybody's lips is gonna be . . . Roxie! The lady . . ."

Nick waved his hand for her to stop. "Hold up, you forgot to say *your* name instead of Roxie's!"

"Ugh, did I do that? Sorry," Skye said, smiling to herself. She'd made that mistake on purpose. If there was one thing she'd learned from her mom, it was that boys liked to feel as if you were lost without them. She took a deep breath and started over.

"The name on everybody's lips is gonna be . . . *Skye*! The lady raking in the chips is gonna be . . . *Skye*! I'm gonna be a celebrity; that means somebody everyone knows. They're gonna recognize my eyes, my hair, my teeth, my boobs, my nose. . . ."

That girl was born to be a star, thought Nick as he watched Skye absolutely kill the monologue. He was *so* relieved that they'd made up, because he really did like her. Her style, her clothes, her sassiness—he loved it all. Skye was fabulous! And finally, they were strictly friends, which was a load off his mind. It had become a little too hard to hide the fact that he was gay. Especially when she had found that horrible DVD in his bag—*Mandingo Madness*. Jesus, that was embarrassing. The thing that worried Nick the most, though, was that Skye had never asked him about it. It was *killing* him, but what could he do? If she was willing to sweep it under the rug, then, dammit, so was he.

Watching her up there, throwing her boa around like the diva she was, Nick couldn't help getting excited about her party. It was a dream for him to get all dressed up in a sharp pin-striped suit and a fedora. He'd already had the perfect suit for the costume, too—he'd simply had it tailored back in D.C. when he took his cousin to the prom.

Nick had already planned to ask Regina to be his date for the party. From the second he met the adorable filmmaker-to-be, he had known they'd be friends for life. He'd just arrived in New York City from Washington, D.C., and, not knowing anyone, he'd decided to join a top secret support group in SoHo for gay, lesbian, bi, and transgender teens. At one of his first meetings, he'd met Regina—a really sweet girl who had a feeling she might be a lesbian. When they realized they were both Armstrong tenth graders, Nick and Regina had decided their friendship was obviously meant to be! And their bond ran even deeper than anyone suspected—Regina was the only person in New York who knew Nick was gay, and vice versa. And they'd sworn to take it to the grave (a good thing, since Nick's Greek Orthodox parents had sent him to live with his butch, carpenter uncle in New York, hoping to "straighten" him out; and if that didn't work, they planned to send him to live with his hairy grandma in Greece).

Just then, Nick saw Skye accidentally drop her boa—and remembered that he was supposed to be coaching her.

"Shit, that's the third time I did that!" She stamped her foot and folded her arms across her chest, furious.

Nick jumped out of his seat and climbed onstage, standing next to her. "Here, try it like this," he said, throwing on her boa and taking her place in front of the microphone. Perfectly, he coached her through the monologue, showing her where her hands and feet should be at all times.

Skye stood there with her mouth open, shocked at how brilliantly Nick imitated her.

"Oh, my God, Nick!"

"What?"

"You're totally going to win an Oscar one day."

He smiled and bowed. "Thanks, sweetie. I've just seen *Chicago*, like, four hundred times. You know I love musical theater, girl. And . . ." he abruptly stopped talking, his head cocked toward the theater door. "Do you hear that?" he said.

Skye shrugged; suddenly she did hear something. It sounded like a faraway roar. They looked at each other for a moment, then rushed offstage and over to the door. Nick opened it a crack and saw dozens and dozens of kids clustered together, all trying to get a look through the sliver of window in the door. A bunch of them had their camera phones poised to take a shot.

As soon as they saw Nick and Skye, the crowd attempted to push through the door, everyone talking at once.

"Are you guys filming in there? Yo, where the cameras at?"

"Let us in, we just wanna be extras! We won't say anything!"

"Come on, Skye, you *do* know me, we have the same life coach!"

Both overwhelmed and weirdly flattered, Skye hollered, "Calm down, everybody! Look, we're just rehearsing. . . . It's against MVN rules to film during school. See me in two days, when I pass out invites. Spread the word, okay? Peace!"

Skye and Nick finally pushed the door all the way shut. Then they looked at each other and burst out laughing.

"Oh, my God, now I know what it's like to be attacked by the paparazzi," said Nick, giggling and excited.

"I know, right? I feel so famous! I'm a star, I'm a star!" Skye clapped her hands and jumped up and down, totally giddy. Then, overcome with excitement, she flung her arms around Nick's neck and gave him a definitely-more-than-friends hug. Always the gentleman, he hugged her back, then slowly pulled away.

No longer giggling, Skye cast her eyes up at Nick and pouted, giving him her sexiest "kiss me" face.

"Really, Skye, I just want to be friends," he said quietly. "Is that cool?"

She looked at him for a couple seconds, and then took a deep breath. *It's now or never*, she thought. "Nick, can I ask you something?"

"Sure," he said, his stomach in knots. *Please, don't ask me what I think you're going to ask me*, he silently prayed.

"The night of my party, I found something in your bag. A tape called *Mandingo Madness*. The cover had three naked black men doing jumping jacks on a beach."

Nick felt his knees go weak. "What were you doing in my bag?"

"I know, it was dead wrong. I was drunk, and actually, I don't even remember what I was doing." She shook her head. "But Nick, what was that all about?"

He'd been anticipating this question for weeks, so he had an explanation ready. "You know I live with my uncle, right? That was his bag. He has a film production company, and they make these crazy triple X videos."

"Really?"

"Yeah, I was running late to your party, and I accidentally grabbed it on the way out."

Skye nodded. "Are you sure?"

"You know what? This isn't about me, it's about you," he said, exasperated. "You refuse to believe that I love my girlfriend back home! I'm just a faithful boyfriend, that's all. How many times do I have to tell you?"

"Wait . . . wait, I'm sorry. God, I'm so embarrassed! I didn't mean to hurt your feelings. Forgive me? *Pleaaase?*"

"Okay, fine."

"Friends?"

"Friends." He sighed, relieved that he was in the clear.

"Hey, friend," said Skye, smiling sweetly. "Can I ask you something else?"

"Oh, no." Nick grimaced, pretending to start sprinting out of the room. "What now?"

"No, no no," she said, giggling, grabbing his arm. "It's nothing like that. I, um, wanted to know if you'd be my 'gangster.' You know, be my escort at my Sweet Sixteen. It's no pressure or anything. You'll just hang out with me in VIP and ride with me in the limo and take pictures. It'll be fun."

Nick smiled, flashing his heart-stoppingly perfect teeth. He'd wanted to go with Regina, but if being Skye's date drove home his straightness, then he was down for it.

"Sure, I'll be your gangster." What he didn't say was, *I'd rather be your showgirl.*

Lunch was almost over, and Tangie decided to stop by the theater to walk with Skye to history. She peeked in the window and saw something that surprised her. Skye was sitting in the front row, clapping and giggling delightedly as Nick flounced around onstage, wearing her pink boa.

Her mouth dropped open slowly and her bag slipped off her arm onto the floor. Ever since she and Izzy had met Nick, whom they adored, she'd wondered if he might possibly be gay. His outfits were a little *too* fashiony perfect, and on more than one occasion, he had used the word *fierce.*

"Oh, my God," she whispered. "Oh, my God, it's true. *He is.* And how the hell does Skye not see it?"

She couldn't stop having the giggles, so she hurried away.

As usual, Studio 7 was packed. Every Armstrong dancer knew

that if she wanted to get in a good couple of hours of independent rehearsal after school, they needed to sign up for studio time at the beginning of the day. By about eight in the morning each day, most of the twenty-five slots were taken. But everyone also knew that Ms. Carmen would make special exceptions if your argument were convincing enough.

Roughly two seconds after Skye had asked Tangie to choreograph her grand entrance number, she'd gone to Ms. Carmen and begged for Studio 7 time. "You don't understand, Ms. Carmen," she'd begged. "I only have three days to choreograph this routine and teach it to my girlfriends!"

"Explain this to me, chicken. Why is it that all I've been hearing about is this *Sixteen Candles* show, when you have final Spotlight auditions next Friday? Is MVN gonna give you a dancing gig after you graduate?"

"Well, no. But here's the thing. . . ."

"No, *here's* the thing," snapped Ms. Carmen. "The Spotlight performances are the only chance you have to showcase your talent individually. Do you want to jeopardize that?"

"Of course not! Believe me, I know how lucky I am to even be auditioning for Spotlight—and I've been practicing nonstop. But this is *MVN*. It's a onetime thing, a chance for the entire world to see me dance! Please, Ms. Carmen, all I need is, like, an hour. Or two, at the most. *Pleeaaase?*"

If there was one thing Ms. Carmen couldn't stand, it was whining.

"Fine."

"Really?"

"On one condition. I'll expect you to see you at every single one of my Spotlight master classes until the auditions." The Spotlight master classes were scheduled after school on Monday, Wednesday, and Friday. And Tangie had been to all of them, so far.

"Of course! I wouldn't miss them."

Ms. Carmen pursed her lips as if to say, *we'll see about that,* and added Tangie's name to the Studio 7 sign-up sheet.

And now, Tangie had carved out a tiny space for herself near the far window. She had about five inches of barre and a square four feet of dance space. Like every other dancer in the studio, Tangie'd tucked her iPod mini down the front of her leotard and was listening through her earphones as she danced. *What the hell did folks did in the nineties,* she wondered, *back when you had to bring your stereo and fight to hear your music over everyone else's?*

Skye's grand entrance song was "Don't Cha," but with a twist. Eden's best friend, Marisol, who was an excellent singer, was recording a Skye-centric version of the Pussycat Dolls' hit song for the party, changing the lyrics to *"Don't you wish your girlfriend was hot like SKYE?/Don't you wish your girlfriend was a freak like SKYE?/Don't cha?"* It was hysterical, and perfect for Skye.

Tangie had eight eight-counts to work with and had already choreographed six of them. She, Kamillah and Regina were going to be all dressed up in ultrarevealing 1930s showgirl costumes—lots of feathers, sequins, and cleavage—so she'd come up with a combination that reflected that glamour-puss image. At the same time, though, she had tried to keep it simple enough that Kamillah and Regina, two nondancers, could not only get the steps but look hot doing them, too. For inspiration, Tangie had stayed up all night studying her *Chicago* DVD and old episodes of *So You Think You Can Dance* that she'd taped. After stealing some moves here and there and combining a bit of jazz with hip-hop and Broadway dance, Tangie was sure she'd come up with the sickest, sexiest routine ever!

After practicing for almost two hours straight, Tangie was sweaty, dog-tired, and out of breath. She sat on the floor against the mirror, gulped down a liter bottle of water, and casually took in the room. There were ballerinas rehearsing a piece from *Romeo and Juliet*; a couple of B-boys bouncing around on their heads; a pimply-faced clogger; and a bunch of overly dramatic lyrical dancers flinging themselves around the room (to Tangie, lyrical dancers always looked as if they'd set themselves on fire).

They were all so different, yet so brilliant. And Tangie was one of them! Or was she? She looked down at her almost-D boobs, tiny waist, and curvy hips. Despite her feverish dieting—if she ate one more rice cake, she'd shoot someone—she was still bigger than everyone else in the studio, including some of the boys. Suddenly, a shudder of self-doubt coursed through her body. Was she really good enough to do this? What if Skye had been wrong to trust her with this routine? God, what if she made her best friend look like a fool on national TV?

A gruff voice came over the loudspeaker: *"Studio 7 dancers, you have twenty minutes until closing; twenty minutes until closing!"* Tangie didn't have time for self-doubt. Instead, she started

"Don't Cha" over and performed her routine full out, one last time. Once she got in the zone like this, it was as if no one else existed on earth. It was just Tangie and the mirror, working it out.

How was she supposed to know she was being watched?

The second Tangie hit her ending pose, she looked up in the mirror and saw Trey standing behind her. His deliciously muscular arms were folded across his chest, and he was grinning at her. Slowly, he started to clap. Whipping around to face him, she blurted out, "What are *you* doing here?"

"What you yelling for?"

Realizing her headphones were still on, Tangie ripped them out of her ears and lowered her voice. "How long have you been watching me?"

"Oh, 'bout fifteen."

She became instantly aware that she was soaked with sweat, her hair was a frizzy pouf on top of her head, and she probably smelled. She'd thought he was meeting her *after* practice, once she'd had a chance to shower! Grabbing a towel from her dance bag, she wiped down her face and subtly backed away from him.

He looked amused. "Whatchu doing?"

"What do you mean? I'm trying to clean up, I'm disgusting."

"No, you ain't," said Trey, snatching the towel from her hands. "You a dime, ma. I like it when you're all sweaty. You look like you been working hard."

"I have been." She smiled, wearily. "I'm choreographing a routine for Skye."

"Oh, yeah. She's doing *Sixteen Candles*, right? Everybody's talking about that. She's like a minor celebrity this week."

"This week?"

Trey nodded. "I seen it all before. She ain't the first Armstrong kid to get a reality show; it's no big thing. Right now she's feeling herself and getting all flossy, but next month it'll be about somebody else. If you ain't noticed yet, Dimples, this ain't no regular school." He looked around, then gestured for her to come closer.

Tangie inched forward, and Trey leaned into her ear. "See that girl over there? The pale one with the red mullet and the polka-dot leotard? Last year, when she was a junior, she lied about her age and went on *America's Next Top Model*."

She squinted at the tall, punky-looking redhead practicing her jetés. "Oh, my God! I totally remember her! She was the one that put Ex-Lax in the bitchy Asian girl's lasagna, so she'd have, um, well . . . the runs at their first photo shoot."

Trey laughed. "Say *runs* again."

"*Ewww!*" She giggled, feeling her cheeks burning.

"No, it sounded cute comin' from you." He scratched his cheek, wanting to get down to business. "So, why you avoiding me?"

"I'm not avoiding you, I'm just busy."

"Please, girl. I tried to holler at you after street funk, and you bounced. I texted you during lunch and never heard back. I ain't used to this abuse, ma. What's it all about?"

Tangie shrugged. She couldn't tell him the truth, which was that she didn't know how to act around him. Somehow, whenever Trey spoke to her, her personality mysteriously changed. Maybe things would have been easier if she hadn't known he'd dated *perfection* for four years—or if she hadn't known that, during those four years, he'd hit on half the dance department.

"You still don't know if you should trust me, right?"

"It's not that. . . ." she began. *Oh, well,* she thought, *I might as well say it.* "Okay, yeah, it is that. Look, I know the type of girl a guy like you goes for. And that's not me."

"How you know what I 'go for'?"

"You have a reputation. Don't act like you don't know."

"So? You got a reputation, too."

"Shut up. No, I don't."

"Fine, I'll let you tell it," Trey said, shrugging.

Tangie was dying of curiosity. "Okay, what is it? Tell me."

"You're the cute, sexy virgin with the crazy ass that don't give niggas the time of day." He grinned at her. "At the beginning of each year, there's a list the senior guys pass around rating the baddest broads in each class, and you're right up in there. You and Edie's sis and that punky homeless chick you run around with."

She looked at the floor, feeling her ears get hot. Please, God, don't let it be obvious how flattered I am, she silently prayed. "I still don't get it," she said, lowering her voice. "I mean, you could have any girl in this school."

"I don't want them." He looked her in the eye. "Why it's so hard to believe I'm really feeling you?"

He was right. She was playing this all wrong, acting as if

she weren't good enough for him! If she'd learned anything from Izzy, it was that you never let the guy have the upper hand. *I bet she's never asked C.J. why he likes her,* she thought. *She just goes with it, too cool to care. That's how I need to be.*

So she changed the subject.

"What are you doing here, anyway?"

"I was tutoring Lettuce Harris."

"Lettuce? Is that his name?"

"His name's Tommy, but we call him Lettuce 'cause he don't weigh nothing." He nodded in Tommy's direction. Tommy was *maybe* five feet tall and about ninety pounds—and he was spinning on top of his head, like an out-of-control dreidel. "His tap game is crazy, but he wants to transfer to hip-hop or breakin'. Ms. Carmen's making me tutor his ass. Something about it helping my character."

"He's cute," said Tangie, giggling.

"I might as well tell you, Dimples," he started. "Your choreo is off the chain."

"Really?" She smiled up at him. "You're not just saying that?"

"No, I'd tell you if it was wack. I'm really impressed. Especially with this part." He quickly marked through one of her combinations from memory.

She giggled again. "No, it's like this." She repeated the combination, ending with a show-offy triple pirouette and knocking into him, on purpose. The only time Tangie really felt comfortable flirting with Trey was when they were dancing. It was like they'd finally found common ground.

Everywhere else, she felt as if he was on a totally different level, and it turned her into a bundle of nerves.

"Hold up, don't forget who was tutoring who," he said jokily. "You think you're *better* than me? Is that it?"

"No, not better," she said, trying to channel Izzy's flirty self-confidence. "Just different."

"You're cute when you're talking shit," he said, grinning. "I don't know, man, I think you need a little reality check. I feel a Drill coming on."

"Drill" was a totally fun but exhausting exercise Trey made Tangie do when he was tutoring her. He would shout a list of different dance styles one after another, and Tangie had to hit each style seamlessly, without fumbling even once.

"You're joking, right? Come on, Trey, I'm too tired!"

"A real dancer's never too tired for Drill," he said, leaning against the mirror with his arms folded across his chest. "You ready?"

She smelled a challenge. When it came to dancing, Tangie would always feel competitive—even if it was around Trey. Making a face at him, she shook out her arms and legs and rolled her head from side to side. "Fine, I'm ready," she said, noticing that the dancers in their immediate area were pretending not to watch them.

"Here we go. Five, six, seven, eight . . . Krump!" he yelled, and Tangie krumped, knocking it out for an eight-count.

"Gimme the Matrix!"

She did.

"Betsy Ballerina!"

Seamlessly, she went from Ciara's signature back-bending move to a graceful triple pirouette and double jeté.

"Get hyphy! Okay, now toe-hop! Gimme some Alvin Ailey shit! Lean wit' it! Dutty wind!"

Trey was relentless, but Tangie kept up with him, dancing her ass off. It was amazing, watching her hit off so many dance styles. Most dancers had mastered a couple of genres, but Tangie could do almost any style flawlessly. She was so magnetic that the other dancers stopped rehearsing to watch her. And Trey was soaking it up. His whole point in drilling her just then, in the middle of Studio 7 rehearsal time, was to make everyone see how dope she was—and *recognize*. Trey Stevens didn't mess with any slouches.

"Gimme two eight-counts of Savion Glover," he ordered, grinning as she started tapping—barefoot, no less. "Okay, stop. Stop!"

"*Aarrrghhhh,*" Tangie moaned, dropping to the ground. She lay there flat on her back, her chest heaving. "I . . . hate . . . you!"

"You win," Trey said, pulling her to her feet. "You still got it, Dimples."

She punched him in the arm, pretending to be angry. In reality, she was flattered that he was paying her so much attention.

"Yeah? What do I win?"

He looked at Tangie and smiled slowly. She was sweaty, exhausted, and hot to death. Plus, she was a brilliant dancer. Trey hadn't seen a girl move like that since last summer, at

Missy's video auditions. If she wanted to, Tangie could quit
school and go pro, like, today. She was that fierce.

Without thinking, he grabbed her by the shoulders and
kissed her—in front of the entire studio. Dimly, Tangie heard
somebody gasp, but she ignored it.

"Go out with me," he said.

"Okay," she breathed, realizing she was doing it again, just
blindly going along with whatever Trey said—and not caring.
"Where are we going?"

"I don't know. I just wanna take you out. Tomorrow night.
Where do you live?"

"I . . . in Fort Greene. But . . ."

"Cool. I'll text you later." He grinned at her and kissed her
again. "I gotta bounce."

"O—okay," she said, at a loss for words.

Seeing that she was obviously having trouble processing
this, he added, "I'm not just trying to fuck you, either. I want
you to trust me."

Again, she said, "Okay." Apparently she'd forgotten how to
say anything else.

And then, Trey left. And Tangie was left there, surrounded
by a studio full of dancers who were all whispering about her.
That was when the gossip began to spread. By noon the next
day, it was practically a fact—Trey Stevens and the cute virgin
with the crazy ass were this year's Trey and Eden.

Name: Cedric James Parker
Class: Sophomore
Major: Visual Arts
Self-Awareness Session #: 44

I don't feel like talkin' today.

There's nothing you want to discuss? You, of all people, know that the most compelling art comes from accessing your feelings.

You really want my feelings?

Yes, please.

I hate Trey Stevens. Okay? There, I said it. He's such a clown, yo. I mean, it's really killing me. Take this, for example. Last spring, it was mad hot outside and everybody was chillin' in the park after school. And this cat is obviously surrounded by a whole crew of Serving Treys.

Serving Treys?

Groupies. So, anyway, folks are playin' music and shit, chillin', and then outta nowhere your boy takes off his shirt, like, in slow motion. But that ain't even it. What killed us was when this dude actually poured an entire bottle of water on his chest *and wiggled around like a goddamn stripper. I kid you not. And the Serving Treys screamed like he's Usher.*

Mr. Parker? Are you all right?

I think I just threw up a little in my mouth.

7.

JUDGING MENTALS

UNION SQUARE PARK, the grassy area directly across the street from Armstrong, was officially out of control. Skye was scheduled to pass out her invites at exactly 7 a.m. (thirty minutes before school started), and by six thirty, the park was overgrown with Armstrong kids who were anxiously awaiting her arrival. Of course, most of them had never spoken a single word to Skye—but they all expected an invite to what they knew would be the party of the year, if not the *decade*.

Tangie, Kamillah, and Regina were sitting on a bench at the edge of the park, feeling slightly superior to everyone else. They were probably the only three people—outside of C.J. and their boys—who *knew* they were invited. Everyone else was in a frenzy of anticipation.

The *Sixteen Candles* camera and lighting crews had set up all over the park and were ready to film Skye's invitation ceremony from all angles. Meanwhile, Jenna and Kiki were slowly wending their way though the enormous crowd. Kiki was filming, while Jenna was using her expert wiles to coax students into revealing their innermost thoughts about Skye on camera.

"I mean, she's cute, but I think the weave's mad excessive."

"Shit, I'd do her. Wait, I can't say 'shit,' can I?"

"I don't know if MVN's looking for a new veejay, but I brought an audition tape just in case. Oh, and here's my card."

Union Square East, the street running between the park and Armstrong, was blocked off. Constipated-looking security guards were stationed along the outside of the park, trying to keep the crowd under control. But the longer everyone waited, the more hectic things got.

Finally, at exactly seven fifteen, a strange bleating siren sounded, and a hush fell over the crowd. The security guards quickly removed a bunch of orange cones from the blocked-off street. Good thing, because two seconds later, a vintage Rolls-Royce skidded to a stop in front of the park. A couple of overexcited freshman girls ran toward the car and were quickly intercepted by the security guards.

The back door of the car opened, and out came a tall Latino man, dressed up like an old-school gangster in a three-piece pin-striped suit, a fedora, and a skinny mustache. An anonymous freshman screamed, "Oh, my God, it's Helio Castroneves from *Dancing With the Stars*! That's his paso doble outfit—is he gonna do the paso doble?" The girl was quickly shushed. The gangster reached back into the car for a sexy brown-skinned woman wearing a long, slinky, sequined halter dress; a mink boa; and a glamorous, wavy, bobbed hairdo. When she emerged, he spun her around and dipped her, and the crowd went wild.

"You waiting for Skye?" he called out, and everyone screamed, "*Yesss!*" Standing back to back, the gangster and the glamour girl each took out a plastic toy gun and posed, outlaw style. Then they pulled their triggers, and a huge flag popped out of both guns, reading *Skye's Sixteen Candles!*

At that moment, Skye jumped out of the car clutching a huge stack of invitations. The crowd roared. Skye posed cutely for the cameras, flipping her hair and blowing kisses over her shoulder the way she'd seen Lindsay Lohan do a zillion times on the red carpet. She was in heaven (remembering Jenna's direction, she was careful not to stare into Kiki's camera . . . but she shot a wink in her direction). *And this is nothing,* she thought, bubbling over with excitement. *Wait until these people see my grand entrance!*

Once Skye had sufficiently soaked up enough attention, she put her index finger to her M·A·C Lipglass–coated mouth, signaling everyone to quiet down. Quickly, she scanned the crowd for Regina—and when she saw that she was taking pictures, she started her speech.

"What it do, bee-yatches? Give it up for Andre and Allegra, two extra-dope dancers that'll be doing their thing at my party. Woo-hoo!"

Everyone cheered.

"I really wanna thank all of y'all for coming out to get an invite to my *Sixteen Candles!* The theme is Gangsters and Glamour Girls, if you didn't already figure it out—and it's all about a glam, sexy, 1930s *Idlewild* meets *Chicago* feel. Don't you love it?"

More cheering.

"Now this is a *very* exclusive party, so if you don't get an invite, don't take it personally. It probably just means I don't know you. Okay? One more thing. When I pass out the invites, my sexy little gangster here will give all the boys a fedora, and my glamour girl will give the ladies a boa. Bring these with you to the party, or you *won't get in*. No exceptions. *Comprende?* Oh, and it's a costume party, so I better not see any prep or thug or hipster ensembles, you feel me? It's all suits and gowns and gorgeousness. All right, people, let's do the damn thing!"

The glamour girl shook up an oversize bottle of fake champagne, popped the cork, and confetti exploded everywhere. With that introduction, Skye began calling out names from her list. As the lucky hundred or so kids came forward, there were definite rumblings from the ones she'd left out. Drunk with power, Skye began to holler things like, "Don't be mad; it just means I don't like you!"

Her invitees were pretty predictable, until she called out Izzy's name—surprising everyone in Union Square Park.

Izzy herself said, "What the holy good god*damn?*" She was only there because C.J. had promised to smoke her out afterward if she came with him.

Skye smiled sweetly, quickly glancing over at Kiki to make sure she was capturing this moment. "You heard me right, Izzy. I want to end our stupid beef right here and now. Come on up here, girl!"

Cautiously, Izzy stepped out of the crowd and went to stand in front of Skye, her arms folded across her chest. She looked in equal parts suspicious and curious.

"Listen, I just think we have way too many friends in common not to share the love, you know?" Skye handed Izzy an invitation and a huge white feather boa. She opened her arms to Izzy, but the tiny, punky girl shook her head.

"Nah, I'm good," she said. "Thanks, though. I appreciate . . . the boa."

From the It chicks corner, Tangie giggled a little bit to herself, knowing Skye would never pick up Izzy's sarcasm.

Ignoring Izzy's rejection, Skye grabbed her hand and lifted it up above their heads, as if they were two boxers at the end of a match. Izzy also looked as if she'd just bitten into a lemon. Regina snapped a picture, and the crowd broke out in applause—though the more skeptical onlookers guessed correctly that Skye had staged the entire making-up-with-Izzy scene purely for publicity reasons. In fact, Tangie overheard a petite boy in pink ballet flats (one of the rejected) mutter under his breath, "If you're gonna be two-faced, Skye, better make one of 'em pretty."

As more invitations were passed out, C.J., Black, and Vineet sat on a bench away from the crowd, way too chill (and high) to get all excited about Skye's party. They were also among the first to be invited.

"Oh, my God, Black, no, no, no." C.J. was extremely frustrated. He and Black were knee deep in the same debate they'd been having for months. "Are we really still comparing Lupe Fiasco to Lil Wayne?"

"Lupe's on some next level shit, youknowhatimsayin?" With every word, Black hit his thigh with his fist. He was that serious. "He's conscious, he's intelligent, he's the thoroughest lyricist in the game right now."

"Look, a hip-hop song is equal parts beat, flow, hook, and word, right?"

"I mean, yeah. So?"

"Lupe has the words, but *nada mas*, cuz. Lil Wayne, though? He spits flames all day, *and* his beats is tight. His hooks is tight. His flow is tight. Lupe is a wordsmith, yeah, but he has yet to come with the whole package, and you *know* this."

"Lil Wayne ain't got no chin, and he's five foot five. What now?"

C.J. shook his head, disgusted. "This conversation is officially dead."

"*Yo,*" said Vineet, who'd been quiet, lost in thought, the whole time.

Black nodded in his direction. "Wassup?"

"I just realized what Skye means by 'gangster.' She's talking about one of them cats from back in the day that used to chill in juke joints and drink gin and shit."

"Yeah," said C.J. "What'd you think she meant?"

"I thought she meant *gangsta*. Like thug. I thought I was gonna have to dress up like Fiddy."

Black looked at him. "You didn't really think that, man."

Vineet refused to think he was alone in this. "Ceej, did you get what *gangster* meant?"

"Yo, your ignorance is truly comical, son." C.J. laughed, giving the aspiring deejay a pound. "Stick to the ones and two, baby."

"Hey, Vineet," said Black. "Whatchu think of Skye's producer, Jenna Aliabadi?

"What, I gotta like her 'cause she's Indian?"

"It ain't even like that. That girl is *bad*, dog. You see her?"

Vineet craned his neck and finally saw the producer whispering something to Skye and Izzy, a clipboard in her hand. She looked up, glancing over in his direction—and just like that, Vineet was lost. He saw the whole thing in slow motion, Jenna's long, glossy, black hair slowly flipping back behind her shoulder, her wet, red lips breaking into a small smile . . .

"Oh, my God," whispered Vineet, his mouth suddenly going dry. "That's my wife. That's my *wife*."

As if Jenna didn't already have enough on her plate that week, she now had to deal with a fifteen-year-old drummer/deejay following her around like a cocker spaniel.

Regina was in film-geek heaven. Since she was old enough to watch *Pulp Fiction*, she'd been writing screenplays, making minidocumentaries with her video camera, and studying Martin Scorsese movies, dreaming about the day she'd become an award-winning filmmaker. The first black Filipina to win the audience award at Sundance. The first Guerrero kid to top the box office charts. *Twenty years from now,* she thought, *I'll look back on this as the moment it all started.*

Regina had been shadowing Kiki for two days, and this was the first time the MVN camerawoman had actually let her shoot film by herself. To Regina's delight, Kiki suddenly passed her the camera while she was shooting Skye's invite ritual. And now, she was standing behind Regina, helping her direct the shot.

"Every kid in my filmmaking department would kill to shoot even two seconds of *Sixteen Candles*," whispered Regina. "I still can't believe you're letting me do this."

"Why not?" Kiki shrugged. "Seriously, you're so advanced for your age, Regina. Judging from your technique, I would've thought you've been directing for at least five years."

"Wow . . . I mean, thank you." Regina could feel her cheeks burning behind the camera. She was glad Kiki couldn't see her face.

"Okay, now, pan over to the left a bit, so Skye's off center," Kiki said, lightly putting her hand over Regina's and steering her. "Good, good. See how nice the lighting is there?"

Preoccupied with the way her skin tingled where Kiki touched her, Regina took a second to answer. "Yeah, it's beautiful! How did you see that?"

"Just practice." Kiki stood back, silently observing her tutee. "I think we can take a break for a sec. We have enough footage of this setup."

"Cool," said Regina, handing her the camera. Now that she didn't have the protection of the camera, she felt oddly exposed. She didn't know what to do with her hands. Kiki noticed her wiping her hands on her jeans, and she smiled a little.

"You okay?"

"Yeah, yeah." *Say something,* Regina told herself. *Say something, you idiot.* "Um, can I ask you a question?"

Kiki smiled. "Of course, go ahead."

"How old are you? You seem so young to be an MVN camerawoman."

Kiki giggled and ran her hands through her floppy shag haircut. Mesmerized, Regina watched as her hair easily fell back in place, the ends flipping up perfectly. She was adorable. "Actually, I'm only twenty-one."

"*What?* Are you serious? But how . . ."

"I started NYU at seventeen and began interning at MVN the same year. I just moved up really quick, I guess." She blushed. "You could do the same thing, Regina. You're *so* talented—all it takes is an internship at the right production company or network, and you're good. If you want, I can see about any openings at MVN."

"You'd do that for me?"

She shrugged. "Yeah."

"Why?"

"I guess I just . . . I just like you, that's all." Kiki's almond-shaped, velvety-brown eyes caught hers, and Regina felt her thighs go wobbly. She'd never felt this *electric.*

Jesus, where was Nick when she needed him?

"So Skye has a quote-unquote *brilliant* idea for our grand entrance routine," Kamillah said to Tangie. All the invites had been passed out, and while the lucky guests were squealing with what-are-we-gonna-wear excitement, the uninvited were hunting down Jenna and Kiki to explain on camera why they'd never liked Skye anyway and thought she was an untalented psycho slut.

"She wants you to teach me and Regina the choreography during the Random Get Down today," she continued. The Random Get Down happened in the hour or so after school ended, when Armstrong kids congregated outside in Union Square Park and watched the most show-offy actors, dancers, musicians, and singers get together for impromptu, free-for-all jam sessions.

"You're really trying to learn a routine in front of all those people?" Tangie asked.

"Um, no?" Kamillah looked two seconds from tears, which was shocking to Tangie. "When I said I couldn't dance, I wasn't playing. I can't believe Skye's doing this to me. I'm gonna look like Michelle from Destiny's Child in front of everyone that ever lived."

"I don't get it, though. Why does she want us to practice in front of an audience?"

"That's the point, T. She *wants* everyone to see us." She lowered her voice a little bit. "It's all about getting publicity for Skye, you feel me? Jenna and Kiki will be there, too, filming us."

"Oh, my God. That's so look-at-how-cool-we-are." Tangie winced, covering her face with her hands.

"Right? Skye is getting mad full of herself, yo. If anyone laughs at me tomorrow, I'm kicking them in they ass. Watch."

Tangie was about to ask if Regina had agreed to the public

practice when she saw C.J., walking alone across the park away from school. Really, it was the perfect time to ask him about the mural. All during the previous day she'd tried to build up the nerve to talk to him, but had chickened out every time. Tangie knew she was running out of time—the party was in three days; could C.J. even paint the mural on such short notice?

Quickly, she made up an excuse to get rid of Kamillah and ran across the park, catching up with C.J.

"Hey," she said, slightly out of breath.

C.J. turned around; seeing her, he couldn't hide his surprise "Oh. Hey. Wassup?"

"Um, nothing."

They stood there for a second, nervously fidgeting. There was *Sixteen Candles* commotion happening all around them, but neither one noticed. C.J. looked at her expectantly.

God, why does he have to be so damn adorable? thought Tangie, realizing that this was going to be even harder than she had thought. Looking at him, with his caramel eyes, mile-long lashes, and sexy, delicious mouth, she was brought back to the moment, almost a month before, when it had all gone down.

They were in her bedroom, she was wearing a gross leotard, but it didn't matter—they were *talking*, after a summer of fighting. Five years of stops and starts and unbearable sexual tension just erupted, and he kissed her for the very first time. And then they were all over each other, locked in that passionate kiss for what felt like hours. But the best part was that, after years of drama,

C.J. finally told her he loved her—and with every molecule of her being, she knew it was true. And so she said it back. In her heart, she knew that at last they'd be together . . . until, surprise! C.J. spent the very next night with Izzy.

The bastard.

Fabulous, she thought. Now I'm pissed all over again.

"So, we're speaking now?" The corners of his mouth turned up a little. But she wasn't having it.

"No, we're not. I'm just doing Skye a favor." Tangie stood there, furious and silent. Moments passed.

C.J. was confused. "Um, Tangie?"

"Yeah?" she said, glaring at him.

"You gonna do an interpretive dance here, or what?"

"No, I'm just getting my thoughts together."

"Cool, cool. Well, I'll be over here. . . ." He tried to walk away, but Tangie grabbed his arm and dragged him back.

"Don't be stupid, C.J., I have to ask you something."

"Lemme ask you something, first. You gonna stay mad at me forever?"

She looked at him long and hard. "Yeah."

"That's mature," he said. His body language immediately switched from cool to annoyed. He pulled his Yankees cap low over his eyes. "So, you said this was a favor for Skye."

She nodded.

"What's the favor?"

But Tangie wasn't ready to go there yet. "You know what, C.J.? I wish you hadn't even said you loved me."

He exhaled, digging his hands into his jeans pockets. When he finally looked back up, his eyes were intense. "Whether I said it or not, you know the truth," he said. "You know what's up." He looked at her long and hard until Tangie felt her face grow hot.

What did *that* mean? Was he saying he loved her again? In an instant, she went from wanting to claw his eyes out to wanting to throw herself into his arms—but she didn't. She didn't because she would've died if he had pushed her away.

"C.J. . . ." she began, and then stopped, the words disappearing. Gazing into his eyes, she'd totally forgotten what she was supposed to ask him. It wasn't fair! Why was it that she could have fun with Trey—and actually *like* him—but that when she stood in front of C.J., she couldn't even remember what Trey looked like? No matter how bumpy their past had been, C.J. was in her heart. And there wasn't a damn thing she could do about it.

"Um, C.J. . . ." She tried again, feeling like an idiot.

"Tangie, Tangie . . ."

"Stop it!"

"What? I thought we was just saying each other's names."

"I don't think . . ."

"That's okay, baby, you look good." He grinned at her, and she punched him in the shoulder.

"Ugh, why are you making this so hard?"

"*Me?* Are you *serious?* You're the one came over here demanding that I talk to you and then said a whole bunch of nothing. Oh, but only after saying some ill 'why'd you say you loved me' shit."

She knew he was right. Taking a deep breath, she concentrated and remembered why she had wanted to talk to him in the first place. "Oh, yeah. Okay, Skye wanted me to ask you to do something for her."

"I liked it better when you was tongue-tied."

"No, it's nothing bad. She wants you to draw a mural for her party. Me, Kamillah, Regina, you, Black, and Vineet—we're all on her court or whatever, and she wants a painting of all of us in vintage thirties outfits, to hang behind the dance floor. Can you do that?"

"Hell, fucking no! I absolutely refuse to . . ."

She folded her arms across her chest and narrowed her eyes.

He smiled at her. "Of course I'll do it. No doubt."

"Good." Now that her objective was accomplished, Tangie wasn't sure what to do next.

"So, um, your boyfriend . . . is he on this court, too?"

"My *what*?"

"I'm sayin', I gotta know, if I'm gonna draw this thing."

"That's irrelevant."

"No, R & B dudes beefing is irrelevant."

"How did you even hear about us?"

"Come on now, T. Everybody knows." C.J. backed away from her, about to leave. "I thought you'd gotten smarter about your wannabe-thugged-out ballerina, but I guess I can't always be right."

"He's *not* a ballerina! How many times do I have to tell you that?" She knew it was a dumb thing to say, but she was caught off guard.

"Okay, he's not a ballerina."

"He asked me out on a date, by the way."

"Oh, word?"

Tangie nodded, feeling smug.

"Here's some advice. Don't do that ill honking thing in the back of your throat. . . ."

"I have allergies!"

"It's just not sexy," he said, shrugging. "That's all I'm saying."

"I hate you, C. J. Parker." That's what she said, but the look on her face told the real truth.

He grinned at her, his dimples showing. Then his expression grew serious. "Just be careful with that ballerina, Mud Butt. Just be careful."

At first, Tangie was too surprised to respond. He had just called her Mud Butt! That was the gross nickname he'd come up with for her in eighth grade, when a hideous case of diarrhea had kept her home from school. If she hadn't known better, she'd have thought they were back to being the old Tangie and C.J. again.

But she did know better.

"Not that I owe you an explanation," she said, "but he's not my boyfriend. And why do you care? It's not like I'm all up in your business about . . ."

"Izzy."

"Exactly."

"Here she comes."

Tangie whipped around and saw Izzy sauntering over to them in that slow, seductive-yet-tomboyish way of hers. And they both knew they were trapped.

"Cedric James and my TMI twin!" She came up between them, threw her arms around their shoulders, and kissed their cheeks. "Now, *this* is a very good look. I can't believe y'all are speaking!"

"Wassup, Izz?"

"Chillin'. Hold up, look at this." She whipped out an invitation to Skye's party. "Can you believe this? T., I know this is all you."

"Izzy, I *swear* I didn't make her invite you."

"My ass, you didn't." Izzy looked slightly annoyed.

"But will you go? Please? It'll be fun."

"I seriously doubt it, but maybe, for you. *Maybe*," she said. "If I go, though, will you do something for me?"

"Anything! What is it?"

"I got all warm and fuzzy watching you two finally talk! Listen, you're my best friends, and I want us all to get along. I don't know what went down with you, but obviously you're over it." Izzy smiled. "I want all three of us to go out. Tonight."

"Um, I don't know. . . ." Tangie was horrified. She couldn't think of anything she wanted to do *less* than be a third wheel on a date with Izzy and C.J.

"Come on, girl! *The Exorcism of Emily Rose* just came out, and I'm dying to see it—and I know you like scary movies."

It was true. Tangie was a huge horror movie fan. She looked at C.J., and he shrugged.

"I mean, yeah," said C.J. "I guess we can go."

"Cool, it's playing at Eleventh and Third," Izzy said, checking Moviefone on her BlackBerry, "so I'll see y'all then, okay?"

At the same time that Izzy was scanning movie times, C.J.'s BlackBerry started beeping. He saw that Melanie O'Donnell was texting him.

HEY, C.J. . . . CAN YOU AND WILL GATES STOP BY MY OFFICE SOMETIME TODAY? I HAVE A CONTRACT FOR YOU TO SIGN. IT'S ALL HAPPENING!!

C.J.'s cheeks became instantly flushed with excitement, but he tried to play it down. "Um, I gotta go, y'all."

Izzy saw that C.J. looked anxious all of a sudden. "Where you going? Are you okay?"

"Yeah, I'm good. I just . . . I gotta go handle some business. I'll see y'all tonight, though. Peace."

And then he was gone.

"I wonder what that was all about," said Tangie, watching him disappear into the *Sixteen Candles* crowd.

"Who knows? C.J. can be so shady," said Izzy. "My question is, what am I supposed to do with this boa?"

Tangie was surprised to see Izzy smile a little. Was she actually pleased to be invited? For all of her toughness, deep down, it seemed that maybe Izzy really did want to be accepted.

And then Tangie noticed something else about Izzy. She was wearing an oversize concert T with a slouchy belt. The shirt had started to slip off her shoulder a bit, revealing a scratch surrounded by a blotchy purplish bruise.

"Izzy, what happened to your shoulder? Are you okay?"

"Oh, yeah, I walked into a wall. So stupid." Her hand flew up to her shoulder, covering the bruise. "Whatever. So, when were you gonna tell me you and Trey were kickin' it again?"

Tangie's mouth flew open. What? Did everyone know they were sort of talking again? And even more important—what was up with Izzy acting all cagey about her shoulder?

She wondered if she should be worried about her.

Name: Skye Carmichael
Class: Sophomore
Major: Drama
Self-Awareness Session #: 47

Skye? What are you doing?

Huh? Oh, I'm just taking a quick sensory picture—we learned how to do it in Characterization class. [Skye closes her eyes, inhales deeply, then exhales with a whispery "aaaah".] *Basically, it's an exercise actors do to remember exactly how they're feeling in a certain moment. And lately I've been doing it, just so I can remember what it's like to feel like a normal, unfamous person. Because once my episode airs, I'm gonna be the biggest reality star of them all!*

You're a remarkably gifted actress, Skye. I would've thought you'd want to become famous for your talent.

Well, duh, that's a given. But everybody knows just being talented doesn't count anymore. It's all about that buzz . . . having a dope MySpace page, getting a reality show, dating Brody Jenner. Look at Nicole Richie. We're exactly alike, if you think about it. She's beautiful, she comes from a famous family, she's a style icon. And, just like me, a reality show made her a superstar. Oh, and guess what? I just found out MVN's hooking me up with her ex-fiancé, DJ AM, to host and spin at my party!

It's kinda scary how similar we are. Actually, I'm a step ahead of her, 'cause I was never chubby.

8.

SQUASHED BEEF, FRIENDSHIP, AND ENCHILADAS

SKYE WANTED TO DIE. She, Eden, and Alexa were sitting on the leopard-print sofa in the Carmichaels' enormous living room, hosting a very important male model audition. Even before she had her theme, Skye had known that for her grand entrance she wanted six buff, badass model boys to carry her into the club over their heads, à la Mariah in her "It's Like That" video. Oh, she'd be so glamorous, decked out in a slinky, sparkly designer gown with a huge white boa and diamonds dripping everywhere. It sounded like a brilliant idea until she actually had to audition the models.

Skye had wanted to host the audition with all her friends, but Jenna had insisted that she interview the boys with Alexa and Eden instead (star power always helped kick the episodes up a notch, since the very best ones featured kids with famous parents or siblings).

What the producer *didn't* know was that when Alexa drank, she tried to molest every man that crossed her path (this included her dog-walker, Skye's life coach, the swarthy concierge at the Plaza Hotel—*everyone*). So, watching a parade of shirtless, muscular eighteen-year-olds flex and flirt was like Christmas to Alexa.

"Okay, thank you, Juan Carlos—we'll be in touch, " said Skye, blowing a good-bye kiss to a stocky Puerto Rican underwear model who looked like a sleepy Daddy Yankee. He tripped a little bit on the rug as he walked out. "Regina, can you let the next boy in?"

Busily listening to Kiki explain some boring camera technique, Regina completely ignored Skye.

"*Regina!*"

"What?"

"Can you please let in the next boy?" *Regina's obsession with that no-concealer-wearing camerawoman is really getting old,* thought Skye.

"Oh, yeah, sorry." Sneaking a glance at Kiki, she giggled a little and hurried over to the French doors separating the living room from the foyer. Regina opened the door, and in came a blue-eyed, black-haired, six-foot-tall drink of water. He walked up to the carpet in front of the sofa and stood there, his thumbs hooked in his belt loops, his pouty red mouth curved in a sexy half smile.

Skye's mouth immediately dropped open. He looked exactly like a tall, insanely buff Nick. *Oh, my God, he's so hired,* she thought to herself. She tossed her hair and stuck out her tiny chest, knowing that her nipples were alluringly pointy because of the air-conditioning in the room. (Alexa had read somewhere that cold temperatures reversed the aging process, so she kept the apartment freezing. For the first time ever, Skye was thankful.)

"H—hi," she said, barely breathing. "I'm Sk—"

"Hello, *dahhhling*," interrupted Alexa, purring in her weird half-British, half-bitchy accent. She stood up and offered up her hand. Clearly unsure of what to do next, the man awkwardly bent down and kissed it.

"Hi, everyone. I'm Kenny," he said, straightening.

"Kenny, if I were *half* my age I'd make love to you for three days straight and then happily bear your mulatto love child."

Skye choked on her Sprite, and Eden had to hit her on the back until she stopped coughing. She shot her sister an exasperated "what is she *doing*?" look, and Eden squeezed her hand sympathetically. As horrified as Skye was, a warm and cozy feeling washed over her. The only time she and her sister bonded was when it was about Alexa's insanity.

"Oh, my God, *control yourself*, Alexa," pleaded Skye through clenched teeth. She turned to the man. "Hello, Kenny. So, tell us a little about yourself."

"Uh, I'm a model. I like weight lifting, playing on my Xbox, and writing poetry. Oh, and I was an extra in *Mean Girls*."

"Really?" Eden was both impressed and annoyed. Here she was, busting her ass in Armstrong's drama department, while this idiot could say he acted in a Lindsay Lohan movie. "Which part were you in?"

"The house party scene? I'm fourth from the left in the

kitchen. It came on HBO the other day, and I paused my scene and took a picture with my camera phone. Here, I'll show you."

Jenna signaled Kiki to stop filming, and she walked over to Eden. "Okay, sweetie, I'd love you to start talking to Kenny about Lindsay Lohan or something. I just want to have some footage of you, a former child star, talking to Kenny about Lindsay, a former child star. It's a great angle to have, you know. These episodes always hinge on the famous family members—it helps drive home that fact that Skye comes from a superprivileged family, that she's not a quote-unquote *regular* girl. It gives the viewer a reason to look up to her. Got it?"

"*Totally,*" said Eden in her faraway, airy voice. She flashed Kenny a gorgeous smile, brushed her bangs out of her eyes, and began chatting him up about the slutty redheaded starlet. Meanwhile, Alexa was licking her lips and rubbing her legs together like a horny grasshopper, gazing up at him through her false eyelashes.

So gross! thought Skye.

She was furious. Fine, she understood that having her famous mother and sister around would make her episode cooler—but it hurt her feelings. Just once, she would've liked for something to be about *her*. And then she started feeling a knot in her throat. She wanted to call the whole thing off, go running out of the room. Would anyone even notice? Suddenly, she felt her cell vibrating in her lap. She checked the screen and saw that it was Tangie.

"Guys," she began, not caring that she was ruining the take, "I need to get this. Can we take five?"

"Oh, no problem," said Jenna, waving her away. "We already have tons of footage of you conducting the model interviews. We'll just shoot Eden and Alexa till you come back."

"Fabulous," muttered Skye, storming past Kenny and slamming the French doors behind her. She sat on the marble floor of the foyer and snapped open her cell.

"Thank God it's you," breathed Skye, almost in tears. "I'm in the middle of shooting my model auditions, and no one's paying attention to me, and I'm in *hell*!"

"Wait, it's that bad? I'm sorry it sucks, I thought it was gonna be fun."

"Fun, my ass. Eden and Alexa are ruining everything. And Regina and Kiki are like two seven-year-olds at their first slumber party. In two seconds they'll be braiding each other's hair and giggling over Bobby Valentino or something."

Tangie giggled, but she was barely paying attention. She had so much to tell Skye! Skye still didn't know that Trey had asked her on an unofficial date. And Tangie *definitely* needed to holler at her before she went out with Izzy and C.J. tonight—Tangie was nervous as hell, but Skye would know how she should act. God, they had *so* much catching up to do, but there never seemed to be any time. It felt like they were growing further and further apart. And *Sixteen Candles* was not helping—Tangie hadn't gotten two seconds alone with Skye since the filming began.

"Hey, I have to tell you something. I don't think you're gonna like it, but here goes. . . ."

"Oh, God. What? Nick thinks I'm a fugly troll."

"What? No!" That was just like Skye, to make it all about her. Tangie took a deep breath. "Trey asked me on a date. A *real* date, not a tutoring session." When Skye didn't respond, Tangie kept going. "I know that before, you thought he was just using me—but it's not like that. Maybe it was, but not anymore. I think he really likes me. And Izzy said . . ."

"*Izzy* said? She knew about this?"

"Well, yeah. I wanted to tell you, but you've been so busy with filming and stuff, and she was just there."

Skye started breathing harder. This was all she needed. She was reduced to a bit part in her own episode, and now her own best friend was confiding in some crazy freak she had just met. She felt like she was disappearing, like she didn't even exist.

"Skye? What do you think?"

"Listen, as Nicole Richie said in *The Truth About Diamonds*, I'm not judgmental, but I can judge mentals."

"What does that mean?"

"I already told you how I felt about Trey. I think you're making a huge mistake, but whatever. Do your thing."

"Oh, my God, don't be like that. I want to be able to talk about this stuff with you—we're *girls*, Skye. You're my best friend."

"Yeah? Don't let Izzy hear you say that."

"What, now I'm not allowed to have two close friends?"

"Do what you want. I gotta go. Jenna can't start this scene without me."

"Skye, don't be like that. I . . ."

"I'm not mad, I just gotta go. I'll talk to you later, babe."

Skye hung up, the tears she'd been fighting spilling down her cheeks. Dammit, she thought, my audition is ruined, and now my makeup is, too.

Happy Birthday to Skye!

Gonzalez y Gonzalez, a Mexican bistro in NoHo, was Tangie's favorite restaurant in the world. The ridiculously delicious salsa, hilarious waiters, and crazy, party-friendly decor (think colorful lights, flashing sombreros and Day-Glo piñatas—olé!) always put Tangie in a good mood. But tonight, the rah-rah atmosphere was making her feel claustrophobic. Or was it the fact that she'd been sitting between C.J. and Izzy all night— first at the movies, and now at dinner? She hadn't been this stressed since her Armstrong auditions.

And so, Tangie did what she always did in high-pressure situations. She talked. A lot. And *fast*.

Izzy didn't seem to notice. She had brought her fake ID, and she'd been drinking margaritas the whole time.

". . . And I mean, it was *so* nuts. I'm, like, trying to teach Regina and Kamillah this dance at Random Get Down, when everybody in the school's in the park, right? Oh, and Kiki's *taping*, by the way. And the thing is, they're not really dancers— not that they *suck* or anything; I'm saying, they're actually kinda good, especially Regina—but they just don't have train- ing. So, it's like, Kamillah hears these beats that aren't even *there*, right? And for the millionth time, I'm, like, 'Kamillah, you cross over on the *two*,' but she just ignores me, and then finally, this boy in metallic gold leggings comes up to us and goes, 'Excuse me, sweetie? I think somebody returned your rhythm to the Lost and Found.' Oh, my God, Kamillah was *so pissed*, but me and Regina were *dying*. . . ."

"No, he didn't!" Izzy collapsed into giggles. She loved to hear anything unflattering about Kamillah. "Oh, that's some funny shit. Yeah, I actually saw you guys over there, doin' your thing. You looked good, girl."

Tangie grinned, happy that Izzy was complimenting her in front of C.J. "Thanks. It definitely hasn't been easy, but I think we'll be tight by Saturday night."

"I saw Trey with y'all, too," Izzy added, her eyes twinkling. She felt totally comfortable chilling with her two best friends, and evidently didn't feel the need to censor herself. "What, did he help you choreograph the routine?"

Tangie held her breath, glancing at C.J. Apparently, he wasn't paying attention to either one of them—he was absent-mindedly sketching something on a napkin, lost in his own world. "Um, yeah. He helped me a little, but whatever."

Izzy raised an eyebrow.

In response, Tangie tightened her mouth and quickly shook her head—sign language for *I'm so not trying to talk about this right now!*

Taking the hint, Izzy got the picture and changed the subject.

"Yo, *The Exorcism of Emily Rose* was off the hook!" she said. "I always think horror movies about, like, possession and spiritual stuff are so much scarier than, like, *Saw* or *Hostel*."

"I know, right? Like *The Exorcist*—did you ever see that?

When the little girl gets possessed by the devil and her head spins all the way around?" Tangie shuddered. "Seriously, it's the scariest movie I've ever seen."

C.J. said nothing. Secretly, he was terrified of horror movies and would've been much happier seeing *King Kong.*

"Speaking of horror," said Izzy, "I still can't believe your girl invited me to her party."

"What, are you too edgy for *Sixteen Candles?*" mumbled C.J., still doodling.

"No, it's just that everybody knows me and Skye don't get along," she said, slurping down the rest of her margarita. Izzy's fake ID had been working brilliantly for two years. "So, Tangie, how'd you get her to invite me?"

"I swear, I didn't! I really just think she's just tired of all the drama. She wants us all to be friends."

"Friends, my ass."

"So, you goin'?" C.J. finally tore his eyes away from whatever he was sketching, but still didn't really acknowledge Tangie. It was the way the night was going. C.J. and Tangie each talked to Izzy, and Izzy talked to each of them, but the two ex–soul mates barely said a word to each other. Just a few *uh-huh*s and *yeah*s so Izzy wouldn't ask any questions.

"I don't know." Izzy shrugged and her cheeks flushed a little. For a second, her armor was gone, and Tangie got a glimpse of the sweet, innocent fourteen-year-old girl she might have been had she not been forced to grow up fast. And then it was gone. "For real? The only reason I'd want to go is to rock a kick-ass outfit."

"That reminds me, I'm gonna need help with mine." Tangie dipped a tortilla chip into Gonzalez y Gonzalez's delicious salsa and popped it into her mouth. Her diet flew out the window when she was nervous. "God, this party is all anybody at school can talk about. I'm kind of sick of it, you know?"

"I'm just happy folks have stopped talking about me," said Izzy, running her finger along the rim of her margarita glass. "In the past month, I've found out I used to be a starving Ethiopian baby on an infomercial, that I lived in an apartment Jay-Z bought for me, that I aborted Jamie Foxx's baby . . ."

She and C.J. shared a private look, and then Izzy, tipsy now, collapsed in giggles, flinging an arm around his neck. Grinning sexily, he said, "Slow down, Iz," and then slid the margarita glass away from her. It was a small gesture, but it was intimate—there was no mistaking Izzy's and C.J.'s connection.

Something kicked in, and Tangie became instantly, outrageously jealous. And *competitive*. She wanted C.J. to feel as kicked in the stomach as she did.

"So, um, what do you think I should wear on my date with Trey tomorrow?" It was petty, but Tangie didn't care. It worked.

Stunned, C.J. instantly refocused his attention on Tangie.

"Hmmm, it depends. I mean, are you doing your cutesy, good-girl thing? Or are you tryin' to bring that *fire*?" Izzy asked.

"Why don't you just wear your leotard?" It was the first time C.J. had spoken to Tangie directly.

"What?"

"You know your leotard has a history of driving dudes bonkers." He shot her a knowing look and grinned. Tangie wanted to scream. Why did he have to refer to that night—*the night*—when he had said he loved her? She had been sweaty, gross, and clad in her stupid leotard, but it had still been the most passionate night of her life.

He knew what he was doing, and it sucked.

"Wait, what?" Izzy was slurring a little bit. "I wanna hear the leotard story!"

"There's no leotard story," said Tangie, quickly.

"Okay, then. Tell me this. What's *up* with y'all two?" Izzy slammed her hand down on the table, jangling the silverware. "Is there a beef? *Was* there a beef? What's the deal, for real?"

Tangie and C.J. glanced at each other and then looked at Izzy. They said nothing.

"How do you even know each other?" Izzy continued.

"Tangela was Skye's best friend," said C.J., "and Skye's my cousin, so when I started going to their school in sixth grade, we started rolling together. Like a tiny clique."

"Okay, so you go *waaayy* back."

"Yeah, way back. I knew T. when the Olsen twins was just toddlers." It was his nickname for her 34-D boobs. *I will not smile,* Tangie told herself. *No matter what, I will not smile.*

Izzy bounced in her seat. "So I got you two together and we're all family now, right?"

"Team work makes the dream work," muttered C.J. sarcastically.

Izzy grabbed both of their hands in a clumsy, drunken show of solidarity. "Then, let's get *real*. Tell me what y'all beefed about."

Tangie sighed, tired of faking it but still not about to tell the truth about their relationship. "What did we fight about, C.J.?"

"Honestly? I don't even remember. It was some old 'he said, she said' bullshit. It don't matter." He looked at Tangie and she nodded, and it was immediately understood that they would pretend to be cool for Izzy's sake.

"Yeah, it was a million years ago," Tangie said, waving her hand dismissively.

"Then let's put this behind us," slurred Izzy, waving her margarita glass in the air, "and toast to squashed beef, friendship, and enchiladas!"

They all laughed at her craziness, and, in spite of themselves, C.J. and Tangie raised their glasses and clinked them against Izzy's.

"I really love you guys. I mean, like, really, *really* love you. I don't have . . . you're the only . . ."

Out of nowhere, Izzy's phone began blaring. She pulled it out of her pocket and peered at the screen, and suddenly, all the color seemed to drain from her face.

"Oh, um, I gotta take that. I'll be right back." Stumbling a bit, she struggled to get out of her chair.

"Whoa, be easy, be easy," said C.J., starting to stand up. "I'll go with you."

"No!" she yelled. "I mean, no, I'm cool. I'll be right back."

And then she was gone, Tangie and C.J. staring after her. For a moment, their issues were forgotten.

"What was that all about?" asked Tangie.

"Man, I have no idea."

"I hope she's okay. There's so much about Izzy that we don't even know." She reconsidered this. "I mean, so much *I* don't know."

"You know as much as I do."

"Yeah, right," she said. "I haven't seen her naked."

"So uncalled for," said C.J., shaking his head.

Tangie shrugged, looking down into her Sprite. There was so much she wanted to ask him. Did he really like Izzy more than he liked her? Did he love her? And if so, was it because she was cooler, sexier, and more experienced? *Well, duh,* thought Tangie. *Of course it is!*

After a couple of moments of silence, C.J. finally spoke up. "So, you and Trey, huh? You really doing this?"

"Doing *what*?"

"I don't trust him, T."

"And I don't care." She sipped some water. "I finally get a boyfriend and you 'don't trust him'? I watched you run around with a million girls over the years and never said a word. It's not fair!"

"If you're trying to get back at me for something . . ."

"Why is it always about you? Why can't I just like him?"

"Because he's superwack, Tangela! I actually saw him kiss his pecs once." C.J. dropped his tortilla chip. "Look at me, I can't even eat. I'm *nauseous* right now. God, how can you even take him seriously?"

"The day you break up with Izzy is the day that'll be any of your business." Tangie looked at her hands.

"She ain't my girlfriend," he said through gritted teeth.

She'd heard C.J. say this so many times it was almost funny to her by now.

"C.J., I hate lying to her. It feels awful. Are we ever gonna tell her about us?"

"You know what, Tangie? Ain't nothing to tell." C.J. was hurt, so he said what he knew would hurt her, too.

Tangie felt as if she'd been kicked in the stomach. "Really? Okay, then."

They sat in silence until Izzy came back a few minutes later. She looked sober—sober and oddly wired, as if she'd just gulped down three Red Bulls.

"You all right?" asked C.J.

"Yeah. I gotta go meet somebody," she said, pulling out cash for her portion of the bill. "An old friend. You got the rest of this?"

"Yeah, but . . ."

"I gotta run." She gave Tangie a kiss on the cheek and quickly hugged C.J. "See you at school, okay?" And then she was gone.

C.J. and Tangie were left behind, feeling weird, awkward, and sad. They paid their bill and left, then stood outside Gonzalez y Gonzalez in the warm late-September night. It was about nine thirty, but Broadway was still crowded, bustling with people.

Tangie spoke first. "Well, nice seeing you."

"Yeah."

"I wish . . . I wish things were different."

C.J. nodded. He was silent for a while, just looking out at Broadway. And then he walked away, leaving a trail of cigarette smoke in the night.

9.
B-GIRL BARBIE

FOR DAYS, KIKI HAD BEEN promising Regina that she'd show her the room where *Sixteen Candles*'s fabulous episodes were edited. Finally, after school on Thursday, Kiki surprised her. She told Regina that they were going to film Skye practicing her grand entrance with the sexy male models, but there was a little stop she had to make first.

After school, the two girls hopped in a cab and headed uptown. Ten minutes later, they were dropped off in front of MVN's sparkling, mammoth office building in Time Square. Before Regina could ask any questions, Kiki handed her one of her old MVN IDs to show the security guard (since the two girls looked as similar as cousins, the morbidly obese security guard barely blinked an eye). The next thing she knew, the elevator doors opened on the forty-fourth floor, and Kiki was leading her down a hallway, covering Regina's eyes with her hand.

"Welcome to *Sixteen Candles*'s editing room!" Kiki yanked

her keys out of the heavy door and shut it quietly behind them. Regina looked around, her eyes bulging. There she was, standing in the room where all of MVN's hottest reality shows were created. In this small space, all the footage Kiki had been shooting for four days would be cut and pasted together and turned into a thirty-minute episode! Regina was in heaven.

She was surrounded by millions of dollars' worth of editing equipment—stacks and stacks of DVDs, monitors everywhere she looked, and uncomfortable-looking swivel chairs that had bruised the butts of MVN's various award-winning editors. Of course, Regina ultimately wanted to be a director—but she knew that the best filmmakers understood all areas of film production. So she could barely contain her excitement.

"Oh, my God, this is so *dope*," gasped Regina, clasping her hands together under her chin. She looked like a six-year-old on Christmas morning. She paced through the room, stroking buttons and running her hands over the monitors until Kiki pulled out a chair next to hers and asked her to sit down.

"Here, I'll show you how we edit down all this footage." Kiki slid a tape into the VCR, and they watched Skye and Alexa shopping for invitations at Kate's Paperie.

"How did you learn all this? Most camerawomen don't usually edit, right?"

"No, of course not. But here's a secret—MVN is so damned cheap, it's not even funny. You end up doing twelve different jobs."

"That must really suck."

"Yeah, but honestly? I just love it," said Kiki, smiling. "And me and Jenna are such a good team, too. I'm good at making the shots look interesting, and Jenna—man, she can get kids to say the craziest stuff."

"How does she do it?"

"She's just really chill when she's interviewing. When you feel like someone's your friend, you'll say anything. That's when we get the really evil, hilarious stuff that makes the shows so juicy."

Regina nodded, scooting her swivel chair closer to Kiki to get a better look at the screen. But then she stopped paying attention altogether, because Kiki smelled so *good*—fruity and spicy and slightly musky. Regina wanted to be able to spray that scent on everything she owned. Distracted now, she zoned out on Kiki's tutorial and just looked at her. Kiki was tiny and curvy, with the cutest pixie haircut and sick style. (Regina couldn't help wondering how Kiki's flowy, cool-looking embroidered Mexican halter top and skinny jeans would look on her!) And her *mouth*. It was so full and pouty, and Regina loved how, when Kiki smiled, one side curved up higher than the other.

Regina didn't realize she was staring until Kiki finally glanced away from the screen and caught her in the act. Mortified, Regina immediately sat up straight and nodded, pretending to pay attention.

"Regina?"

"Yeah?" She gazed at the monitor, refusing to look in Kiki's direction. Suddenly her palms were sweating, and she felt her heart thumping wildly in her chest. *Please just pretend you didn't see me staring at you,* she silently pleaded. *Just spare me the agony!*

No such luck.

"I saw you looking at me," said Kiki, quietly.

Regina's stomach sank. "No, I wasn't! I was . . ."

"Don't worry about it. It's okay." Kiki smiled a little. "I've been looking at you, too."

Regina swore she heard a choir of angels singing in the distance. "Really?"

"You remind me of myself five years ago. I don't pretend to know your . . . situation, but I know that when I was in high school, I never dreamed of telling anyone I was gay. I don't think I even told myself until I was in college."

Regina's mouth went dry. *How did she know? And if this total stranger could tell, was it obvious to everyone else?*

"I had an awful identity crisis," continued Kiki. "I mean, I always pictured lesbians as really tough looking, with bad barbershop buzz cuts and Birkenstocks. "

"Rosie O'Donnell," Regina whispered quietly, looking down at her hands.

"Exactly!" Kiki burst out laughing. "And that wasn't me. It's not you, either." She tucked her finger under Regina's chin and tilted her face upward. "Listen, you can be open with me. *I get it.* Okay?"

Regina nodded, feeling a huge weight being lifted from her. For some reason, she felt like crying. "Okay."

They looked at each other for a moment, all kinds of

possibility hanging in the air. Before anything more interesting could happen, though, an intercom went off.

"Kiki Jackson to the front desk, please."

The moment was broken.

"Oh, shit," Kiki said, jumping out of her seat and grabbing her bag. "I hope they didn't figure out I snuck you up here. I'll be right back, okay?"

Suddenly Regina was in the room alone. The skin on her arms where Kiki had touched her was tingling. She was trembling and sweating—what had just happened? She wished Nick had been there. He'd have known what to do in that situation. She shook her head, trying to get her bearings. *Pull yourself together,* she told herself. *Make yourself busy until she comes back.*

Absentmindedly, she searched through the DVDs on Kiki's desk. She came across one marked *Confessionals*. This must be the recording of Jenna's one-on-one interviews! she thought. She wondered whom she'd already talked to. Regina kept staring at the DVD, running her finger along the label, until the curiosity was like an itch at the bottom of her foot, driving her crazy. A few moments passed, and then she peeked out the door to see if anyone were coming, popped the disc into the DVD player, and pushed PLAY.

And there was Skye, perched on her tiger-print love seat, rocking a tiara and talking shit.

". . . A good friend would let me have my moment, right? Instead, she's running around bragging about this senior she likes, throwing it in my face all the damn time. I'm like, shut it, *okay? She's lucky I*

don't kick her off my court. God, he's such a dick. After he shits on her, she'll feel bad for ruining my Sixteen Candles *experience. Oh, and, can I just say? Her recent fashion choices have been very wrong. She's just not dressing for her body type. Hello? Big butts and miniskirts are a major* don't!*"*

Regina's mouth dropped open. How could Skye say those things about Tangie? She was absolutely horrified . . . and wildly intrigued. She knew she should stop the tape before Kiki came back, but she *had* to see who else had spilled their guts on camera. Before she had time to rethink it, she pushed FAST FORWARD. She stopped when she saw Kamillah. She was sitting on a bench in Union Square Park, looking very un-happy in a kente-cloth dashiki and matching head wrap.

"Whatever to Black's whole thing about reality shows reinforcing 'angry black man' and 'loudmouth black bitch' stereotypes. He's got mad nerve trying to ban me from doing Sixteen Candles *when I know for a damn fact that he TiVos* Survivor *and* Project Runway. *Look, I love him, but his super-African mandingo shit is strictly wack. That's why I kissed Vineet at Wendy's last weekend. How ya love that?"*

"Oh, my God, oh, my God . . ." whispered Regina, beside herself. Vineet? *Oh, hell, no, this stuff* so *can't make it on the episode,* she thought. Holy shit, her entire clique would fall apart in seconds! Nothing would ever be the same again. These confes-sions were just too scandalous. Still, she absolutely couldn't stop watching.

After fast-forwarding a bit more, she landed on Tangie, who was sitting cross-legged on a studio floor, her curls pulled back into a messy bun atop her head. She looked . . . mad. In fact, Regina had never seen her look so pissed.

"Her head's totally exploded with this Sixteen Candles *thing, and it's like we all have to bow down to her. And she's so jealous of me and Trey. The thing is, she's used to getting all the guys, and now that a popular boy likes me, she's bugging out. God, right now I really hate her. All she cares about is publicity and being a star. And yeah, she's popular, but how many people really, truly like Skye? I'm one of the few, and she treats me like shit.*

"Oh, and FYI? I have some information that would really, really embarrass her, but since I'm the better person, I'll just keep it to myself."

Regina's eyes were practically bugging out of her head. When had Tangie gotten so vindictive? And what was this secret information? *Kiki was right,* Regina thought. *Jenna really does get kids to talk crazy!* She realized that she'd just put herself in the really awkward position of knowing that her friends had said these things. If she didn't do something to stop this footage from airing on the episode, would the outcome be sort of her fault?

She clutched her stomach, suddenly feeling queasy.

But before she could decide what to do, she heard footsteps in the hallway. She quickly ejected the DVD, sliding in the one she had been watching with Kiki.

By the time Kiki walked through the door, Regina had broken out in a cold sweat. She felt as if the guilt were all over her face like prepubescent acne, but thankfully, Kiki didn't seem to notice.

"So," she said, sliding into the chair next to Regina. "Where were we?"

"Um, can I ask you a question?"

"You know you can ask me anything."

"Remember when Jenna was telling us she'd be taping one-on-one confessionals over the week?"

"Yeah, of course."

"Um, how many of those confessionals do you use in a regular episode?"

Kiki laughed. "Well, your friends turned out to be real bitches, so we'll probably use as many as we can!"

Regina felt the blood drain from her face. What the hell was she going to do?

At exactly eight twenty, the front-door buzzer went off in Tangie's apartment.

"*No!*" Tangie yelped in surprise, dropping her mascara wand on the floor, where it left an inky smudge on the carpet. Trey was ten minutes early! She bolted out of her room and down the hallway, pressing the talk button on the intercom.

"I'll be right down!" she called. She did not ask Trey to come upstairs. Her father didn't know about her date (he had believed her ridiculous lie about going to a math club dinner and fund-raiser). And she'd rather jump in the East River than introduce her depressed, silent blob of a father to Trey.

She sprinted into the bathroom to check herself out in the full-length mirror one last time. An hour earlier, Izzy had come over and put together her First Date Ever outfit for Tangie—a delicate Empire-waist top from bebe with a denim mini and superhigh Nine West wedgies. It was cute and sexy without looking desperate, and the ensemble highlighted Tangie's legs. *And* she was wearing her wild, shoulder-length curls loose instead of up in a dance department—regulated bun. Tangie looked good, and she knew it!

Shouting, "I'm gone!" she grabbed her little polka-dot purse and flew out the door. Seconds later, she was standing outside her brownstone facing Trey.

"Hi," she said, smiling. God, she was nervous. Her palms were already sweating, and she and Trey hadn't even left Brooklyn.

"Hi, gorgeous," he said, kissing her on the cheek. He was the gorgeous one; in his crisp Ralph Lauren polo with the collar popped, he looked Kanye West fresh. "You're lookin' mad cute, Dimples. I'm sayin', I might not be able to control myself."

"Oh, stop it," Tangie said with an awkward giggle—the flirty, plastic one she used only around Trey.

"Here, I brought you something," he said, handing her a pink gift bag.

Tangie couldn't have been more shocked if Trey had said he'd flown to her house on a spaceship. She'd never gotten a real gift from a boy!

"You brought me something? *Really?* What is it?"

"A present, kinda. I don't know, I thought you should have somethin' to help you remember our first date."

Tangie beamed, taking the bag from him. "Are you

serious? You really didn't have to do that."

"Not a problem, I'll just return it," he joked, reaching for the bag.

"No!" she giggled (there it was again), flattered. She reached inside the bag and pulled out a beautiful black Barbie doll . . . B-Girl Barbie, to be exact. She was decked out in a jersey, a red-and-white bandanna, cutoff jean shorts, and itty-bitty felt Timberlands. "Aww, she's the cutest thing ever. I can't believe you!"

"I saw it and thought of you. It kinda looks like you, right? But without the curls." He smiled. "So, you ready?"

"Where are we going, by the way?"

"You'll never guess."

"Hmmm. The movies?"

"No, but I'm really tryin' to see that *Emily Rose* joint? I love a scary movie, yo. I see 'em all the time; that's why I got a night-light."

"That's so funny—I saw *Exorcism of Emily Rose* last night!"

"Word? Who'd you go with?"

"My friends, Izzy and C.J."

Instantly, Trey's ears pricked up. C.J.? That was the dude Skye had said was the love of Tangie's life, he thought. She had also said Tangie was just messing with him to make C.J. jealous.

Trey didn't like the fact that she had gone out with C.J. the night before. He didn't like it at all. But for now, he just filed it away under the category of Things to Investigate Later.

"Cool, cool. But we ain't going to the movies." Trey grabbed her hand. "Trust me, though, you'll have fun."

Tangie grinned at him. She couldn't believe he'd actually bought her a *gift*—it was so romantic! It was perfect. The night had already gotten off to a fabulous start.

And it was about to get even better. Tangie had assumed they were taking the subway, but Trey walked her to his car. No one in New York drove! It was a fancy Lexus, his sixteenth-birthday present. And the best part? He was a perfect gentleman, opening the door for her and everything.

They drove over the Brooklyn Bridge as the sun was setting—it was gorgeous. Tangie was unbearably nervous in spite of the fabulous setting. She was fine with Trey when they were dancing in the studio, but she never really knew what to say to him otherwise. Luckily, this time he did most of the talking. In fact, he talked so much—about his plans after graduation, his workout routine, the agents that already wanted to sign him-that all Tangie had to do was nod and smile.

They drove up ritzy Madison Avenue through the shopping district until they got to Fifty-ninth Street. Then Trey made a sharp left and turned toward the Plaza Hotel, one of the oldest, fanciest, most *exclusive* hotels in Manhattan.

"Trey! What are we doing here?" Tangie said as Trey handed his keys to the valet. He opened her side of the door and pulled her out.

"I'm taking you to a penthouse party. You know Ana Claudia and Daniela Rosario, right? They have these dope-ass joints, like, every month . . . but you gotta know somebody to get in, it ain't no 'just anybody can come' type thing."

Tangie's eyes widened. "But . . . but, Trey, I've never even met them!"

"Chill, girl! You're with me. Come on, we gonna turn this shit out."

Tangie looked cool as she walked with him into the ornate Plaza foyer and rode up in the plush, gilded elevator, but she was actually fending off a major panic attack. Ana Claudia and Daniela Rosario? Who *hadn't* heard of them? The gorgeous Brazilian twins were superpopular seniors, heiresses to the multibillion-dollar Claudio Rosario fashion empire—and their hotel parties were both legendary *and* impossible to get invited to. While their parents traveled the world, the twins lived in a sprawling penthouse on the Plaza's top floor. Ana Claudia was a ballerina, Daniela an opera singer—and together they were trouble.

Tangie and Trey were now standing outside the penthouse door, which was practically vibrating from the thumping bass. Tangie was in full-on panic mode, though she was trying to look cool. "But I don't know them, Trey. And they didn't invite me. What if . . ."

"What if nothing," Trey said, wrapping his muscular arm around her shoulders and hugging her to him. His body was rock hard, *perfect*. "You with me, Dimples. Anywhere I'm good, you're good."

She didn't have time to answer, because the moment knocked, Daniela Rosario answered the door. "Trey mothafuckin'

Stevens!" she tra-la-laed in a pitch-perfect, opera-trained high C (which sounded odd coming out of a person wearing a gold lamé caftan over a white string bikini). "You better get your hot ass in here, baby!" she screamed and grabbed him by the arm, dragging him into the penthouse. Tangie followed, feeling like some kid Trey had been was babysitting.

Once her eyes adjusted to the darkness, she caught a glimpse of the penthouse and was blown away. The living room was spectacular. With its sparkling crystal chandeliers, plush overstuffed sofas and grand, gold-framed paintings, it looked like some Parisian palace. In the main room, someone had pushed the sofas against the wall, and folks were dancing like maniacs to Rihanna's "Pon de Replay." Everywhere she looked, she saw twelfth graders from school, as well as people she'd never met, making out, laughing, drinking, taking weird pills. And it seemed like *everyone* was trying to get to Trey. It was total mayhem.

Tangie had never felt so out of place. Why would Trey take her to an exclusive senior party on their first date? He knew she didn't know a soul. This was *his* crowd, a private party, and she felt as wrong as black socks and sandals.

She turned to ask him where the bathroom was, but he was already deep in conversation with a bunch of girls who had surrounded him. Each one was prettier than the last. Tangie felt like sinking through the floor. Suddenly her outfit felt tragically young, like something from GapKids. Her cheeks felt hot, and she didn't know where to put her hands. She looked over at Trey, eyes pleading, but he was in full storytelling mode. *Please talk to me!* she screamed in her head, wishing he could hear her. *Just talk to me, only me! Ignore those stick-figure sluts—I'm your date!*

Totally abandoned, Tangie wandered over to a coffee table stocked with sodas, vodka, gin, tequila, beer, and orange juice. She poured herself a Sprite, thinking that maybe she'd feel cooler holding a red plastic cup. As she took a sip, her eyes darted around the room and she noticed a group of girls whispering and pointing at her.

She knew what that was all about, of course. They wanted to check out the girl who Trey had decided was fly enough to walk in Eden the Great's shoes. Tangie wondered if they were disappointed.

Just when she was two seconds from running for the hills, the unbelievable happened. Ana Claudia Rosario herself wandered out of the whispering group of girls and linked her arm through Tangie's.

"Hey, sweetie, I'm Ana Claudia; I'm so happy you're here, we've heard so much about you, come on, let's get you a real drink." She talked so fast that her words seemed to melt together into one vodka-soaked, run-on sentence. Without waiting for Tangie to respond, the gorgeous Brazilian led her into the kitchen.

Surprisingly, it wasn't as packed as the rest of the penthouse. For the first time in fifteen minutes, Tangie felt as if she could exhale. While Ana Claudia poured twelve different liquors into a little red cup, she leaned against a counter, trying to get her bearings.

"So, Tammy—wait, it's Tammy, isn't it?"

"Tangie."

Ana Claudia burst out laughing for what felt like three hours. When she finally recovered, she said, "That's what I meant. Here, take this." She handed Tangie the red cup and watched her intently, as if she were looking at her under a microscope.

"I have to tell you, we've all heard *so* much about you. Like, everybody's talking about this new chick Trey's hollering at. Don't get me wrong, he talks to lotsa girls—even when he was dating Eden—it was so sad—but we knew you were different, 'cause he was seen in *public* with you. And now he's bringing you to one of our *parties*? Shit, girl, you're *in* there."

Tangie had no idea how to respond to this, so she blurted out the first thing that came to her. "He bought me a Barbie."

"What?"

"Nothing. Uh, thanks for the drink." *He bought her a Barbie?* Jesus Christ, she needed to pull it together. Humiliated, she took a sip of her mystery drink and immediately wanted to vomit. Ana Claudia's concoction was disgusting—and it went right to her head. Suddenly, she started to feel warm, loose, liquidy, like she was made of maple syrup.

Ying Yang Twins' "Whisper Song" turned into Omarion's "Touch," which always reminded Tangie of the first time she had seen Trey dance—he had been rehearsing alone in a studio, she had been watching him, and he'd invited her in. They'd ended up dancing together and, just like that, he became her tutor! *That seems like a million years ago, like the 1970s*, thought

Tangie, feeling all squishy from whatever her hostess had given her to drink. Ana Claudia was chattering on and on about wanting to buy a red Fendi Spy bag, but Tangie was floating, unable to focus. She was feeling good; her face melted into a goofy smile, and her body began moving to the beat.

Abruptly, Trey burst into the kitchen, hollering, "You know this is our song, Dimples!"

He kissed a squealing Ana Claudia on the cheek, then grabbed Tangie and twirled her around. "Let's go do this thing, girl!"

Excited that he was finally paying attention to her (and loving the fact that he remembered their moment in the studio), she followed him to the dance floor. He pulled her into the middle of the ecstatic, out-of-control crowd, and they started dancing.

But Trey and Tangie's dancing was *waaay* different then everyone else's dancing. Together, they made the rest of the party look as if they'd never even heard music before. Their chemistry was so incredible that, within seconds, people had started to form a circle around them. Smoothly, Tangie and Trey transitioned into the famous choreography from the video, the part where Omarion and his girl danced together down the street. The funny thing was, they didn't look like they were copying anybody—the way they flirted and popped and grooved with each other, it was as if they'd made up the routine on the spot. And the crowd around them went nuts. People screamed so loud they drowned out the music.

When "Touch" ended, everybody broke out in messy, drunken

applause for the brand-new couple. Trey and Tangie stood there, sweating and breathing hard and grinning at each other. Basking in the crowd's attention, he spun her around three times and dipped her—and then, in front of every Armstrong senior who mattered, he kissed her full on the mouth.

When Tangie came up for air, she was shocked. For the first time, she realized that this *was* real, that he *did* actually like her. She looked at Trey, the gorgeous, perfect boy, and then looked at the crowd of people, in which girls she didn't know were complimenting her—and suddenly she felt *electric*. It was as if the air around her and Trey was crackling, buzzing. She'd never felt so sexy and important. The chick guys wanted and other girls wanted to be.

I get it now, she told herself. I get why celebrities get addicted to the spotlight, the applause, the cameras.

She didn't want the feeling ever to end. . . . It was the most exciting, delicious, spectacular moment she'd ever had.

Until she noticed Eden. Skye's glamorous older sister was leaning against the wall, eyeing Tangie with a suspicious expression. Across the room, she mouthed, *Can I talk to you?* Tangie nodded and then made her way over to where Eden was lurking.

"Hi, Eden," she said, feeling social power for the first time ever. She wasn't afraid of her.

"Hey, sweetie," said Eden in her breathy, faraway voice. She always sounded as if she'd just awakened from a nap (it was all the Valium she took "for her nerves"). "You looked amazing out there."

The compliment was so unexpected that at first Tangie didn't know what to say. "That's so sweet. Thank you."

Eden nodded, brushing the bangs out of her eyes. "I know Trey makes you feel like you're on top of the world. And I'm not gonna lie: it's exciting being with a guy that so many girls want. But how about I save you some trouble, okay? He doesn't love anyone but himself. And he can't keep his penis in his pants for *any* girl, no matter how cute she is." She giggled airily. "If he cheated on me, then no one's good enough."

Tangie flinched, feeling completely deflated. She opened her mouth to speak, but nothing came out.

"Listen, just have fun with him. But don't catch feelings."

"But . . . but we like each other," Tangie said, her voice sounding small and pathetic.

"I can see why he likes you, you know. You *kill* on the dance floor. You're the perfect prop—you make him look good." She took a sip of her drink. "And for a guy as conceited as Trey, that's all that counts."

Tangie wondered if that were true. Eden was actually making sense, and that bothered her more than anything. How dare she try to ruin her moment? And yet she still felt as if she had to be deferential to her. While growing up with Skye, Eden had kind of been like Tangie's big sister, too.

"I don't . . . why are you telling me this?"

"I'm trying to help you out, sweetie. Be careful. The end won't be pretty."

Eden gave her a feathery kiss on the cheek, then floated away. For the rest of the night, Eden's words *you're the perfect prop,* sounded over and over in her head until she thought she was going insane.

It wasn't until later, when Trey dropped her off at her doorstep like a perfect gentleman and gave her the sweetest good-night kiss, that she forgot Eden's warning. Tangie didn't care what anyone said—she was Trey's girl. Things were going to be different this time.

The Carmichael sisters were just *haters*, plain and simple.

Name: Tangela Marcia Adams
Class: Sophomore
Major: Dance
Self-Awareness Session #: 7

So, Miss Adams, how are things with Trey?

I think I really, really like him! Oh, we had the best date last night. You should see him dance. You should see us dance together! I think we make a really cute couple. I mean, I guess we do.

You don't sound so sure.

Well, it's something my friend Skye's big sister said to me the other day. She kinda said all Trey cares about is himself. And that he really only likes me because I'm a good dancer and I make him look even better. Her exact words were that I'm the "perfect prop."

That's not very nice. Do you believe her?

I've been thinking a lot about it, and I don't know. Me and Trey don't really have anything in common besides dance. We talk a lot, though—actually, he talks, and I listen.

Does he ever ask you about yourself? You know, your thoughts, the things you like?

Mmm, not really. But maybe that's not true—maybe I just don't like talking about myself too much. I should be more out-going, I guess. You know something? There's one other thing that bothers me, and I haven't brought it up to anyone.

What is it?

He calls me Dimples all the time. It's like his nickname for me, which is so cute. But . . . I don't have dimples! Isn't that weird?

10.
SHE'S SO LUCKY

IT WAS FRIDAY, THE DAY BEFORE Skye's Sweet Sixteen bash, and her anxiety was at an all-time high. To prepare her party personality, she and Regina went on a top secret *Sixteen Candles* mission. After Characterization class, they'd snuck into the drama department's enormous, off-limits props closet (the day before, Skye had flirted with the maintenance man until he gave her a key). And now, surrounded by hundreds of miscellaneous theater accessories—a complete Marie Antoinette costume, Salvation Army furniture, fairy wings, 1960s Supremes wigs, clown shoes, and so on—Regina and Skye were engaged in some very hush-hush party preparation.

Skye was an actress; the best actresses came to the set prepared, rehearsed, and knowing *exactly* how to play the scene, and she was approaching her party the same way—she intended to practice being Skye as much as possible before the MVN cameras broadcasted her every move to the entire world.

So, Regina was taping Skye as she acted out certain key party moments—things like looking surprised when she saw her new Happy Birthday car, a gift from her parents, or blowing out her candles, or posing for pictures in the VIP area. After filming, the two would play the tape back and dissect her every move. If anything looked crazy, weird, or unsexy, Skye would work on it and remember to do it right the next night.

Yes, it was cheesy—and yes, if anyone had found out, she'd have killed herself—but Skye was *not* about to let MVN catch her looking wack.

Regina held the digital video camera up in front of her until Skye was centered in the screen. "You ready?"

Skye nodded. "Yeah, yeah, yeah; let's just hurry!" Free period was over in fifteen minutes, so they were in a serious time crunch.

"Okay," Regina said, holding up her thumb. "Skye dancing at her *Sixteen Candles* party, take one."

Skye raised her hands above her head and began wiggling her hips in what she thought was a sultry, but not slutty, way. She closed her eyes and smiled. Then she lowered her hands down to her sides, looked over her shoulder, and started doing the Beyoncé booty-shake.

"Okay, we've got enough," said Regina, rewinding the tape. Skye ran over to her, and together they watched her sexy dance. Immediately, Skye felt her stomach turn.

"Holy fucking shit, I look like a tired, hungry stripper! Is that how I dance? Oh, my God, I'm not dancing at my party. That's it, forget it."

"Wait a minute. Why don't you just change it up a little? Don't raise your arms, maybe?"

"Next to Tangie, I'll look ridiculous." She squinted at the screen and then yelped in horror. "Please tell me I don't *always* make that face when I dance?"

"What face?"

"The 'ooh-baby-I'm-so-hot-right-now-I'm-on-*fire*' face?" She licked her finger, touched her shoulder and made a hissing sound. "Like that? J. Lo makes that face when she dances. Ugh, it's so desperate!"

Regina agreed, but she thought it was best to keep quiet.

"Forget it, let's do a different scene. Let's film me looking surprised when I see my new car for the first time."

She ran over to her mark; Regina rewound the tape and gave her the thumbs-up. Skye counted backward from five and then exclaimed, "Oh, my God, is that mine? For real? Daddy, thank you so much. . . . Oh, I love it!" She jumped up and down, clapping her hands and laughing. "I'm the luckiest girl in the world!"

This one, Skye *loved*.

"Okay, I've redeemed myself," she said, watching the tape. "Damn, I'm a good actress."

"Yeah, you are," said Regina. "Okay, are we done? We only have, like, three minutes."

"I think we're done!" squealed Skye, running over to the mirror. She turned to the side and sucked in her nonexistent stomach. She'd been dieting for a week. *I can't imagine what a bride must feel like on her wedding day*, she thought, fluffing up her hair. She turned to face Regina. "You know what? You look gorgeous."

Regina looked up, surprised. She could count on one hand the number of times Skye had ever complimented her. "Really?"

"Yeah, you've been glowing all week. Like you're having really good sex, which I know you aren't." She giggled. "What's going on?

"I don't know. Nothing!"

"Are you wearing that Stila bronzer I told you about?"

Regina shook her head, smiling to herself. It was Kiki. Every time she thought about her, which was every second, she felt all flushed and excited. "I think I'm just excited about the party."

"I know, I can hardly stand it. I just wish it were tomorrow night," Skye said, turning to face the mirror and fussing with her hair some more. "I'm as anxious as a virgin on prom night."

"That's pretty damned anxious," muttered Regina.

"Has Nick said anything about me?'

"Like what?"

"You tell me, babe. I know how he talks to you." She saw Regina's confused expression in the mirror. "I mean, we're totally just friends, but I still like him. I can't help it."

"*What?* Wait; I thought you were over him, Skye."

"Come on," Skye said, turning back to face her. "You know me better than that. I love a challenge. And I'm really not about to let some long-distance bitch win over me. Are you nuts?"

A very bad feeling was coming over Regina. This was not good at all. Last time Skye had thrown herself at Nick, he'd narrowly escaped being outed. When he told Regina that Skye had found his *Mandingo Madness* DVD, she had been horrified. If anyone discovered Nick was gay, his parents would send him to live with his great-aunt in Greece, and Regina would lose the only person on the planet she could confide in!

"You really should take it slow with him." Regina packed her camera inside its carrier and stood up. "I just don't want to see you getting hurt again. He's really devoted to his girl-friend."

"That's what makes him even sexier," said Skye, looking all dreamy-eyed. No matter what his situation was, she was deter-mined to change all of it the following night. She'd look so damn irresistible, he wouldn't be able to keep his hands off her.

She actually felt kind of sorry for his long-distance girl.

Tangie was sitting on one of the three chairs outside Ms. Carmen's office, waiting to talk to her. She wasn't alone—three other girls were also waiting with her. She recognized Gigi Cho and Allison Mosbacher from her street funk and jazz classes, but she'd never met Nessa Otumba. It didn't matter, because they all knew exactly who she was. Overnight, she'd gone from being Tangie Adams, sophomore dancer in need of booty-liposuction, to Tangie Adams, reality-show costar and Trey Steven's girlfriend. And now the snooty Skinny Bitches who never spoke two words to her in dance class were loving the hell out of her. In fact, Tangie and her almost-famous friend Skye were all they could talk about.

Tangie knew they were only talking to her to get gossip, but she didn't mind. She was still on a high from the Rosarios' party, and nothing was going to ruin it.

"Okay, Tangie, you *must* tell us all about Skye's *Sixteen Candles* extravaganza tomorrow night," said Gigi, an elegant but scary-skinny Chinese ballerina. She'd befriended Tangie for about two minutes on the first day of school, then promptly dropped her when she realized Tangie hadn't trained at a major New York City dance academy, like National Dance Theater or Joffrey Ballet School.

"What do you want to know?"

"First of all, who's performing?" asked Nessa, a long-legged, ebony-skinned goddess from Ghana. Her Russian leaps were legendary.

"Obviously, Smoove Killah," replied Allison, a fantastic lyrical dancer whose father was a cutthroat Wall Street tycoon. The bossy know-it-all lived and breathed dance department gossip. "I mean, Eden's dating him, right? Or will there be a surprise guest?"

"Oooh, this is the most exciting thing to happen at Armstrong in forever!" squealed Gigi, jumping up and down. "You're so-o-o lucky to be going! I hate you!"

"Tell me Trey's going with you," said Allison, grabbing Tangie by the arm. "God, he is so beautiful. My best friend Charlotte's boyfriend's ex-girlfriend takes Vocal Arrangement with Daniela Rosario, and she said you and Trey danced like fucking *pros* at their party last night."

"Thanks," beamed Tangie. She still got tingles thinking about that moment.

"That choreo from 'Touch' is the sickest," gushed Nessa. "Do we know who did it?"

"I'm pretty sure it was Rich and Tone," said Allison. "They choreograph tons of stuff for those R & B guys. I bet Trey knows them—he's so connected."

Gigi nodded. "His career's gonna be off the chain when he graduates."

"I know, right?" Allison sighed, wistfully. "Tangie, I totally appreciate your hustle, girl. Very, very smart of you."

"What do you mean?" Tangie frowned.

"Why can't she just be with him 'cause she's feeling him?" Nessa shot Allison a look.

"I'm not saying she isn't! It's just that you'd be *insane* not to use his connections. We all know it takes much more than talent to win . . . and Tangie's one step ahead of us all right now."

"All I know is, I could never not date a dancer," announced Gigi. "They kiss better, they hook up better—I don't know, they're just sexier."

"Last year I messed with a sax player, right? We snuck into Butter with my fake ID, and I danced solo all night long. He couldn't even handle a damn two-step." Nessa shook her head. "And he was a terrible kisser. See this scar? He bit me and broke the skin."

"See? A dancer would never chew your lip off." Allison looked at Tangie. "I bet Trey can kiss. This girl in my friend Bree's homeroom said . . ."

Gigi elbowed Allison in the ribs.

"Uh, never mind."

"What?" Tangie flinched. "She said what?"

"Just that he was good," Allison said quickly. "I mean, you have to know he's been with a lot of girls in our department."

"Yeah, but now he's into *you*." Nessa smiled at her sweetly. "It's, like, so obvious."

"You have nothing to worry about. I mean, he cheated on Eden like it was his *job*, but I really think he's a new man." Allison nodded authoritatively, her big, bushy curls bouncing. "I honestly feel that getting in trouble for the Missy video really made him grow up."

They were silent for a minute, thinking about all of this.

"Anyway, what's Skye wearing tomorrow night? Is she doing wardrobe changes?"

"No doubt she'll get a gorgeous BMW at the end," said Gigi, giggling. "Have you noticed that the kid gets a McBeamer in every episode? Tangie, do you know if MVN has a contract with them?"

"You're so *lucky* you're gonna be there!" Gigi looked like a little kid anticipating her first birthday party. "You have to give us all the details on Monday, okay? Promise?"

Before Tangie could say anything, Ms. Carmen's door opened, and a petite redhead walked out, wiping her eyes. As she grabbed her bags from the floor, Tangie noticed she had a major leotard wedgie.

Sticking her head out of the office, Ms. Carmen said, "Tangie, you're next, Pumpkin."

Tangie waved good-bye to the girls, and Gigi blew her a kiss. *They told me I was lucky about fifteen times,* she thought, shutting the office door behind her. What, was she some charity case?

"So, what brings you to my office, Sugarplum?"

"I, um, wanted to talk to you about something. . . ." began Tangie.

"If it's about this *Sixteen Candles* party, I'd rather talk about something else. Like the war." She rolled a pencil back and forth along her desk. "My students are so preoccupied with that party. It's a huge distraction."

Biting her lip nervously, Tangie said "Well, um, that's why I'm here."

Ms. Carmen rolled her eyes. "Lord. What is it?"

"I wanted to tell you that, um . . ." She took a deep breath before continuing, anticipating her teacher's freak-out. "I can't make tonight's Spotlight master class, because, well, I choreographed a routine that me and my two friends are performing at Skye's party, and tonight is our final rehearsal."

Disappointment and anger flooded Ms. Carmen's slightly wrinkled but still pretty face. "You do realize that, two days ago, you promised you'd make all the rehearsals."

"I know." Tangie looked at her hands, ashamed. "And I feel awful, but . . ."

"Tangie, you were one of *very* few students selected to audition for Spotlight. That's cute and all, but in the end, no one remembers who was selected to audition. What matters is *making* Spotlight. Let me refresh your memory on why this is important. Each department only picks three Spotlight Students per grade. You'll get to perform a solo at Fall Fling. And, come twelfth grade, you'll have a greater chance landing Spotlight at the final senior showcase, where the most important casting and talent agents in New York City will see your work. Nod if you get what I'm saying."

Tangie nodded sadly.

"Now, explain to me how your friend's reality show will do more for your dance career."

"Here's the thing, Ms. Carmen. I got to choreograph my very own routine—and millions of people all over the world watch *Sixteen Candles*! Who knows? Maybe, say, Ciara's choreographer will see it, remember me, and after graduation, ask me to go on tour with her! Or dance in her videos! You never know, Ms. Carmen."

"That's right, you never know. You never know if your part on *Sixteen Candles* will end up on the editing-room floor. You never know if your friends will bomb and make you look like a fool." Ms. Carmen's coffee-bean-colored eyes were blazing. "I'm telling you this because I care about you. You've been slacking, Pumpkin, and it's not cool. Those master classes are to help your chances at Spotlight auditions, and you're ignoring them. I asked you to find another tutor, and you haven't done that, either. Have you?"

Tangie shook her head. "But me and Trey dance all the time together. I know you don't like him, but he's really a good guy once you get to know him. And he's been teaching me so much."

Ms. Carmen shook her head. "I'm so disappointed in you, Tangie. I gotta be honest. And I don't see you improving. I see you flirting with Trey in class. And it's your career, in the end. Not mine." She stood up from her chair. "We're done here."

Tangie could feel the tears coming. "But, Ms. Carmen, after the party, I swear I'll be back on track. You'll see. I'll kill auditions next week. I didn't come to this school to fail."

"We're done here," Ms. Carmen repeated, opening her door.

When she walked out past Gigi, Nessa, and Allison, Tangie couldn't even hold her head up. She was ashamed. She had gone from being the luckiest girl in the world to being a huge disappointment.

Trey had heard C.J.'s name a little too much that week. First, Skye had told him that Tangie was in love with this fool, and then he found out that they went to the movies together. It was eating away at him, and he didn't know what to do about it.

Trey was the kind of guy who liked to know his competition. Before auditioning for a spot in his junior high school talent show, he had spied on the other break-dancer's rehearsal. He had nothing to worry about, of course, (the boy had a gimmick that involved dry-humping a Cabbage Patch Kids doll), but having *proof* that he could squash him had helped his tryout immensely.

That was how he felt about C.J. Now, Trey knew he had Tangie wrapped around his finger, no question. But he was still curious about the guy who, according to Skye, had been Tangie's first love. What was he all about? And what kind of hold did he have over Tangie? No matter how fly C.J. was, Trey *knew he'd* win—he had everything over a penniless fifteen-year-old drug dealer from the projects. But he still wanted to know what he was up against.

So, Trey went on a little spying mission. Nothing crazy—he just wanted to see how C. J. Parker operated. He'd done some undercover digging and discovered that C.J. took one-one-one weed appointments behind the bleachers during the underclassmen's lunch. It was funny—ever since the previous year, when Trey had heard that some graffiti-obsessed freshman had the best shit, he'd been meaning to stop by, but something had always distracted him (lunchtime had usually been his and Eden's prime fighting hour). Now he had a reason.

So, Trey skipped Advanced Tap to go see C.J. under the bleachers. He just wanted to have a few friendly words with him, figure out where his head was at and if he still liked Tangie. More than anything else, Trey wanted to make it very clear to this fool that she was now *his*.

As soon as he rounded the corner behind the bleachers, Trey saw C.J.—but something made him stop in his tracks. C.J. was leaning against the wall with a guy dressed like a Black Panther, in a beaded dashiki and bell-bottom jeans.

"So, you think it went good, right?"

"Melanie O'Donnell was *loving* your ass, partner. When you

pulled out that portrait, she was like a twelve-year-old at a Pretty Ricky concert."

"I know, right? I know." C.J. chewed on his lip. "It went good, but I had a bad feeling about it, too. I keep worrying it's gonna get out, somehow."

"Son, nobody's gonna find out. I'm quiet, and Izzy's quiet— and no one else knows!"

"But what if it does get out? It's like, it just really hit me. I could get *expelled*, yo. That shit is not a game."

This was the part where Trey's ears pricked up. *What* could get C.J. expelled?

"But weigh the consequences," said Black. "You get kicked outta school, but so what? Your nude sketch, a random homework assignment, made the *cover of OutKast's greatest hits album*, one that's absolutely going multiplatinum. Everybody's gonna be talking about it . . . you'll probably even get love in *The Source* or *Vibe* or *XXL*. So, yeah, Armstrong would be a wrap, but you'll have so much juice, you won't need this school."

C.J. was quiet for a long time, thinking. "And honestly, the reason I came to Armstrong was to get my career started as an artist."

"That's all I'm sayin', cuz."

"I could go to a regular school around my way. Find an agent, and sell my shit for, like, five to ten g's apiece. . . ."

"That's what I'm talkin' about. Work for your *damned* self, fuck the man. Keep it *funky*, homie. Our people gon' rise!" He raised his fist in the Black Power salute.

"Okay, but on the flip side . . ."

"Here you go."

"Seriously. I got my grandma to think about. I truly gave that woman hell for a good three years—she thinks I'm fully on the straight-and-narrow tip. If I got expelled, it'd kill her."

"Listen. Nobody's gonna know it was you. Your alias is Donatello, and nobody knows who that is. Okay? You're straight."

"I know. You're right, I'm good." C.J. laughed a little, but his brow was furrowed. "I was just trippin'."

Trey slowly backed away, wanting to burst at the seams. He had all the information he needed. He didn't really know what to do with it at the moment—so he filed it away for future use.

Something was telling him it would come in handy one day.

11.
WIFEY

IT WAS SATURDAY MORNING, and Smoove Killah, the international rap star, was driving Eden back to the Carmichaels' penthouse apartment in Chelsea, after spending the night in his $5,000-a-night loft at the Soho Grand Hotel. They were riding in his tricked-out Phantom, a car designed to impress. Eden never loved Smoove more than when she was riding in the passenger seat of his spectacularly divine whip, knowing they were making heads turn. But today, not so much. Today, she wanted to kill him.

At first, Eden thought she had misunderstood Smoove over the earsplitting music blaring from his sound system.

"Wait, what did you say?" Skye reached over and turned the volume down.

He shrugged and shook his head. "I told you—Smoove can't do his thing at your sister's party. I got a conflict."

She studied his face, searching for some sign that he was kidding.

"I ain't kiddin', Edie-Bird," he said, as if reading her mind.

"But . . . but I don't understand! You promised me a week and a half ago you'd do it. The party's *tonight*, Smoove! MVN's filming this! The producers have every second of this party accounted for! How the hell are we gonna find someone else now?"

"I dunno, baby. You smart—you'll figure out what to do."

Eden covered her face with her hands, totally distraught. She felt bad for letting Skye down, of course. Ever since she could remember, her little sis had always wanted everyone to think she was the prettiest, flyest, girl around (at bedtime, their nanny had used to have to chant, *Mirror, mirror, on the wall, Skye's the prettiest six-year-old of them all* three times before she'd close her eyes). And this party was just the latest stop in Skye's constant quest to prove herself to the world. And if Skye didn't have a hot performer—or worse, if she had some tacky, one-hit-wonderette like Lumidee—the poor girl would be ruined.

Even worse, though? Eden secretly felt that her very solid standing as Armstrong's golden girl would be tarnished if people found out she couldn't get her boyfriend to perform at Skye's Sweet Sixteen party. *Holy fucking shit,* she groaned inwardly. *Shoot me now.*

"Smoove, you can't do this. What the hell could be more important than this party? A party that'll be all over MVN, by the way?"

He shrugged. "Wifey."

"What do you mean, 'Wifey'?" Eden looked at him. "Pearl?"

"Yeah."

Eden didn't know which was more crushing, the fact that Smoove referred to his ex-fiancée as Wifey, or that he was backing out of the performance. "But . . . but I don't get it! Why would she care if you did an episode of *Sixteen Candles?* I mean, you don't tell her what to do in her career, so she can't . . ."

"Whoa, whoa, whoa, shawty! No woman tells Smoovie-K what to do, you feel me? It was definitely *not* like that. No, she just, um, strongly suggested that I not take the gig." He stopped at the light and then looked at Eden. "She's pissed because she saw the shot in *Page Six*. The one of us walkin' out of La Esquina."

A couple of weeks earlier, a paparazzi shot of Smoove and Eden leaving a chic restaurant had appeared in the *New York Post*. Which would've been cool if he hadn't been publicly attached to Pearl. Eden knew about Pearl, of course. But on their first date, Smoove had assured her that they weren't in love anymore, and that they only stayed together for the sake of their careers (they'd done too many guest appearances in each other's number one hits to suddenly split). Like an idiot, she had believed him. But now, all of a sudden, he was referring to Pearl as *Wifey?*

"I just don't understand why Pearl would care about this. You two aren't even together anymore."

Smoove was silent.

"Right?"

"Well . . . that depends on how you look it at. Per se."

"Oh, my God." Eden covered her face in her hands again, moaning at her stupidity. She was so humiliated that she couldn't even look him in the face. Why had she believed Smoove? Was she that gullible? After all, he was a damned hip-hop icon—everyone knew that those guys were the biggest playas ever (well, outside of athletes). She should've known.

She should've known, but . . . then again, there was the way he looked at her. The way he touched her. Smoove made her feel like the most important, exciting, and glamorous girl in the world. He took her to the fanciest restaurants and clubs in Manhattan—she had even hung out with Mischa Barton one night. He had bought her a diamond toe ring from Jacob the Jeweller. He had even jetted her off to Bermuda the previous weekend.

I mean, out of all the girls he could have, she said to herself, *he picked me . . . me!* But what had he picked her to be, exactly? The girl he ran around with when his real girlfriend got too boring or crazy? That was not cute. Smoove might've been the superstar, but did he know who *she* was? She was Eden Carmichael, a former star her damn self, and she wasn't going to take this treatment.

Number one, no one fucked with Eden. Number two, no one but Eden was allowed to fuck with Skye.

"So, you're really gonna back out on me, on my sister, like this? At the last minute?"

"I told you, shawty. It ain't like I wanted to back out. I just ain't got no choice. You understand, don't you?"

"Fine, you can't perform." She was talking very slowly and very softly, in a really threatening way, as she had seen Meryl Streep do in *The Devil Wears Prada*. "But I'm sure you can get one of your friends to take your place, right? I mean, you were in that *Fast and Furious* piece of shit with Bow Wow. And what about your guest sixteen bars on that Dipset song? Can't you get one of them?"

"Wow. I'm really feelin' you, boo, but it's *crazy* mad short notice. Do you even know what those niggas' schedules look like? I'm sayin' . . ."

"What did I tell you about using that word?"

"Schedules?"

"No, the N-word."

"Oh. My bad. Those *dudes* have schedules, man. Bow Weezy and the Dipset crew definitely don't got time to do some kid's birthday party. You gotta understand that."

Eden narrowed her eyes as she looked at him. "This is what I understand. I understand that if you don't get somebody— somebody *famous*—to perform tomorrow night, I'll tell Pearl all about the time you let me into her apartment to try on her Roberto Cavalli gown from the 2003 Grammies."

The Phantom screeched to a halt. Smoove looked at her, his face turning a queasy shade of khaki, and said, "Okay, okay, fine. I'll work it out. Dat nig—I mean, dat *dude* Smoove gonna work it out. Don't worry, I got this. Okay?"

She whipped out a Bobbi Brown compact from her bag and began nonchalantly reapplying her lip gloss. Smirking a little, she said, "Yeah, that's what I *thought*."

* * *

Skye and her parents were at the Lexus dealership on Eleventh Avenue in Manhattan, and things were not going well. Her father, the acclaimed Broadway producer Junior Carmichael, was trying to persuade the dealer to lower his price on a very cute 2005 SC 430, but he wasn't having any of it.

"Do you understand, Mr. Jimmy, that this car is my child's sixteenth-birthday present?" Junior was speaking in what he felt was a reasonable tone. The truth was, his deep baritone echoed through the dealership, making him sound like Darth Vader.

"I understand," said Jimmy.

"And do you understand that not only this vehicle, but your *dealership* will be shown on MVN networks all around the world—giving you tons of publicity?"

"I understand," said Jimmy.

"And do you understand that I've won five Tony Awards, and my wife has a star on Hollywood's Walk of Fame?"

"I understand," said Jimmy. "Last month, I sold vehicles to Shaquille O'Neal, Brad Pitt, and Prince William, the future king of England. None of them were discounted, sir. Either you take the car, or you don't. But I'd love for you to make a decision soon, as I have a Tae Bo lesson in twenty minutes."

Mr. Jimmy walked back into his office, and Junior Carmichael looked as if his head were going to explode into tiny pieces. After calling him every filthy name he could think of, the producer stormed after the pompous dealer. He was followed, of course, by Jenna and Kiki (who were filming the whole thing).

Meanwhile, Skye was two seconds from a full-throttle nervous breakdown.

"*Alexaa!*" she wailed to her mother. "What am I gonna do? This guy hates Daddy now, and I'll never get my car! Do something!"

"What do you want me to do, darling? Daddy's taking care of it." Alexa was examining her cuticles and couldn't have cared less about Skye's car. Her daughter had made them get up at 7 a.m. to get to the dealership by eight, and Alexa had had to skip her morning cocktail. She was cranky and wanted a Bloody Mary.

"Just go in there and make sure he's being nice," said Skye, fighting back tears. "Please? Come on, I have to have a car for my surprise tonight."

Alexa said nothing, but continued to pick at her cuticles.

"*Go!*" Skye screamed at the top of her lungs.

"*Fine!*" Alexa screamed back, and she stomped into the office.

Skye spun around and looked at Tangie, her face melting into sobs. Tangie nodded sympathetically and gave her best friend a hug. Skye would've been a complete basket case if Tangie hadn't agreed to go to the dealership with her. With the party only twelve hours away, everyone in the Carmichael household was stressed to the zillionth power. And Tangie was the only person who knew how to calm Skye down.

"Tangie, I'm gonna lose my mind," Skye said, wiping her eyes.

"It's okay, sweetie, you're gonna be fine. You know how crazy your parents are."

"But what if I don't get my car?"

"You're gonna get your car! Don't worry." Tangie grabbed Skye by the shoulders and shook her gently. "Listen to me. Three hundred people who worship you are coming to your party tonight. You're gonna look totally fabulous, and everything'll go perfectly."

"Yeah?"

Tangie knew exactly what to say to perk Skye up. "Yeah! And you know what else? All week long, all anyone could talk about was how *lucky* you are, and how *jealous* they are that you're about to be a reality star."

"Really?" A wide smile slowly crept across Skye's face. "Yeah, I guess I am lucky. Tangie, I can't believe my party is tonight. It's so surreal!"

"Seriously." Tangie shook her head. "Remember how we used to play teenager back when we were kids? We'd put on your mom's heels and drink ginger ale out of the bottle, pretending it was beer."

Skye giggled. "And French-kiss my B2K posters."

"Back then, I never imagined you'd be on TV. It's incredible." *I also never imagined I'd be going out with Eden's gorgeous ex-boyfriend*, she couldn't help thinking.

"I know, right? I just wish we could see the episode, like, tomorrow. I can't believe we have to wait a whole month! It's killing me." Skye shook her head. "I just hope I look pretty, that's all. And that my blow-out stays straight. My night'll be *ruined* if I sweat out my roots."

"Um, Skye? I wanted to ask you about the limo situation tonight."

"Oh, yeah. So, we got this enormous, totally tricked-out stretch limo to pick us all up—you, me, Regina, Kammi, C.J., and the boys. Oh, and Jenna and Kiki, of course. He's starting the pick-up at seven thirty, so be ready."

Tangie bit her lip nervously. "Do you . . . do you think there's room for one more person?"

"Who, Izzy? No, she's totally coming. I told you, I'm really committed to welcoming her into our clique. I mean, the girl is a full-on Armstrong obsession—it's a cute look for us, you know?"

"No, I was talking about Trey." Tangie held her breath, waiting for the drama to start.

"Ex*cuse* me?"

"I was wondering if I could bring Trey."

"Hell, fucking no."

"Skye, he's my *boyfriend*." She paused, realizing it was the first time she had said it out loud. It sounded weird. Forced, somehow.

"Did he tell you that?"

"No . . . no, but it's understood. I mean, it's obvious from the way he treats me that he's my boyfriend."

"Give me an example," said Skye, her hands on her hips.

"Okay, listen to this. It was so cute! On our first date, he bought me a Barbie doll." She realized that that sounded ridiculous, so she added, "It was B-Girl Barbie."

Skye looked at her for a moment and then burst out laughing. "He's your boyfriend 'cause he bought you a *Barbie*? Did you whip him up a cupcake in your Easy-Bake Oven?"

"Don't be like that. It was really sweet," Tangie said, sounding unconvinced. In the light of day, B-Girl Barbie really did seem idiotic. "I guess you had to be there."

"Yeah, I guess so. Tangie, don't bring that fool. Please."

"Why?"

"Because it's my party, it's my big day, and I don't want anything to ruin it." Skye stamped her foot like a child. "You know how much this party means to me. And you know how much I hate Trey. I don't care if you think he's your man, I know he's a jackass. And if you bring him, I'll have a terrible time, and it'll be your fault."

Tangie could feel her heart rate quickening. "You know what? I'm so tired of this. Why do you care if I hang out with Trey? It's not like he broke up with you; he broke up with Eden."

"It's not about Eden. It's about you. I don't want to see you get hurt, Tangie. You're being really stupid. He's a player, and everyone knows it." Skye leaned back on some car. "Look, *please* don't bring him, okay? I just want to have a good time."

Tangie stood there, stony-faced and furious. Because it was Skye's big day, she agreed not to bring Trey. But she couldn't help thinking that her supposed BFF was being really selfish and evil about the whole thing. Of course, Tangie didn't want to consider the obvious, which was that maybe Skye and Eden were right about Trey. Maybe he *was* a cheating player who'd only break her heart. No, the thought of that was too painful.

On the subway ride back to Brooklyn, Tangie remembered something Kamillah had said about Skye and karma. Kamillah was convinced that, because of the way Skye treated them after her Back to School party drama (dropping everyone for three weeks, then getting all chummy again only because she needed help for *Sixteen Candles*), something would go wrong with her Sweet Sixteen extravaganza. Skye couldn't get away with treating her friends like that and not have it come back to her, somehow.

Even though she knew it was wrong, right now Tangie hoped Kamillah's little premonition would come true.

12.
BRINGING SEXY BLACK

UNFORTUNATELY FOR TANGIE, the "Sorry, Trey, but you're not coming with me to Skye's party" conversation did not go very well. Actually, on the surface Trey took it like a champ, but she could tell—by the limited knowledge she had of him—that he was not happy.

Their phone conversation went like this.

"Hi, Trey."

"Hey, Dimples. You ready for tonight?"

"Yeah, but . . . um . . ."

"Wassup?"

"I talked to Skye about you coming with us in the limo, and—let's just say, she wasn't really cool about it."

"Yeah, she's still salty over the whole Eden thing, but whatever."

"I know, I know. It's so stupid. . . . I mean, it was *months* ago."

Trey was silent for a while, and then he said, in an

oddly cold voice, "Tangie, who's riding in the limo with you?"

"Oh, just our friends. Skye, Kamillah, C.J. . . . ."

"Word?" Silence. "Oh, okay."

Tangie could tell Trey wasn't thrilled about not riding with her, and at that point, she just didn't have the heart to tell him Skye didn't want him at the party, either. Skye would just have to suck it up. After all, it wasn't as if Tangie had liked all of *her* boyfriends. But she had always put up with them, even the one that scratched his balls in public.

"You know what? Just 'cause we're not riding together doesn't mean you can't come. Just meet me there, later."

"Naah. I'm good."

"What? What do you mean?"

"I'm really not pressed to go to my ex-girlfriend's little sister's birthday party."

Tangie flinched. "Well, yeah, but it's MVN. It's *Sixteen Candles*—this'll be the biggest party of the year. Plus, I'm performing."

"Sorry, it's a wrap for me. But jump in a cab and come over afterward, if you want."

"I can't do that, Trey. It'll be midnight!"

"Oh. Well, I'll get at you tomorrow, then. Text me later."

Tangie hung up, miserable and hurt. She'd been so looking forward to performing her grand entrance routine in front of Trey—after all, he had helped her teach Kamillah and Regina the choreography. She couldn't believe he had just blown her off like that.

Since she was the last one the limo was picking up, she had

an hour to psych herself up for the party. She packed her favorite lip gloss (Revlon Raisin Glaze), her favorite gum (Orbit Cinnamint), and her cell phone into her tiny gold metallic party bag, checked the mirror for any makeup mistakes (there were none), and told herself she was going to have a fabulous time, with or without Trey.

But when Tangie climbed into the long, sleek, black limo, her heart sank yet again. Everyone was separated into groups of two. She was the only single, the odd person out. Sitting in pairs were Skye and Nick, Kamillah and Black (though they weren't speaking), C.J. and Izzy (daggers in her heart!), Regina and Kiki (they had been attached at the hip lately), and Jenna and Vineet.

Wait, Jenna and *Vineet*?

"Hey, y'all," exclaimed Tangie, hoping her peppy voice masked the miserable way she felt.

"Get in, bee-yatch!!" Skye held a champagne glass up in the air, spilling a little on the seat. The birthday girl looked drop-dead gorgeous in a silver satin halter-topped gown (she had asked her dad to get an advance copy of *Idlewild*, and she'd had it copied from one of Paula Patton's dresses in the movie), a dove grey mink stole, and Alexa's diamond tiara. Her usual stick-straight weave fell in soft, rippling waves around her face, and she wore false eyelashes and a fake beauty mark above her upper lip. Despite her pristine appearance, Skye was well on her way to wasted, and had clearly forgotten about her spat with Tangie at the Lexus dealership.

Tangie sat down on the only empty seat, which was next to

Izzy, and quickly took in the scene. She'd never been in a limo before, but from what she'd seen on TV, this one was super-ritzy. Everything from the leather seats to the plush carpet was a rich, creamy shade of beige, and there were chilled bottles of champagne and wine glasses on built-in shelves in the wall. A spinning, multicolored disco ball cast a funhouse glow over everything—including the flat-screen television (which was playing *The Hills*). Some krunk song Tangie'd never heard was blaring from the surround-sound speakers, and her friends were chair-dancing their hearts out. The girls were all decked out in their glamour-girl costumes (courtesy of Brown's Broadway Costume Shoppe's 75 percent discount)—sequined Old Hollywood—era gowns with retro pinned-up hairstyles and vampy red lips. The boys were dapper-to-death in three-piece suits and fedoras. Everyone's personality was cranked up to ten, and there was a nervous, excited energy crackling in the air, as if everyone were anticipating something earth-shattering.

And yes, everyone was definitely paired off. Skye was in full seduction mode, falling against Nick's shoulder when she laughed, whispering in his ear, and ruffling his perfectly floppy curls. Generally, he just looked uncomfortable, his plastered-on smile never wavering. To their left sat Kamillah and Black, who were *not* happy. Kamillah had her arms folded across her chest and was pouting, while Black was deep in conversation with C.J. across the limo. No doubt Kamillah was furious about Black's inappropriate ensemble—instead of a gangster costume, he was proudly rocking an Afro wig and a T-shirt that said *Bringing Sexy Black!* (the exclamation mark was shaped like a black power fist). The only reason Skye had even let him come was that he wore the fedora! Next to the miserable couple were Regina and Kiki, who were giggling hysterically over private jokes. The oddest pair of all, Jenna and Vineet, were sitting next to them. While Jenna barked out orders to the club manager on her cell phone, Vineet stared at her like a lovesick kid. Occasionally, he'd touch her hair or attempt to hold her hand, and she'd slap him away impatiently.

Tangie made a mental note to ask Kamillah about that later.

And then there were C.J. and Izzy. Tangie had to admit they looked adorable. Dressed in a fringed minidress, patent-leather Mary Jane stilettos and a homemade, feathered headdress, Izzy had taken the glamour-girl theme and given it her own funky, Izzy spin. Meanwhile, C.J. had on his signature Bape kicks with his suit. Tangie looked at him and immediately started to sweat—she'd never seen him so dressed up. Somehow, he looked just as comfortable in a suit as he did in a white T and jeans. The boy was too sexy for words.

"What it do, mama?" said Izzy, giving her a kiss on the cheek. She linked her arm through Tangie's and whispered in her ear. "Can you *believe* I'm in a whip with these bougie bitches?"

"Thank God!" Excited to see her, Tangie squeezed her arm. "I really thought you weren't gonna come."

"You know what? Me and Ceej were at that Halloween costume store on Eleventh and Broadway looking for a toy gun to go with his costume—we're working a Bonnie and Clyde moment, can you tell? Anyway, we had so much fun that I was like, *fuck it*. You only live once, right?" She looked over at C.J., but he was deeply involved with his BlackBerry (to Tangie, it was obvious that he was doing everything he could to avoid looking her way).

"Anyway," continued Izzy, "that beef with Skye is so damn old I'm, like, bored to death with it."

"It's about time!" Tangie smiled at her, but the smile didn't reach her eyes. Hearing how much fun Izzy and C.J. had had only put more of a damper on her already sucky mood.

"Where's Trey at?"

"Oh, he couldn't make it," shrugged Tangie. "He had to do something with his parents, I'm not sure what."

"I'm sorry, baby. We'll have fun, though. Right, Ceej?" Izzy elbowed him in the side, and for the first time, he looked up at Tangie. And he was visibly in awe.

Tangie had on an outfit her mom had worn in a Dance Theatre of Harlem performance—a slinky gold mermaid-shaped dress that accentuated her curves, with matching T-strap heels and fishnet stockings. Her hair was wild and curly, and she'd stuck a huge red rose behind one ear. Tangie looked like one of those glamorous black socialites in old photos from the Harlem Renaissance.

To C.J., she was a goddess. Totally overwhelmed by her beauty, he did a double take and then dropped his BlackBerry. It was a cute move coming from C.J.—he was usually so damn cool all the time.

"Hey, T. You look . . . you look good."

She smiled her first real smile of the night. "Thank you.

You, too. Love the pocket square, it's a great touch."

"I had to get my grown man on, right?"

"Show her your rifle," said Izzy, knocking her shoulder against his.

Reaching under the seat, C.J. pulled out a toy rifle. He tucked it under his arm and cocked his fedora to the side. Izzy posed with her back to his and lifted a rubber gun in the air, blowing on the tip.

"Omigod!" screamed Skye. "Somebody, take a picture of C.J. and Izzy. They look just like Bonnie and Clyde!"

Regina took a picture. Squealing with delight, Skye gave Izzy a high five. Izzy rolled her eyes, but the party girl didn't notice. Skye was loving her decision to squash her beef with her former foe. Socially, she had decided it was smarter to join forces with such an exotic, controversial figure than to fight with her. The It chicks plus Izzy equaled *fierce*!

Kamillah whispered in Skye's ear, "Tangie looks mad sulky. Did you tell her not to bring Trey?"

"Yeah, but so what? It's my night."

"That's superwack, man. Now she has to sit there watching Izzy and C.J. all night long?"

"I'm being a good friend. Trey is a piece of shit, and you know it. I'm saving her years of grief." Skye adjusted her tiara.

"I guess you're right. Boyfriends suck, anyway. I *hate* Black right now. In two seconds, I'm gonna snatch off that Afro." Kamillah sounded jokey, but really, she couldn't believe that Skye was so indifferent to the position she had put Tangie in.

"Whatever. Just ignore him." Skye was barely listening to

her—she was in full party mode. "Pour me some champagne, girl! Woo-hoo! I'm trying to get *kruuunk*!"

Meanwhile, Vineet executed a big, dramatic yawn, stretched, and put his arm around Jenna's shoulders. "I like your girl's video camera," he said, gazing into her eyes. "I'm a huge fan of those, especially in the, ahem, bedroom. Knowhatimsayin'?"

The thirty-one-year-old producer, wife, and mother of two rolled her eyes at him. "Not even if you were hung to your *knees*, little boy."

Across the limo, Kamillah had squeezed in between Regina and Kiki. The two girls were in the middle of an intense discussion about whether or not scripted TV shows were dead.

"Well, let's see what Kamillah thinks," Regina said to Kiki. She turned to Kamillah. "Do you think reality shows are pushing out scripted shows? I mean, I just think there's a lot of quality stuff right now, like *Lost* and *Heroes* and . . ."

"You don't wanna ask me, kid; my favorite show is *The Simple Life*," Kamillah snapped, itching to get to what she wanted to discuss. Lowering her voice to a whisper, she said, "Listen, I just had a revelation over there. I think Skye's jealous of Tangie."

"What are you talking about? No, she's not."

"Yeah, she is. A hundred percent. Tangie's hot shit at school right now 'cause of Trey, and it's killing her, 'cause this was supposed to be her big moment."

"Hmmm. I guess I *kinda* see what you . . ." Regina began, and then stopped herself, glancing over at Skye. It would be a major scandal if Skye overheard them. And then, suddenly, she was reminded of the confessionals tape.

"Hey, do you remember what you said in your confessional interview with Jenna?"

"Um, not really," said Kamillah. "I barely remember what I said that day. Jenna is so sweet, man—it was like we'd been girls for years. It felt more like gossiping than an interview."

Exactly the problem, Regina thought. "Listen, do me a favor. Don't say anything else to Jenna. And don't repeat what you just said about Skye and Tangie to anyone."

"Why?"

"Because we're being taped every second, Kammie. You never know what'll end up on the episode."

"Whatever! Jenna's the sweetest. She wouldn't fuck us over like that."

Regina and Kamillah looked over at the producer, who was watching Skye as she knocked back her second glass of champagne and asked Nick if he'd like her to flash a boob.

Jenna was taking notes on her every move: Sixteen Candles Special Edition: *Skye Gone Wild!*

By the time the limo reached Club Tropicana, on Thirty-second Street and Tenth Avenue, Skye's party had been under way for at least twenty minutes. Which was a good thing, since Skye wanted her court to be fashionably late.

So as not to ruin Skye's grand entrance, Skye, Nick, Jenna, and Kiki snuck in through a side door. Everyone else walked up the red carpet that led up to the club's front door. Along the sides were legit photographers posing as paparazzi, snapping all the guests' pictures as they piled inside. Regina, Kamillah, Izzy, and Tangie posed with the guys, feeling superfamous.

Before admitting them to the party, a hulking doorman demanded to see their Skye-assigned fedoras or boas. Then a perky blond girl with a clipboard checked their names off a list and stamped their hands. The security was no joke! After practically being strip-searched, Tangie, Izzy, C.J., and the rest of the crew finally entered the club. And for a good two minutes, they all stood in the doorway, too awestruck to move.

No one had ever been to a party this . . . big. It was like a circus. The entire club was decorated to look like a glamorous cabaret from the 1930s. Cocktail waitresses dressed like showgirls roamed the crowd, serving up nonalcoholic cocktails called Blue Skyes (a mix of blue Gatorade, Sprite, and lime juice) and cigars made of fudge. A silent, flickery, black-and-white short film of Skye, wearing a bobbed black wig, was being projected on the walls in a continuous loop. It featured her backstage in an old-school dressing room, seductively changing from a dark velvet robe into a skimpy showgirl costume as she winked and flirted with the camera—and somehow, the film had been treated so it looked about eighty years old.

When did she have time to shoot that? wondered Tangie in awe. On the left was a photo booth where people could pose for vintage-looking black-and-white photos in front of different backdrops. Around the club were different faux gambling stations, where kids played poker, roulette, and blackjack for raffle tickets (the crowd's favorite was a Shoot the Gangster carnival game, where the winner received an oversize, bubble-bath-filled champagne bottle). Everywhere you looked were platters of candy, delicious finger food, chocolate fountains, and tiny ice-cream sandwiches. Go-go dancers wiggled at all four corners of the club, dressed in the same sequined, skimpy showgirl outfits as the waitresses, bumping and grinding and tossing raffle tickets out at the overexcited crowd.

But the centerpiece of the room was C.J.'s mural. Hanging on the wall across from the packed dance floor was a huge, stylized painting of Skye and her court—but they were decked out as gangsters and their gorgeous glamour girls, all hanging out in a smoke-filled speakeasy. Some were were clinking their glasses together, others were dancing or playing dice—but they all looked *cool as hell*. It was truly a piece of art. The mural was also the first thing people noticed when they came in—and not just because it was so sexy, but because the likenesses to Skye and her friends were dead-on. Somehow, C.J. had managed to capture their essence perfectly without even getting his subjects to pose—and in only three days.

Minutes after Tangie and company walked in, a manager asked them if they were Skye's court, then ushered them up to the VIP area, which was a balcony overlooking the dance floor. It was already teeming with Skye's closest friends from her drama classes, a few CSOs (celebrity spin-offs) whom Eden and Skye had spent their whole lives vacationing with in Aspen and Saint Barths—including Evan Ross, son of Diana Ross; Sosie Bacon, daughter of Kevin Bacon; *The Closer*'s Kyra Sedgwick;

and Jillian Hervey, daughter of Vanessa Williams. None of the CSOs were dancing, of course. They were too busy flossing. And security guards were everywhere, so the VIPs had to be very discreet when sipping vodka from their Evian bottles.

Izzy looked around and frowned. "This is truly some uppity bullshit. Come on, y'all, let's go downstairs." Just as she grabbed Tangie's and C.J.'s hands and headed for the stairs, the blond clipboard girl ran over to Tangie.

"Are you Tangela Adams?"

"Yes. Is there something wrong?"

"No, no, no . . . it's just that Skye's ready for her grand entrance. So, can you round up Kamillah and Reginald . . ."

"Regina," said Tangie, correcting her.

"No, my name's Candace."

"Huh? No, I meant . . ."

"Whatevs. I need you all to follow me backstage. We're in a hurry, because one of the male models carrying Skye is suffering from steroid withdrawal, and we only have a twenty-minute window before the seizures start." She threw her hands up in frustration. "*Now* he tells us."

So, Kamillah, Regina, and Tangie raced behind Clipboard Chick, winding through the crowd. They slipped into a backstage bathroom to change into their identical showgirl costumes—glittery, low-cut white leotards with short fringed skirts and huge ostrich feathers—and rushed out into the wings. Peeking behind the red curtain, Tangie looked out into the crowd and felt her first pang of nerves. *Look at all those people,* she thought. *They're all waiting to laugh at how big my ass is, I just know it.* As she scanned the crowd, her eyes stopped at Izzy and C.J., dancing. Well, maybe *dancing* was a strong word, since C.J. refused to dance (he believed that it was impossible to look hard while busting any kind of move). So, as Izzy ground up against him seductively, he simply bobbed his head and kept his cool.

Tangie felt a pang of jealousy that was like a kick in the stomach. Now, more than ever, she wished Trey were there—not only because she felt like the only girl there without a date, but also because she really wanted him to see her perform. He always looked so proud, so blown away when she danced. And Tangie would've *loved* for C.J. to see the look on Trey's face at that moment. Was that so wrong?

Tangie glanced at Kamillah and Regina and saw that they seemed a little shaken. Just then, she realized that it was her job to make sure they felt calm and confident, or else this routine could go really wrong.

"Okay, girls, Clipboard Chick said we had six minutes before the DJ announces us," said Tangie, feeling like a football coach before the big game. "Are we ready to kill it?"

They did not look ready. Kamillah, usually bristling with cocky attitude, had broken into a sweat, and poor Regina's eyes were bugging out of her head.

"I can't do this," whispered Kamillah. "I . . . Tangie, I'm so not ready. Go on without me, y'all. Save yourselves."

Tangie grabbed her by the shoulders. "Pull yourself together, sweetie! You're an actress, so you're used to performing, right? This is *nothing*. I know you'll be amazing."

"What about when that motherfucker said I needed to walk it out?"

"Fuck him," said Tangie, who never usually said the F-word. "How about we run through the routine real quick? Regina, you ready, sweetie?"

Eyes still wide with terror, Regina looked at Tangie and nodded tensely.

"Okay, line up behind me. Five, six, seven, eight . . . and *one!*"

The girls marked out the choreography as Tangie counted the steps. Midway through, Kamillah tripped over nothing and fell to the ground. Without missing a beat, Tangie helped her up, dusted off her costume, and assured her that that was good luck. "Seriously, Kammie, a sucky rehearsal always means a kick-ass performance. I promise."

In the deejay booth across the club, DJ AM faded out Amerie's "One Thing" and grabbed the mic. *"What it do, New Yaawwwk!??!!"*

The crowd screamed.

"How're my gangsters and glamour girls feelin' out there? So, look, we about ready to officially pop this thing off. I want y'all to put your hands together for three lovely ladies from Skye's court, Tangie, Kamillah, and Regina, who are gonna help us introduce the birthday girl! And shout out to Marisol, for singing a very special version of the Pussycat Dolls' 'Don't Cha'!! Let's do this, people!"

The three girls ran onstage and stood in place behind the heavy red curtains. Tangie smiled encouragingly at Kamillah and Regina and blew them each a good-luck kiss (she noticed a single, terrified tear running down Kamillah's cheek and was shocked to realize that the tough Harlemite was so vulnerable). Seconds later, they heard the first couple of notes of "Don't Cha," sung by Eden's BFF, Marisol.

The curtains opened, and a burst of confetti was released from the ceiling, as Tangie, Kamillah, and Regina, their backs to the audience, began doing a seductive shimmy. One by one, they looked over their shoulders, winked, and threw their boas out into the crowd—creating a cool-looking ripple effect. The audience was hollering and clapping and loving every minute of the sexy, tongue-in-cheek routine. When the song got to the chorus—*"Don't you wish your girlfriend was hot like Skye"*— Tangie, Kamillah, and Regina mouthed the words and pointed at the door, on the word *Skye*. The entire crowd turned around, and to their delight, saw six drop-dead-gorgeous male models in tuxedos carrying Skye high above their heads.

She was holding a sparkler in her hand and beaming, her smile lighting up the room. As the crowd parted for her, Skye looked out at her adoring fans, blowing kisses, waving, and posing for the cameras. A zillion cameras went off, flashing from every direction—and in that moment, Skye became a star.

When the hunky male models finally made it through the crowd, they smoothly deposited Skye onstage. She raised her arms above her head in a wide *V* and threw her head back, like a true diva. Tangie and the girls posed around her for a quick photo op, and then sexy-walked offstage, to tremendous applause.

The house lights dimmed, and a single spotlight shone on Skye. A microphone stand slowly rose up out of the floor. In the background, everyone could hear a piano playing "All That Jazz," the theme song from *Chicago*. And then, DJ AM announced on the microphone, in an old-school radio announcer's voice, *"Gangsters and Glamour Girls, may I present to you . . . Skye Carmichael, as Roxieeeee Hart!"* Like a true pro, she stood there with her head down until the applause died out. Only then did she look up at the crowd with her sparkly, grayish-green eyes and begin her monologue.

"All my life, I wanted to have my own act," she began, in a high-pitched, breathy, exaggerated New York accent. "It's such a special night . . . and you're such a great audience! And I really feel like I can talk to you, you know? So forget what you read in the papers. Forget what you heard on the radio, because I'm gonna tell you the truth. The name on everybody's lips is gonna be . . . *Skye!* The lady raking in the chips is gonna be . . . *Skye!* I'm gonna be a celebrity; that means somebody everyone knows. They're gonna recognize my eyes, my hair, my teeth, my boobs, my nose. . . ."

Skye gracefully transformed herself into a beautiful young starlet, right in front of her captive audience's eyes. Her monologue was a raging success, and the applause lasted a good five minutes. She stood onstage soaking up the cheers, the attention, the love from the audience—it was better than any high she'd ever experic   .d (better than Red Bull, weed, hooking up, anything). And when she was done, she curtsied a zillion times before giving her thanks.

"Thank you, everybody! I want to thank you all for coming out to celebrate my sixteenth birthday! I'd especially like to thank the girls in my court—Tangie, Kamillah, and Regina—for their incredible performance!" The girls peeked out from the wings and waved. "And a huge thanks to my parents, Alexa and Junior Carmichael, for putting this whole thing together." A spotlight shone on her parents, waving from the VIP balcony. "And now, a big shout-out to my 'gangster' tonight, Nick Vardolos! Nick, come on up here!"

Nick was clearly caught off guard. He looked around, wondering if she were serious, and then ran up the stairs to the stage.

"Isn't he fine?" she said, and the girls in the audience screamed. Somebody said, "Girl, he a fine white boy!" Together, they did look amazing. Skye, high from the performance and more than a little tipsy, gave him a huge hug, and then, shocking everyone, threw her arms around his neck and kissed him. Acting purely on reflex, Nick pulled himself away from her.

The crowd gasped in shock. Thanks to Clipboard Chick's quick thinking, the curtains abruptly closed, shielding Skye and Nick from the audience. DJ AM quickly put on a hot song, and everyone started to dance. For now, the moment was saved. But the damage was done. In two seconds, Skye had gone from feeling as if she were on top of the world to wanting to die of humiliation. Somehow, Tangie and Kamillah managed to usher her back to the dressing room for her wardrobe change, while a horrified Nick grabbed his best friend and confidant, Regina, and dragged her off in the opposite direction.

The funny thing was, the drama had only just begun.

In the dressing room, Skye was inconsolable. She'd been crying tipsy, humiliated tears for fifteen minutes, and no one could calm her down. She was laid out on a chaise, surrounded by Tangie, Kamillah, Regina, and her mom. Penny, Alexa's hairstylist and makeup artist, was perched on an ottoman, waiting for Skye to stop crying so she could fix her eyeliner. Used to *Sixteen Candles* midparty meltdowns, Kiki was perched calmly on the dressing table with her handheld video camera, filming Skye's every move, while Jenna directed her.

And after fifteen minutes of weeping, cussing, and throwing everything within reach, the birthday girl finally realized she was being taped. She sat up, impatiently shrugging off her mom's incessant stroking of her hair.

"Get out, get out, get out!" she screamed, pointing at Kiki. "What are you doing? You can't tape me like this!"

"I'm sorry, Skye, but you signed the contract," said Jenna, sounding firm. "We're allowed to film you everywhere but the bathroom, remember?"

"Then I'm going in the bathroom!"

"You can't," snapped Alexa, grabbing Skye's arm. "Your father's been in there for twenty minutes! He *knows* he has irritable bowel syndrome, so I can't *imagine* why he insisted on ordering those smoked barbecued ribs before we got here. . . ."

"Oh, shut up, Alexa," Skye wailed.

"Listen, sweetie," began Tangie, sitting down next to Skye

on the sofa. She was still pissed about the Trey situation, but she sucked it up for the time being. "It's really not as bad as you thought. No one really noticed that Nick didn't kiss you back."

"But what did you do that for, anyway?" Kamillah was back to her old brassy self, after the success of Tangie's routine. "How many times does the boy have to tell you he's into his girlfriend in D.C.? It's not that he doesn't like you, he's just in love with some other chick!"

"I don't care, it doesn't even matter anymore," Skye said, her tears finally slowing down. She hopped up from the sofa and poured herself her third glass of champagne. Jenna shot Alexa a look clearly asking why she was cool with her underage daughter drinking right in front of her.

"Oh, it's fine," said Alexa. "I'd rather my girls drink in front of me than out in the streets."

That's the stupidest thing I've ever heard, thought Jenna. *Hope this Dina Lohan wannabe isn't surprised in a couple years when her darling daughter goes to Promises rehab clinic instead of Princeton.*

"My party is ruined," said Skye, sipping her champagne and staring off into space, big mascara tears streaking her cheeks. "I just wanna go home."

"Okay, for real? This is enough," said Tangie, storming over to Skye and taking the champagne from her. "This is a fabulous party. Everyone's having the time of their lives, your Roxie Hart monologue was fierce, and we did a great job on our routine; right, Kammie?"

Kamillah smiled happily and did a quick, rhythmless

booty-shake. She'd never seriously danced in front of a crowd before, and everyone was saying the girls had done a great job—Kamillah had even been complimented by a couple of Armstrong dancers (arguably the pickiest critics in New York).

"DJ AM is amazing," continued Tangie, "and everyone's dancing like crazy. You look beautiful. *Everyone* looks beautiful. . . . It's the most glamorous, off-the-hook party anyone's ever been to. So, forget Nick; this party isn't about him—it's about you. Let's get into your second dress and go back down there and *do* this thing!"

Something in Tangie's speech made Skye perk up a little. "You're right. This is a fucking fantastic party. And I do look good." She stood up and peered into the huge lighted mirror, wiping away her tears. "Okay, let's get to work. Penny, I need a new face, ASAP. And Kamillah, can you pass me dress number two?"

Penny and Kamillah sprang into action.

"Alexa? I need to ask you something," said Skye, stepping into her *very* strapless, *very* red Michael Kors evening gown.

"Yes?"

"Can I please wear your mink shrug? It'll look good with this dress." Skye had been eyeing her mom's luxurious, expensive-looking shrug all night.

"How many times do I have to tell you? You're allergic to mink. Absolutely not." Alexa stroked her mink in the mirror behind Skye. "Now, if everything's okay here, I'm gonna go dance. Adios, people!"

For the first time in the week that Jenna had known Skye,

she felt sorry for her. She wasn't a high-strung, bossy brat for no reason—her mom was a callous, conceited nightmare.

"Girls, I'm gonna be a minute," said Skye, "so can you do me a favor? Go tell everybody that my parents are giving me a present in private, and I'll be out soon. I just can't have anyone thinking I'm back here crying over some asshole."

"Of course," said Tangie. "You sure you're gonna be okay?"

"Don't I look okay?" Skye grinned at them and winked. "Seriously, I'm fine. Go! Go dance and party and be the baddest bitches out there. I'll be down in a second."

With that, her friends left. But they had a feeling this wasn't the last they'd heard about the Nick-Skye disaster. The wrath of Skye was never short-lived.

13.
THE SECOND FIRST KISS

BEFORE THEY LEFT THE BACKSTAGE dressing room, Tangie and Kamillah switched back into their glamour-girl dresses (they certainly weren't trying to parade around half naked all night). While Kamillah went back to the VIP balcony, Tangie went downstairs to find Izzy. The music was amazing, and Izzy was the only girlfriend she had who loved to dance as much as she did.

The second she stepped out the floor, she caught her breath. Standing in front of her by the bar, was Trey. He was wearing a crazy red Cab Calloway zoot suit, and he looked gorgeous. When he saw her, a huge smile came over his chocolate-smooth face, and he held up the peace sign.

Overcome with happiness, Tangie ran over to him and, without thinking, gave him a huge, public hug. Ever since he had ignored her in front of his friends the first week of school, she'd been really hesitant to show any sign of public affection. Terrified of doing the wrong thing and looking stupid, she usually just followed his lead, waiting for him to acknowledge her first.

But right now, she was too thrilled to care about all that.

"What are you doing here?"

"I wanted to surprise you, Dimples," said Trey, straightening his hat after the hug.

"Well, you did. I really thought you weren't coming!"

"And you know what?" he said, putting his arm around her waist. "You absolutely killed your routine, girl."

"You saw me? *You saw me?*" Tangie jumped up and down like a little girl. This made her whole night.

"You didn't really think I'd peace-out on your performance, did you? Your boy's an asshole, but he ain't a dick. "

O-*kay.*

"Did you really think I was good? Did I hit all my marks? How did Kamiillah and Regina do?"

"Yo, y'all looked sick as shit. But you . . . whew!" He stepped back and clapped for her. Giggling, Tangie did a sweeping curtsy. "Seriously, you're *fire.* You know you on point. But yo, keepin' it hood? You gotta give your boy some credit for helping with the choreography," he said jokingly. "I'm just sayin'."

"No doubt," she said, smiling. "Thank you. I couldn't have done it without your help the other day."

"It's all good," he said, kissing her on the cheek. "So, uh, how was the limo ride over?"

It was a weird question. "It was fine, why?"

"Oh, no reason, no reason." His eyes darted around the

crowd. Tangie wondered who he was looking for. "Who you been hanging with so far? I mean, just the girls, or what?"

Tangie looked confused. "I don't know. Just my friends, I guess. Why?"

Trey rubbed his chin and nodded. "Nothing. Just makin' conversation."

She felt things getting awkward, and she didn't know why. Had she done something wrong? Maybe she shouldn't have hugged him like that in front of everyone. She racked her brains for something to say. "Um, you want something to drink? They have these Blue Skye drinks; they're so good."

"Yeah, let's go get a drink. We can't dance yet—these fools ain't ready for us."

Trey slipped his arm around Tangie's waist and led her over to one of the cocktail waitresses. Meanwhile, C.J. was watching them from the VIP balcony.

I cannot believe Tangie likes a dude who'd wear a strawberry-colored suit, he thought, tuning out Black's incessant complaining about Kamillah. And then, shocker of all shockers, Trey randomly looked up over his shoulder and locked eyes with him. C.J. raised an eyebrow, and Trey shot him a small, somewhat evil grin. Then he grabbed Tangie's hand, and the couple disappeared into the crowd.

What was *that* all about?

Since Kiki couldn't film Skye getting dressed, she went back to the party and found Nick and Regina, who were having the time of their lives (Nick had quickly gotten over the Skye embarrassment when his favorite song, Gwen Stefani's "Hollaback Girl," came on). The party was so *exciting*. Everywhere you looked, there was something happening—cocktail girls breaking into impromptu go-go dances, groups of kids screaming with delight at the roulette table, a huge flat-screen TV showing celebrities like Diddy, Eva Mendes, and Sarah Jessica Parker (all friends of Skye's parents, of course) wishing Skye happy birthday. Every half hour, confetti dropped from the ceiling—and a tiny photo of Skye was printed on each tiny confetti flake.

Regina had seen all of the *Sixteen Candles* episodes, and she knew Skye's would be the best. Of course, it still had to be edited and put together, and Kiki was busy telling her all about the process—among other things. They were sitting on a tiny banquette in the VIP balcony, oblivious to the party all around them. One thing led to another, and soon Kiki was telling her entire life story. She told Regina all about coming out, and how hard it was to get her parents to understand that it wasn't a choice, it was just who she was. To Regina, it was as if Kiki were reading her thoughts and feelings. Aside from when she and Nick hung out at their LGBT teens group, it was the first time she had actually felt *good* about herself. She wished she could be with Kiki all the time. It was like she was made for her—they looked alike, they were both filmmakers, and they both had the same heritage. Everything felt so *easy* with her!

"So, now that I have a break from filming Skye," said Kiki, "do you want to do a quick confessional?"

Regina froze. *So much for everything being easy with her,* she thought. The memory of the confessional DVD had been eating away at her ever since she'd snuck a look at it. She desperately wanted to ask Kiki not to use it, but how could she do that without looking like a snoop?

"Do we *have* to do a confessional right now? We're having so much fun!"

"Well, you're the only one from Skye's inner circle we haven't interviewed," said Kiki. "How about if we did it without Jenna? She really doesn't care, as long as I get the footage."

"Well . . . okay."

"It would be supercute to get you like this, all dressed up. You look beautiful, by the way."

Regina blushed down to her toes. And in that moment, she knew she'd do whatever Kiki said. They got up and went, searching for a quiet place to do the interview. Finally they found a tiny nook backstage, where all the lighting was set up. It was a great spot to film—the music was slightly audible in the background, and the heavy red velvet curtains were a great backdrop.

Kiki set everything up. "Okay, so tell me what you think about the party?"

Regina sat up straight, her eyes wide and glassy. "I'm having a great time. Everything is great. Skye's great. Our performance was great."

Giggling, Kiki said, "How about using a different word than *great*? Why are you so nervous, Reggie?"

"I'm not! I just . . . it's just that I don't want to say anything that'll come back to bite me in the ass later."

"You think I'd do that to you? Come on, I thought you knew me better than that."

"Yeah, but you still have to do your job." Regina swallowed. "And your job is to make this a juicy episode."

"True. But we have enough juice, don't worry." Kiki adjusted the levels on her camera.

Regina was silent.

"What's wrong?"

"The juice." Regina took a deep breath, suddenly too aware of everything around her. She felt the bass pumping in her chest, she smelled the sickly-sweet scent of the Blue Skye cocktails—nausea churned through her stomach. "If I tell you something, promise to still be my friend?"

"Of course. What is it?"

"I saw the DVD. The confessional DVD . . ."

"What? When?"

"It was after the front desk called you downstairs." Regina clasped her hands together in her lap. "I knew it was wrong, but I was just so curious! Look, Kiki, you can't use that stuff. I don't know how Jenna got them to say all that stuff, but it's really horrible, and if it makes it onto the episode, I don't think they'll ever speak to each other again. These are my only friends in the world, and I just don't want our whole group to explode. . . ."

"Okay, okay, calm down. It's okay." Kiki put the camera down on a shelf behind her and gave Regina a hug.

"You're not mad? I mean, I looked at that stuff behind your back."

"Listen, I know how film-obsessed you are. I didn't think

you were sitting there with your hands folded on your lap while I was gone." She smiled a little. "But Regina, I have to use that footage. The testimonials are a huge part of the show—Jenna will know if they aren't there."

Regina shook her head. "But do you know how bad they are? I mean, do you remember the stuff they said?"

"I barely pay attention to what the subjects are saying while I'm filming. I'm looking at the light, the dimensions, adjusting the sound quality . . . stuff like that."

"Please, Kiki?" Regina was two seconds from getting on her knees and begging. "Isn't there anything you can do?"

Kiki sighed, chewing her bottom lip. There was no *way* she could get rid of that footage—she'd be fired if anyone found out! And working for MVN was the best thing that had ever happened to her. But then there was Regina. She looked into her eyes and realized that she couldn't tell her the truth, that there was nothing she could do.

"I'll . . . I'll figure something out," Kiki whispered.

"You promise?"

Kiki nodded, but didn't say anything.

Regina's heart leapt, and so did she. Delirious with relief, she flung her arms around Kiki's neck and hugged her. At first, it was a friendly embrace—but then, it turned into something else, and Regina started getting that hot feeling again, like fire in her veins. Terrified, she let her arms fall away from Kiki and stepped away. They stood there, looking at each other.

"I can't do this, Regina," said Kiki. "I want to, but I can't. I'm, I'm older than you. And . . ."

"I know," said Regina. She was shaking uncontrollably. She wanted to laugh, to cry, to run—a zillion different emotions were racing through her, and yet she didn't move. And then she couldn't, because Kiki grabbed her face and kissed her.

Regina had been kissed once before, at her eighth-grade dinner dance. The person who'd kissed her was named Floyd, and he had sucked her bottom lip so hard it was purple for four days. She hadn't gotten get what the big deal was. Tonight, she did. And in that moment, she forgot all about the tape, the potential scandal, and everything. She was lost in her second first kiss, the kiss she'd always remember, the one that chased away any doubts she had had about being gay, leaving behind a new, clear-headed certainty that she was what she'd always suspected—a full-blown, lady-loving lesbian.

Skye stepped out on the dance floor in her stunning red dress and her mother's diamond tiara, looking so diva-licious that no one would've guessed she'd been halfway to a mental hospital a mere ten minutes ago.

Within seconds, she had crowds of admirers surrounding her—mostly people she'd never seen before—complimenting her outfit, fawning over her monologue, and generally bigging her up. It was everything she'd always wanted: not only was she the center of attention, she was *easily* the hottest girl in the room. Skye should've been thrilled, but all she could think about was being publicly dissed by Nick. Where *was* that ridiculously sexy Greek bastard?

She made her way through the crowd, posing for pictures,

dancing a little, and throwing an "Oh, my God, your 'glamour girl' costume is *fire!*" here and there. She played the part of the happy-go-lucky party girl to perfection. Every time she felt her face fall a bit, she'd think, *what would Lauren Conrad do?* No matter what crazy drama was happening in the *Hills* star's life—two-faced friends, evil boyfriends—L.C. always managed to come out looking perfect (Skye suspected it had something to do with her dope black eyeliner).

Skye was a dangerous combination of furious, humiliated, and drunkedy-drunk-drunk. But her actress genes kicked in, and she managed to pull it off. She did such a brilliant job, in fact, that everyone was shocked by what happened next. For days afterward, when folks talked about where they had been when it happened (most of them making it up so as to seem in on the drama) they'd inevitably say something like, "One minute she was chillin', and the next minute she was crazy-out-of-her-mind *bonkers!*" And that was a pretty accurate description of her meltdown.

Ludacris's "Pimpin' All Over the World" was playing, and she was dancing with a group of girls from her Musical Theater 201 class. Suddenly, she spotted Regina and Nick walking through the crowd, arm in arm. Skye's entire face changed. She stopped dancing and pushed her way through the crowd toward Nick.

Meanwhile, Jenna and Kiki were nearby, filming a geeky kid with a reddish fro and glasses saying, "I'll remember this party for the rest of my life. Even on my deathbed, probably." Jenna saw Skye storming across the dance floor and immediately sent Kiki to follow her.

The birthday girl finally got to Nick. She stood in front of him, blocking his way.

"What. The. Fuck," she said, trembling. Dangerous-looking purplish-maroon splotches had erupted on her cheeks.

"Skye, I'm sorry you're upset," said Nick, aware that a crowd was forming around them. He stepped closer to her, lowering his voice. "You wanna talk about this somewhere else?"

"No, I don't! Right here is just fine. These are all my friends, right?"

"That's right, girl!" said some chick in the crowd.

"I just don't understand," Skye said, slurring her words and swaying. "I don't understand how you could lead me on for an entire month, and then play me out like that—*in public*. This is *Sixteen Candles*, you mothafuckin' *bastard*! What's your long-distance D.C. bitch got on me, huh? Do you see what I look like?" She gestured toward her face, then slapped her ass. "You wanna give all this up for some needy, clingy girl that doesn't even *live* here? Then be my guest, Nikolas Vardolos."

"Look, let's just talk about this. . . ."

"No-o-o!" she screamed, totally out of control now. "I don't wanna talk anymore. Regina, how can you be his friend? Where's your loyalty? I'm outta here, my party is ruined!" Crying again, she tried to push past Nick, but he grabbed her arm. Working off some crazy reflex, she grabbed a Blue Skye out of somebody's hand and threw it in his face. Nick was soaked, his gorgeous floppy curls plastered to his blue-tinted face.

The crowd gasped in horror and excitement.

"Oh, *hell*, no," said Nick, lunging for Skye, but Regina jumped between them, as swift as a defensive linebacker.

The crowd gasped again. Kamillah appeared just in time, saying, "Let's give her some air, y'all," and, for the second time that night, dragged Skye back into the dressing room.

Jenna was so happy she almost burst out in a triple handspring. *This one's gonna win me a Emmy,* she thought, giving Kiki a thumbs-up.

DJ AM, fully used to crazy shenanigans going down at parties and clubs, immediately got on the mic and said, "Break it up, folks, break that ish up! We're here to party, so let's party!" Then he put on TI's "Bring Em Out," and the dance floor exploded. Skye and Nick's showdown was forgotten for the moment.

While Kamillah was calming Skye down and getting her into her third dress of the night, the different cliques in the VIP room were not feeling each other. Skye's CSO friends hung out in a cluster by the banquette, taking turns making out with each other. Skye's fellow Armstrong actresses were the worst—they were incredibly loud, shouting over the music and cracking annoying jokes, each one trying to out-drama each other. And her glamorous L.A. cousins spent most of the time in the bathroom, occasionally returning to the VIP area to sulk on a banquette and rub their noses.

Meanwhile, Tangie was determined to have fun and dance, even if the boys weren't. C.J. and Black were bobbing their heads to the music and freestyling, while Vineet was chasing

Jenna all over the club (the enterprising deejay-wannabe ended up introducing himself to DJ AM, who offered him a job interning with him at gigs all over the city). And for some reason, Trey hadn't wanted to dance all night long. He was in a weird mood. On the surface, he was giving Tangie attention—holding her hand and getting her drinks and such—but his mind was somewhere else. She couldn't figure it out. For the first time, Tangie realized she really didn't know anything about him outside of dancing. She could read every single one of C.J.'s moods, but with Trey, she was at a total loss.

It sucked. She'd been so excited that he had showed up and watched her performance, and now she wished he hadn't come at all.

Izzy was tired of watching Trey ignore Tangie, so she dragged her out of the VIP area and down to the main floor, where they danced for six songs straight. At one point, the two girls ran into Regina, Kiki, and Nick—by now, he'd dried off and fully recovered from Skye's insanity (later, he told Regina that he had secretly *loved* being the center of all the drama)—and they all snapped in a circle, laughing and joking and posing for Kiki's camera. Tangie was having the best time of all, until Kiki let them peek at some of the footage and she saw her hair. In the humidity, her curls had gone wild with frizz. Horrified, Tangie excused herself and ran for the bathroom.

The line was ridiculously long, so she pulled her hair into a ponytail and decided to head back to the dance floor. On the way, she passed C.J.'s mural. There was a crowd of people in front of it, getting their pictures taken—and she could see why. The painting was absolutely breathtaking.

She was mesmerized. Even though the painting was funky and stylized—more a caricature than anything else—his drawings of each of them were spot-on. Especially Tangie (but then again, he'd been sketching her for years). As she stared at the mural, the party seemed to disappear—the thumping bass of the music faded away, the loud chatter ceased, and the crowds around her vanished into thin air. She just felt tingly and peaceful and, simply, happy.

Tangie had always had this reaction to C.J.'s art, ever since they were kids and he drew her for the first time. They were in sixth-grade social studies, and Mrs. Sinclair was going on and on about the revolutionary war. When she turned around to write on the board, LuLu McKenna passed Tangie a folded-up piece of paper from C.J., who was sitting in the back. She opened the note and saw that it was a sketch of her and C.J.— as George and Martha Jefferson, except for the fact that George was holding a can of spray paint, and Martha was raising her fluffy skirts a bit, showing off her pink ballet slippers. It was hilarious and adorable, and God, how could she *not* have fallen in love with him that day?

Just as Tangie was wondering if C.J. remembered that drawing, she heard a voice behind her say, "You like it? I don't know, man, I heard the artist is mad full of himself."

Tangie grinned. It was C.J., of course.

"You said it, I didn't," she replied, turning around to face him. He was still wearing his fedora, cocked at an angle. He looked like a movie star.

Tangie wondered if it were physically possible for thighs to melt.

"Hey," she said, breathlessly.

"Hey."

"C.J., this is . . . this is truly beautiful," said Tangie, glancing up at the mural. "But I guess everyone's been telling you that, huh?"

He shrugged. "Yeah, I guess. But, really, folks have been asking me who the girl with the curls is."

"Shut up. Really?"

"Yeah." He looked up at the mural as if he'd never seen it before. "It's 'cause I drew you the best. I guess it's 'cause I know you, um, on a different level than everybody else."

"You always make me look so much prettier than I am in person."

"Naah. I just draw what's real." He turned to face Tangie. "I got you memorized."

She sucked in her breath, her stomach flip-flopping like crazy. She desperately wanted to look away, but couldn't. And then, she starting grinning like a kid with her first crush, and he smiled back at her—oh, that dangerously sexy, tingle-inducing smile—and the air between them seemed to crackle with electricity. Finally, she had to force herself to speak, just to break the tension.

"I was . . . I was just thinking about that picture you drew in Mrs. Sinclair's class. . . ."

"The George and Martha joint?"

"Yeah." She smiled. "Doesn't that seem like yesterday?"

He laughed a little. "Actually, what seems like yesterday is the time you came to that block party around my way. . . ."

"Oh, God," she said, laughing. It was her real laugh, not the weird tittering giggle she did around Trey. "I was, what, twelve? And I'd never been to your neighborhood before, and I was nervous your friends would think I was this prissy, stuck-up girl that talked white. . . ."

"They *did*. Until 'Thong Song' came on, and you lost your damned mind. Remember that?"

"To this day, I swear I don't know what happened," she wailed, covering her face with her hands. "I loved Sisqó so much, you know? That song just moved me. I swear, it's like I blacked out or something."

"You blacked out? T., you did a handstand, and then you hopped around on your hands with your underwear showing."

"They were cheerleader spankies!"

"Whatever, yo."

"Your great-aunt was so upset, she made you take me home." She giggled. "But we went to José's Chicken Shack, and you had chicken nuggets and chicken chow mein, and I had pizza."

C.J. shook his head. "You know something's gotta be suspect about a fast-food joint sellin' pizza, chicken, and Chinese food."

It was a good moment. They were talking and laughing as if nothing shady or wrong or hurtful had ever gone down between them.

"You know, sitting back there in Mrs. Sinclair's history class, the George and Martha day?"

"Yeah?"

"I knew even then that drawing your face—it'd never get old."

Tangie could feel the smile before it actually happened. "Never?"

He shook his head. And suddenly, it was like some crazy magnetic force was pulling them together. Tangie and C.J. stepped closer and closer, until there was nothing left between them. They hesitated there, not sure what to do next. And then, surprising them both, Tangie held his face between her hands and slowly brought it down in front of hers.

"What are we doing?" Her voice was a whisper, but strong. "What is this?"

"I don't know. . . ."

Nothing made any sense. Tangie really did like Trey, but when it came to her and C.J., it was like no one else existed in the world. As she stood there, two seconds away from kissing him, she wondered if maybe she really just liked the way being Trey's chosen one made her feel. Seemingly overnight, the cute senior girls had come to think she was cool. Dance department people took her more seriously. For the first time, Tangie was living the life of a confident, popular girl. And it felt good.

But not as good as this. Nowhere near.

Something held C.J. back. He knew that if he kissed her right now, that would be it. With Tangie, it was serious. It was real. And yet, if he started things up with her—knowing full well that, in a couple months, a million copies of his nude portrait of Izzy would be floating around—she might never forgive him.

Tangie sensed it the second he decided not to kiss her, and she pulled away.

"You'll never be ready, will you?"

"It ain't even like that. You don't understand. . . ."

"What was I even thinking? I have a boy—a *man*, almost—who really likes me, and isn't afraid to show it."

C.J. rolled his eyes and laughed humorlessly. "Oh, my God, Tangela, *please*. He don't even know you."

"Yeah, he does. In a way you never will." She turned to walk away, but C.J. grabbed her by the arm and pulled her back to him.

"Does he know you used to sleep in your mom's old ballet slippers every night until eighth grade? Does he know we buried them in Fort Greene Park on your thirteenth birthday? What about your ridiculous ice-cream thing? Does he know you won't eat any desserts that melt? Has he ever noticed that you pull your shirt down over your ass when you're nervous? You ever shown him your secret collection of Happy Meal Shrek toys? *Have* you?" C.J. paused, waiting for her to respond. She said nothing, just looked up at him with wide, shocked eyes.

"Don't insult me, T. And don't kid yourself, either—it's a bad look."

He let go of Tangie's arm, but she didn't move. She stood there, breathing hard, trying to decide whether to run away, slap him, or kiss him until his lips fell off. They both knew he was right, of course. No one would ever know Tangie better than C.J.

She bent her head, feeling hot tears behind her eyes. But then, before she knew it, C.J.'s arms were around her. She burrowed into his strong chest, holding on to him as tight as she could. They were standing upright, but they might as well have been lying down, C.J. on top of her—every inch of their bodies was pressed against each other, his face buried in her hair, her hands clutching his muscular shoulders. They fit together like two pieces of a puzzle; even their breathing was synchronized.

All around them, the music was pumping and the crowd was raging—but Tangie and C.J. stayed locked in their embrace, oblivious to the party. They didn't look at each other, because if they had, they would've kissed, and they wouldn't have stopped there, either—and the last time things had gotten that intense, everything had gone wrong.

It was too bad. Because if they'd come up for air, even once, maybe they would've noticed who was watching them.

14.
DANCE-OFF

AT THE BEGINNING OF THE NIGHT, Skye's guests were hyper-aware of the MVN cameras. It was all about looking fly in their costumes, and no one wanted to get too messy or sweaty. Now, boas and fedoras were flying in the air, blow-outs were getting sweated out, and the boys had thrown off their jackets and unbuttoned their shirts. For the first time that evening, Skye's guests forgot they were at an A-list soiree and got down as if it were a house party in Harlem.

Everyone but Eden, that is. She was pacing back and forth, periodically checking the VIP entrance and glancing at her watch. It was 10:50, and the performer was supposed to go onstage at eleven on the dot. She'd been trying to get Smoove on the phone all night, but he hadn't been answering her messages or her texts. And now she was really worried.

Eden had a terrible secret. She had no idea who was going to perform. *As long as I live, I'll never forgive Smoove for backing out,* she thought, seething with anger. He had promised he'd get one of his friends to do it—but then, three hours ago, he had taken off for Hong Kong to guest-star in a Ludacris video shoot. Still, Eden trusted that Smoove had handled it. She *had* to trust him, because the alternative—that Skye had no performer for her *Sixteen Candles* episode, and that her big sister would forever look like the nobody who couldn't get her big, fancy, famous-ass boyfriend to hook her up—was too horrifying to bear. And all night long, when Skye's friends asked about the performance, Eden had flashed one of her devastatingly perfect smiles and murmured something like, "It's a secret, silly. But you just wait—it'll blow your damn mind."

She checked her watch again. It was 10:57. Freaking out now, she ran over to the Green Room, a special backstage waiting room for celebrity guests. A gruff, hugely fat security guard stopped her.

"Where you think you goin', miss?"

"I'm Eden Carmichael," she said, impatiently. The security guard didn't budge, so she added, "Hello? Skye's sister?"

What a strange way to identify herself. Usually it was the other way around.

Clipboard Chick peeked her head out of the Green Room. Was this woman *everywhere*? "Um, let me see if I have you on my list of people cleared to go into the dressing room." Her eyes scanned the first page of her clipboard, than flipped to the second and the third. "I'm sorry, ma'am, you're not there. Did you say Edith Carmichael?"

"*Eden!* Eden Carmichael. Don't you know who I am? I was Kendra on *Family Chatter*."

"Oh, I remember you! Wow, you look exactly the same—haven't changed one bit! I remember . . ."

"That's truly awesome, but I need to get back in that dressing room. Look, it was my responsibility to book the performer, but then there was this miscommunication, and I have no idea who's on tonight."

"So sorry, Kendra. I can't let you back there with no clearance."

"It's Eden," she growled, feeling her blood rising. Who was this sad, slithery-looking woman to keep her from going back there? She stormed away, telling herself she'd never forgive Smoove for leaving her high and dry—and for what? For that ratty-weave-wearing, hypnotiq-addicted, so-2002, neo-soul bee-yatch? *I'll kill him*, she snarled to herself.

"Can't you at least tell me who's back there?"

Clipboard Chick smiled sadly and shrugged. "Sorry. Can't." She took a step aside and pressed her earpiece. 'I have to take this, Eden. Listen, just go out into the audience and enjoy the show. You'll have fun."

Sulky, on the verge of tears, Eden spun on her heels and stormed back up to the VIP area. She'd been hiding out up there all night, pretending to talk on her cell phone in order to discourage annoying tenth graders from asking her if Smoove was performing (it was a trick she had picked up from Paris Hilton, who supposedly used her cell as a prop when she didn't want to deal with paparazzi). Looking out at the hundreds of kids on the dance floor, Eden was suddenly overwhelmed by a feeling of panic. *Please, God,* she thought,

I'll do anything; just make sure Smoove comes through tonight.

But then a thought interrupted her desperate prayer. Smoove loved to play stupid practical jokes on the boys in his entourage. What if this was some elaborate joke, and he actually was going to perform himself? Maybe he wasn't really in Hong Kong! After all, it *was* kinda shady that his Luda video shoot had popped up out of nowhere. A wave of adrenaline rushed through Eden as she considered this possibility.

Feeling a tap on her shoulder, Eden whipped around.

"Trey?" She punched him in the arm. "You scared me! What the hell do you want?"

"Nothin'. Just wondering if you'd, uh, seen your cousin."

"C.J.? Isn't he running around with that starving Ethiopian girl? The one that hit off the entire G Unit?"

Trey shrugged, looking preoccupied.

"If you're looking for weed, don't. Don't ruin Skye's party by getting us all arrested. Besides, C.J.'s too smart to sell here, anyway."

"That ain't even it," said Trey, being unusually mysterious. "I just wanted to get at him."

He leaned up against the balcony railing next to Eden. She turned up her nose in disgust and inched away from him. "Where's your girlfriend?"

"Tangie ain't *officially* my girl," he said, sounding annoyed. "We're just talking. I'm actually kinda feeling her, but you know I'm-a do my thing, regardless."

"Wait, I think I see them. Down there, standing in front of C.J.'s mural." She tsked, her hand on her hip. "My cousin is so talented, but that street stuff is gonna end up killing him one d—"

But Trey was gone. Eden watched him bump into about twelve girls on his way down to the main floor.

With a stormy expression, he marched over to where C.J. and Tangie were now sharing a shockingly sexy hug.

Out of nowhere, Eden felt a weird pang of sadness. In all the years she'd dated Trey, she couldn't remember him *ever* having been that jealous over her. Whatever he had with Tangie Adams, it must have been sort of real—or as real it could ever be with as a poseur like Trey.

Whatever, she thought, the moment quickly passing. *Tangie can have him. If she wants to deal with a conceited, cheating jackass who doesn't know the difference between Iraq and Idaho, then be my guest.*

"Okay, now *this* is interesting."

Somehow, Tangie heard Trey's voice over the roar of the crowd and the crazy bass of Snoop's "Drop It Like It's Hot," and she jerked out of the delicious cocoon of C.J.'s arms.

"*Trey?* Hi! I was, um, I was looking for you; where have you been?"

"Oh, word? You was lookin' for me?" Trey was both angry and sarcastic, an unattractive combination. "I'll tell you where I been. I been watching you stand here in front of the entire school, practically *hitting off* this wack-ass Chris Brown knock-off."

"Wow, that's original," muttered C.J.

Tangie was totally taken aback by Trey's anger. She'd never seen that side of him before. "Hold on, I can explain. . . ."

"You think I'm stupid, don't you? I know all about you two."

"What do you mean, you know all about us?"

"Your girl, Skye, she told me everything. Don't try to play me, Tangie, I'm not the one."

"*Skye?* What did she say to you?" Cornered, Tangie turned toward C.J., and he shrugged, shooting her a "don't trip" look.

Trey didn't like all the silent communication between C.J. and *his* girl. "You got a problem, Chris Brown?"

"Look, playa, my patience game on the whole Chris Brown tip is wearing out," said C.J., trying to keep his cool.

Trey cocked his head. "You wanna do somethin' about it, kid?"

"What? You mean, like, a dance-off? You wanna krump it out, tough guy?"

Somebody burst out laughing, and Trey turned purple with anger. Completely uninterested into getting into a fight, C.J. tried to walk away, but Trey grabbed his arm. C.J. jerked out of his grasp and instinctively stepped to him, chest to chest. They were an uneven match—at six feet one, C.J. was about four inches taller than Trey, but Trey was stockier. For a minute, it looked like they were going to kill each other, but then C.J. reconsidered, shaking his head and moving back. It wasn't worth it.

Tangie moved in between them, pushing Trey backward. "This is ridiculous; stop it! Look, I don't know what Skye told you, but me and C.J. are just friends. I wasn't doing anything wrong."

"I saw you," said Trey, getting angrier by the second. "I know you came here with him, and I know you went out with him the other night. And now this."

C.J. stood behind Tangie, watching Trey carefully, hoping to God he wouldn't say the wrong thing. He truly didn't want things to get hectic. C.J. had grown up fighting constantly, all day, every day—he'd had to; it was the only way to prove he wasn't to be messed with. Fighting was a means of survival. But even as a kid, he knew there could be a way out, and it was a combination of school, his art, and his brains. Most of the boys from his block didn't have his kind of talent, and he didn't take that for granted. And he *really* wasn't about to waste it all on some idiot rich bitch who pretended to be from the gutter because he thought it was sexy.

By now, a huge crowd was forming around them, looking back and forth between Trey and C.J., rumbling with anticipation.

The pressure was building, and Tangie felt it. "Let's go talk about this somewhere else." She reached out for Trey's hand, but he jerked away from her.

"Naw, naw. I see how you are. Explain this to me, though. Why you wanna roll with this nigga over me?" He cocked his head toward C.J. and made a sour face. "Do you *know* who my daddy is? You *seen* my crib. You'd rather holla with a project cat who's probably gonna fuck up his one chance to get out the street?"

"*Ooooh!*" said the crowd.

Tangie was furious. "Don't talk about C.J. like that—you don't even know him! He's brilliant!"

"No, it's cool." C.J. put an arm around her protectively. "Where you goin' with this, *Soul Train?*"

Trey looked at C.J.; he was filled with hate. More than anything, he couldn't stand being made to look like a fool. Trey was used to being the hottest one in the room, the guy all the girls wanted, and he did not appreciate being upstaged by some kid from nowhere. Especially one with as much swagger as C. J. Parker. No, he was going to crush this cocky little hustler, and he knew exactly how to do it.

"I know all about your OutKast cover," said Trey, smiling a little bit. "*Donatello.*"

The color seemed to drain from C.J.'s face. His mouth tensed, forming a tight little line. How did Trey know about the cover? *No one* knew! C.J.'s eyes darted around the crowd; he suddenly felt horribly, uncomfortably exposed. Did everyone know?

Tangie looked at C.J., baffled. "What's he talking about?"

"Oh, I can tell you," said Trey, delighted. "This fool is risking getting expelled for selling a piece of his nobody-gives-a-fuck ghetto art to OutKast, for their greatest hits album cover." Trey chuckled a bit, feeding off the attention of the captive audience. "Oh, yeah, and it's a picture of his naked girlfriend—what's her name? Izzy?"

Tangie's mouth dropped open. The crowd gasped, totally scandalized. In a school full of students itching to make it big, there were always a few brave ones who secretly broke the rules by going the professional route. But no one ever outed them—that was considered sabotage, a total player-hater move.

But Trey couldn't have cared less. After all, Eden had sold him out for performing in Missy's video—and now it was incredibly satisfying to be doing it to someone else. Someone he wished to disappear. And where Trey had serious connections at Armstrong (which had garnered him a mild punishment for his crime), C.J. had none—he'd be expelled so fast his head would spin.

Meanwhile, Tangie was utterly confused. OutKast? Izzy's nude portrait? How could all this have happened without her knowing? She whipped around to face him. "Is this true? C.J., is it true?"

He couldn't speak. He stood there, trembling with rage, his blood pressure rising, his hands closing into fists. With every molecule of his being, he wanted to kill Trey Stevens. *Don't do it*, he told himself. *You got too much to lose.*

"Aww, you mad?" Trey stuck out his bottom lip, making a mock–pouty face. "Guess what else. I fucked your girl."

In one quick, powerful motion, C.J. lunged forward and punched Trey in the face as hard as he could. Trey went flying backward into the crowd ("My nose, my nose!" he yelled), and in seconds C.J. was on top of him. "Fake-ass, wannabe hood, motherfuckin' faggot ballerina *pussy*," he hissed through clenched teeth, letting it all out, punching until his right fist ached. Somehow, Trey grabbed him by the neck and flipped him around (it was done very gracefully, like the dancer he was). And in a total bitch move, he kneed C.J. in the balls.

To everyone's surprise, Black suddenly appeared out of nowhere, hollering like Bruce Lee. He tore the Afro wig off his head, threw it into the crowd (a tipsy voice major named Evangeline caught it and wore it the rest of the night) and jumped on top of Trey and C.J., throwing wild punches that landed nowhere. The three of them rolled around on the floor, blood from Trey's nose splattering all over the place. And that was when the security guards pulled them apart.

All three of them were quickly escorted out, the guards holding their hands behind their backs. Calling after C.J., Tangie scurried behind the cluster of burly guards all the way to the exit, but was then blocked by a sour-faced bouncer. "But, I need to—that's my best friend; *where are they taking him?*" She screamed the last five words.

"I need you to calm down and stand back, miss," growled the bouncer. "The guards are taking care of the situation. Go inside and have fun."

Tangie stood by the exit feeling completely helpless, humiliated, and confused. How had things gotten so out of control so fast? Was C.J. okay? And how could Trey have told such a hideous lie about her, in front of all those people? She turned around to go back into the club—and there was Izzy, standing right behind her. Wordlessly, the tiny freshman wrapped her little arms around Tangie, who finally burst out crying. Various girls began crowding around them, whispering and pointing, the nosier ones asking if Tangie was okay. Wanting to protect her friend from further drama, Izzy grabbed Tangie's hand and led her back into the club and into the packed ladies' room. The oversize handicapped stall was empty, so they hurried in before any of the girls reapplying their lip gloss noticed Tangie's tears.

Izzy closed the toilet lid and sat Tangie down. "Shhh, baby," she said, handing her some toilet paper. "Are you okay?"

"N—n—no-o-o," Tangie wailed, wiping her cheeks.

"I saw everything."

"*Everybody* saw everything! And heard everything, too! Oh, my God, I'm so humiliated. . . ."

"No, I mean, I saw you and C.J.," Izzy said quietly. "Before Trey came over."

"Wh—what do you m—mean?"

"You were alone by the mural, and I was gonna see if you wanted to dance. But then C.J. stepped to you first, and then . . . well, I sort of hung back in the cut. And I overheard your conversation."

Tangie looked at Izzy, finally getting it. And then she felt worse than ever.

"Why didn't you tell me, Tangie? I've never lied to you about a damned thing."

Wait—was withholding information lying? Tangie wondered. "Izzy, I'm so sorry," she said, holding her hand over her heart, Pledge of Allegiance style. "I just didn't know what to say about us! Me and C.J.—we were never boyfriend-girlfriend, so it's not like I had any right to ask you not to mess with him, you know?"

"I don't care if y'all weren't an official couple," said Izzy, leaning up against the tiled wall. "I saw you two together. Whatever's there, it's real."

Tangie nodded sadly, too emotionally drained to pretend it wasn't true.

"T., I *never* would've messed with C.J. if I'd known how you felt." She paused, looking down at her hands. "And that picture . . . really, it was just for a class, it's not like we were in the middle of . . ."

"I know," said Tangie, interrupting her. "He told me. I was just upset because it happened the night after me and C.J. had a really good moment, so . . ."

"Did you *do* it?"

"*What?* No, you know I'm a virgin!"

"Just checking."

"Listen, I'm sorry I didn't tell you the truth about me and C.J.," Tangie repeated, her voice shaky. "I guess I just didn't want anything to come between us."

"Girl, please," said Izzy, waving her hand. "I been through some serious, life-or-death shit, okay? It really ain't my style to get dramatic about a damn boy." She thought about that for a second. "Though C.J. is cute as shit."

"I kno-o-ow," wailed Tangie, half crying, half giggling. "The truth is, I can't remember a time when I didn't like C.J. It's just *in* me, you know? It never goes away. But he's just— we never can get it together. And then when I saw him with you, you both seemed so perfect for each other. I was like, Izzy's exactly the kind of girl C.J. should be with. You're like, fly and sexy and not all goody-goody and boring like me. I mean, I've only kissed two boys in my life. And I don't smoke, or . . ."

"So what? Look, me and C.J. were never serious, first of all. We're really just friends that sometimes—well, you know."

"I know, I know. Believe me, I know."

"And second of all, you're a fucking amazing girl. So what if you're a virgin? That's a good thing. You're the kind of girl that, when he's ready, C.J. will be with forever." She fixed her exotic, gold-lined eyes on Tangie. "He was fighting for *you* out there. You get that, right?"

"I'm so stupid," Tangie said, throwing her arms up. "What was I doing with Trey? God, everybody was right about him. Did you hear that terrible lie? Ugh, I can't even *repeat* it. How am I ever gonna go back to school?'

"Every single day somebody asks me if I gave Nick Cannon's baby up for adoption." Izzy rolled her eyes. "You can't care what bitches think about you. Seriously. It's all about you and your girls and what you know is true. Period. Fuck everybody else. Look at Ciara—folks think she's a damned transvestite, okay? And she's out there doing her thing. So don't trip."

"I guess you're right."

"You're beautiful, and talented, and sweet—folks are always gonna wanna tear you down."

"I love you, Izzy."

"I love you, too, girl." Izzy grinned. "We're TMI twins."

"It's weird. I really feel like you're my closest friend. It was always Skye, but things are so awkward with us this year. I don't know why."

"Maybe 'cause she's a bougie bee-yotch?"

"You're terrible," giggled Tangie, staring in the mirror over the minisink, trying to repair her tear-streaked face. "You know, I never understood that rumor about Ciara. She doesn't look like a man to me."

"Well, she does kinda have big hands. And shoulders."

Tangie smiled, finally relaxing a little bit. Suddenly, under the bright fluorescent lights, she noticed the red welt on Izzy's cheekbone. Izzy had covered it up with concealer, but it was definitely there.

"What happened to your cheek?"

Izzy's hand flew up to her face. "Oh, this? Yeah, I accidentally scratched myself. I don't even remember when it happened—probably in my sleep. I'm a crazy sleeper, for real."

First the bruise on her shoulder, now the cut on her cheekbones. To Tangie, it all seemed sort of suspicious. Izzy wasn't a clutzy person at all—she was way too cool to be accident prone. What had happened? Had she gotten into a fight, maybe, with someone from her past? She remembered the urgent phone call at Gonzalez y Gonzalez.

Before she could question Izzy any further, she was interrupted by the voice of DJ AM over the loudspeaker.

"Yo, yo, yo, yo! Listen up, party people! I need y'all to stop whatcha doin' and pay attention, ya heard? We got 2005's flyest hip-hop superstars comin' to the stage right now, and I mean flyyyy. *Skye Carmichael, it's all for you, baby girl—so put your hands together for your birthday surprise!"*

Tangie and Izzy looked at each other, eyes wide, and

then joined the rest of the girls scrambling out of the bathroom.

Skye and Kamillah had missed the C.J.-Trey smack-down completely. They'd been in the dressing room for the past fifteen
minutes. Kamillah was trying to calm Skye after the Nick inci-
dent *and* get her into her third dress of the night.

"Who does that Greek asshole think he is, Stavros
Niarchos?" Skye was in a bra and thong, stomping all around
the room and taking sips from half-empty champagne bottles.
The only other person in the room was Penny. She was sitting
in a corner, having text sex with her boyfriend and ignoring the
entire episode. (She was being paid by the hour; what did she
care if Alexa's bratty daughter lost her mind?)

"This is *my* party," Skye continued. "I'm the fucking
princess, and Nick should've been kissing *my* ass! Does he know
how lucky he is that I asked him to be my gangster? I could've
asked Jared Shamwell, that dope bass player with the
Hamptons house across from Kimora and Russell's! Nicolas
Vardolos is *over* at Armstrong—O.V.A.H.!!"

"Okay, you know what? *I'm* the one over this shit!"
Kamillah grabbed Skye by the shoulders, pushed her down on
the sofa, and threw the dress at her. "Put this on. I'm tired of
you wilin' out. I know *Sixteen Candles*-ers are supposed to have
attitude, but if you notice, Kiki's not here. There's no camera
on you, so there's no point in bringing all this drama."

Skye sat silent for a moment. Now that she was still, the
room was spinning a bit (she'd passed being tipsy about

twenty minutes earlier, and now was full-on drunk). "You're right. Why'm I acting crazy, Kammie? What's the point if I'm not on camera?"

"Exactly! Hello?"

Skye burst into spontaneous giggles, and Kamillah joined her. Penny glanced over at the two girls and rolled her eyes, thankful that high school was a faint memory.

"Now put on your dress, so we can go party," said Kamillah, checking her watch. "Isn't the performer supposed to be on at eleven? We got, like, two minutes."

Skye slipped on her final ensemble, a low-cut yellow satin vintage Balenciaga halter dress with a spray of Swarovski crystal beading along the bottom. The floor-length gown was skintight, as if it had been custom-made for Skye's supermodel-thin figure. Penny finally turned off her Sidekick and arranged Skye's long, blond-streaked extensions in a softly waved, retro updo. Penny finished off the look with some sultry, smoky eye makeup.

"Okay, let's go," said Kamillah, halfway out the door.

"Hold on, something's not right." Skye posed and twirled around in the mirror, her mom's diamond chandelier earrings twinkling. "I don't feel sexy! Something's missing. . . . Penny, what can we do?"

Penny yawned. She couldn't have cared less, and it showed. Frustrated, Kamillah marched back into the dressing room, looking around. She grabbed Alexa's mink shrug from a chair and handed it to Skye. "Here, this is fabulous."

Skye slipped on the furry stole and looked in the mirror, and her mouth dropped open. "I look like a goddess," she whispered, in awe of her own fabulousness. "Kammie, don't I look like a *goddess?*"

Before her friend could answer her, they both heard DJ AM's booming voice introducing the surprise guest performer. *". . . Skye Carmichael, it's all for you, baby girl. So put your hands together for your birthday surprise!"*

Squealing excitedly, the altercation with Nick now completely forgotten, they hurried out onto the dance floor, pushing and shoving until they got to the front, just under the stage (Kamillah did a double take when she saw a lanky Latina rocking Black's Afro wig). Just then, the music of the current smash hit "Like You" filled the club, and the red velvet curtains peeled back. And there was Bow Wow, sitting on the edge of a park bench, rapping the first verse.

But no one heard the lyrics, because suddenly there was a collective, earsplitting scream from the girls in the audience. In the background, some disgruntled boy called out, "We got duped, son—that ain't no Smoove Killah!" A single spotlight shone on Skye, broadcasting her thrilled expression and ecstatic dancing to the crowd. The birthday girl was in heaven. The thumping bass of the music, the energy of all her friends going crazy around her, the out-of-control hotness of Bow Wow—this was the most exciting, important moment of her entire life! *I don't even care if I don't get my car,* she told herself. She started screaming at the top of her lungs.

As if it were even possible, things got a zillion times better. Because Ciara sexy-strolled out of the wings in a gold baby-doll minidress. This time, the boys hollered like crazy (and, toward the back of the crowd, Tangie almost fainted with excitement at seeing her idol). As her boyfriend spat lyrics, Ciara danced all around the bench, teasing him. Every time he reached for her, she twirled away. It was only when she got to the irresistible hook (". . . *we gon' always be together, baby, that is what you told me and I believe it cuz I ain't never had nobody do me like you!*") that she pulled him off the bench and sang to him. Their chemistry was unbelievable. The audience lost their minds, singing along with Ciara and pumping their fists in the air.

Meanwhile, the upstairs VIP lounge was totally empty—everyone had long since bum-rushed the stairs to get down to the dance floor. Everyone, that is, except Eden. As she leaned over the balcony, watching hundreds of sixteen-year-olds screaming for Bow Wow and Ciara, a secret smile crept across her beautiful face. *This is all happening because of me*, she thought, a giddy rush of adrenaline shooting through her. *Smoove really does love me!* She would later tell Marisol that this was the second best moment of her life, after winning junior prom princess.

Bow Wow and Ciara were killing it. Right before the princess of Crunk 'n' B got to the final chorus, she called out in her familiar husky, Southern-tinged voice, "Skye? Where you at, birthday girl? I think we need some help up here—you better come on up!"

Beaming with delight, Skye hiked her dress up to her crotch and climbed up on stage. Jumping in between Bow Wow and Ciara, she sang the chorus with them, waving her hands in the air and dancing as if it were her last night on earth. Pure, champagne-soaked joy washed over her as she looked out into the audience, seeing all her friends having the time of their lives. Who cared if Nick never spoke to her again? Who cared if he played her in front of everyone she knew? Right now, Skye was celebrating her sixteenth birthday onstage with two of the biggest stars in the world; everyone loved her; and she was a *star*.

"I love you guys!" she screamed into the mic, and the crowd roared back, *"We love you, Skye!"* And then she started feeling dizzy. And hot. The room started spinning, and her dress felt five sizes too small.

"Oh, my God," said Tangie, watching the whole thing from the sidelines with Izzy. "What's wrong with Skye?"

Abruptly, Skye stopped dancing and just stood here, swaying a little bit. Angry, bright red blotches broke out on her arms, traveling up to her neck and face. She began scratching uncontrollably. "Oh, my God, oh, my God," she wailed, frantically scratching all over. "What's happening? Somebody, help me!" She squirmed and hopped up and down, turning redder and redder. She began flailing around uncontrollably in an effort to scratch everywhere at once. Trying to help, Bow Wow approached her and she accidentally kneed him in the crotch. He doubled over and fell down on the stage. Kneeling down beside the tiny rapper, Ciara screamed, "Weezy!" and frantically cued DJ AM to cut the music.

"The birthday girl's having some trouble, y'all!" DJ AM hollered. "Can somebody help her? Yo, is your moms in the audience? Skye's moms, where you at?"

Alexa had been sharing a smoke with the coat-check boy by the back door when the deejay called for her. Dropping the cigarette, she ran over to the dance floor and looked up at the stage. When she saw Skye—now a splotchy maroon color—she clapped her hands over cheeks and screamed like the heroine in a horror movie (Eden would later say her mom was channeling her role in 1974's *The Jefferson High School Strangler*). Bursting through the crowd, Alexa charged onstage and grabbed Skye by the shoulders. "This is my mink shrug, isn't it? *Isn't it?*"

"Yes! Yes!"

"I told you, you're allergic to mink!" Alexa turned toward the audience. "She's *deathly* allergic to mink! Sweet Baby Jesus, somebody, call an ambulance!"

Bow Wow and Ciara clearly hadn't bargained on all this drama, so they quietly peaced-out, wondering if they should fire their publicist. Alexa wrapped her arm around Skye's waist and dragged her scratching, wailing child off into the wings, where she laid her out on the floor. Even in her crazed state, Skye found enough strength to holler out, "I love you Bow-Weezy . . . and Ciara, too! I hope y'all stay together!"

Somehow, Tangie, Regina, and Kamillah found each other in the madness and met the birthday girl in the wings. Skye was lying on the ground, bright red, but still gorgeous (she looked like a beautifully dressed cherry Popsicle).

"I called an ambulance; it's coming in, like, two seconds," said Tangie breathlessly. "Mrs. Carmichael, do you want me to go with you guys to the emergency room?"

"No, no, no, it's fine. Just stay and have fun." Alexa was wringing her hands, looking very distracted and overwhelmed. She wasn't used to dealing with this kind of stress—after all, wasn't this what nannies were for? Suddenly remembering that there was a club full of bewildered teenagers out there, she ran out onstage and grabbed the mic.

"Hello, everyone, I'm Skye's mother?" Somebody screamed "M.I.L.F.!" and there was a smattering of laughter. Not knowing what the acronym meant, Alexa smiled, waved, and continued her speech.

"You probably know me from *Shoulder Pads*, the hit Aaron Spelling nighttime drama from the eighties, but then again, maybe you're too young—your parents will know, that's for sure. Anyway, Skye is experiencing a deadly allergic reaction to my mink fur shrug." Hearing that, the crowd erupted in shocked murmurs and gasps. "*I know!*" Alexa went on. "Look, I told her not to wear it but, well, you all know Skye—you can't tell that girl *anything*! Anyway, we're on our way to the emergency room, but please stay. We paid for the space and the deejay till midnight, so you might as well party on the Carmichaels, right? So, keep spinning, AM . . . and, um, will someone knock on the little boys' room and tell my husband Junior that we're leaving? Cheers, darlings!"

Jenna was watching the scene with horror. "Skye can't leave now!" she wailed to no one in particular. "We haven't even gotten to the surprise BMW!" She quickly hissed into her earpiece for Kiki to meet her backstage, where Skye was. They might not get the all-important "Surprise, here's your luxury car!"

scene, Jenna figured, but at least they'd get some sensational footage of Skye freaking out and going to the ER.

Seconds later, a group of EMTs came bursting into the club carrying a stretcher over their heads (in a weird way, it echoed Skye's grand entrance) and found Skye, her friends, her mom, and Jenna and Kiki waiting in the wings. They carefully rolled Skye onto the stretcher and carried her down the stairs. Unfortunately, the only way out was through the dance floor, so Alexa ran out in front of the stretcher, yelling at everyone to make way (thinking on his feet, DJ AM started playing Ludacris's "Move Bitch"). As if in a scene from one of the 1950s epic Bible movies, the crowd parted like the Red Sea, allowing the EMTs to carry Skye down the center. Slipping in and out of consciousness now, she heard the seemingly faraway sounds of people oohing, aahing, and "poor Skye"-ing, and saw people holding up their cell phone cameras.

When they brought her out of the club into the brisk night air, she became more alert. She stirred a little as the EMTs rolled her onto a gurney and loaded her into the back of an ambulance, followed by Alexa, Jenna, Kiki, and Kiki's everpresent camera.

The back doors slammed shut, and Skye opened one eye, looking around. There was Alexa, absentmindedly patting Skye's thigh and putting on her best "concerned mother" face (it could've easily been read as constipation). Sneaky Kiki was pretending to look at previously recorded footage in her video camera, but was filming the whole time; and Jenna was busy interviewing the head EMT.

"Wha—what's going on?" Skye murmured weakly.

"You're experiencing an allergic reaction to animal fur," answered an EMT as he took her blood pressure. Skye immediately perked up when she saw him. His complexion was a beautiful deep caramel, and he had sexy, sleepy eyes and the most *adorable* right-cheek dimple she'd ever seen.

And just like that, she forgot all about Nick, Trey, the party, and everything.

"Just hold on, Skye," continued the EMT, "you'll be fine."

"I'm already fine," she said, her voice flirtatious even as she lay on the stretcher. "Are you a doctor?"

"I'm just an intern. . . . I'm still in medical school," he said, jotting down her blood pressure on a chart. "This is actually my first run. But trust me, you're in good hands."

"I believe you," she said, batting her eyelashes. He smiled at her bashfully. "My name's Corey."

"Corey," said Skye, "you're my hero."

And that was how Skye met the love of her life.

15.
ENDINGS AND BEGINNINGS

THE MONDAY AFTER SKYE'S *Sixteen Candles* party, most of the Armstrong teachers—especially the ones with tenth-grade classes—felt like running from the building in frustration. Absolutely no one was paying attention. All anyone could talk about was the Skye vs. Nick smack-down, the C.J. vs. Trey smack-down (and where had Blackadocious come from?), whether or not Trey's supremely tacky "I fucked your girl" comment was true, the brilliance of Bow Wow and Ciara, and Skye's dramatic mink allergy. The mood was rabidly gossip-hungry. Anyone directly involved in any *Sixteen Candles* drama ducked in and out of classes that day, trying to avoid the constant pointing and whispering. It was truly a circus.

Skye stayed home. Still slightly itchy, she'd been curled up in a fetal position on her pink bed for three days; she was in no mood to process her birthday party. The crazy thing was, she didn't even care. She and her new boyfriend, Alex, had already declared their undying love for each other over while instant-messaging the night before. Let all the haters at Armstrong gossip about the diva antics she had pulled at her *Sixteen Candles* soiree! Tonight, her sexy, connected, twenty-three-year-old future-doctor boyfriend—who happened to be the only son of a top music producer at Island Def Jam—was taking her to dinner at Blue Fin and dancing at Bungalow 8. And everyone else could kiss her skinny butt—including Nick.

Kamillah and Black finally made up, which was a good thing. When Kamillah found out that the police were holding him, Trey and C.J. at the station until their guardians rescued them, she immediately left the party and called her parents. They met her at the station and signed for both Black and C.J. (Kamillah knew there was no way C.J.'s grandmother could (A) physically get there, and (B) find out about this, so she took care of it. Also, while he was being dragged out of Club Tropicana, C.J. told Tangie not to come after him, no matter what—so she wanted to do the right thing for her girl, who was worried sick. Karma points for Kamillah!) The second she saw Black sitting on that rickety metal chair, without his stupid Afro wig, she remembered the sweet, sensitive lyricist she had fallen in love with last year, not the overzealous Black Panther wannabe. Raj Jamison, not Blackadocious. Their passion was reignited almost instantly, and on Monday, Kamillah even wore a delicate sterling silver necklace with a tiny black-power-fist pendant.

By the end of the school day on Monday, Trey Stevens was officially declared MIA. The last time anyone had heard from him, he was wailing, "Too tight! These cuffs are too damn tight!" as he was forcibly removed from the party. There was a rumor that C.J. had broken Trey's nose so badly that Trey would need plastic surgery—and that, on the low, he'd actually opted to have an abs-sculpting procedure as well.

Idiot.

That day at school was tough for Tangie. She got more attention than she would ever have expected. Basically, she spent the entire day telling people that, no, she had not had sex with Trey. The good thing was that most people did believe her—which made tons of dance department girls actually *congratulate* her on being the first young dancer to avoid falling victim to Trey's love-'em-and-leave-'em routine. By the end of the day, she'd even become sort of a cult figure among the Serving Treys.

But now, the hellish school day was finally over. The sun was setting, and Tangie was sitting on the stoop outside her brownstone, waiting for C.J. He had been in meetings all day long with his guidance counselor, the art department dean, and the principal, and Tangie hadn't had a chance to talk to him. In fact, she hadn't seen or spoken to him since the security guards dragged him out of Skye's party. He hadn't returned her calls or text messages all weekend.

But finally he was there. Tangie saw him turn the corner and walk down her street. C.J. was as adorable as ever, but today there seemed to be less swagger in his step. He was definitely dragging a little. When she saw him up close, her breath quickened—his right cheek was swollen and dark purple, and his lip was cut. Gasping, she ran down the stoop and gently hugged him.

"Oh, my God, C.J., look at you! Are you okay? Want me to get you some ice or something?"

"No, no, no, I'm good," he said, laughing a little at Tangie's dramatics. "Stop being such a girl. I'm fine."

Tangie grabbed him by the elbow and helped him sit down on the stoop next to her, as if he were an invalid. The sweet thing was, he let her do it.

They sat on the stoop for a moment, silently watching Brooklyn life go by. Young, bohemian mothers rocking Seven jeans and dreadlocks pushed designer strollers, while an ice-cream truck played the Super Mario Brothers theme over and over. Across the street, a couple of seven-year-olds drew chalk pictures on the sidewalk. There was so much to talk about—but neither Tangie nor C.J. knew where to start.

"So, you're sure you're not hurt?"

"Nah," he said. "But I heard your boy got a broken nose."

"Good! I'm glad. I can't believe he said that we, that we actually . . ." It was too awful a thought to continue with. The humiliation caused by Trey's remark was still fresh in her mind—it was like a paper cut that wouldn't heal. "C.J., you didn't believe him, did you? You know I didn't have sex with him, right? Not even close."

"Come on, now. You ain't gotta tell me that. That's why I lost it." He shrugged. "I couldn't have him put that bullshit out there. Strictly unacceptable."

She looked at C.J., her eyes wide. So, Izzy was right—he

had been fighting for Tangie. "So, you . . . you really did that for me?"

"Somethin' like that," he said quietly. "Yeah."

She kissed him on the cheek. "Thank you."

"Anytime," he said, smiling at her. "Seriously, Mud Butt, what did you ever *see* in that kid?"

What was she supposed to say? *Sometimes I feel in over my head in the dance department, with all those bitchy girls with the super-trained backgrounds and size-0 bodies all around, and it felt nice knowing that the guy they all want to be with wanted me! Or . . . knowing I was the girl Trey picked right after he dated Eden, the most perfect girl ever, made me feel like I was really special. But most of all—after loving you for so many years, and watching you have sex with slut after slut, basically choosing them over me, it was nice to feel like I was somebody's chosen one, for once.*

But Tangie kept all that to herself. Instead, she said, "We just had a lot in common, dancewise. I don't know, it was dumb. Clearly."

"Clearly."

"I talked to Izzy. I told her the truth about us, finally."

"Yeah? I guess we're gonna be one big, happy, incestuous family." He chewed his bottom lip. "I'm kinda worried about her. She's been so cagey lately."

"I know!" Tangie was relieved—she had thought she was the only one who'd noticed. "She has these cuts and bruises, and she's so weird every time I ask her about it."

"Yeah," he said, shaking his head. "We might have to follow her ass around, to see what's up."

They were quiet for a minute, and then Tangie asked the question that had been plaguing her all weekend.

"C.J., why didn't you tell me about your OutKast cover?"

"Whatchu mean, why? I saw how you bugged out over my sketch of Izzy. I thought you'd cut me back for good if you knew it was gonna be multiplied, like, a million times when the CD comes out."

Tangie waved her hand in front of her face. "Honestly? I'm so over Izzy's nude picture. It doesn't bother me anymore. I just don't want you to *lie* to me. Okay? Look at all the time we wasted, acting like immature kids."

"I know, right?"

"So . . . what happened today with your art dean and Principal Fischer?" It was the question they'd both been avoiding ever since C.J. sat down.

He sighed and stretched his legs out. "I was in meetings all fuckin' day long. Basically, it took my guidance counselor, the principal, and my dean four hours to tell me I'm expelled."

"You're *what?*" Tangie felt as if the wind had been knocked out of her.

"I'm expelled," C.J. repeated. "I mean, it's not a surprise. I broke the rule about professional gigs, so it's a wrap."

"But, but . . . Trey did the same thing, dancing in the Missy video, and all they did was make him take an underclassmen dance class! That's not fair! I don't understand . . ."

"Tangie, Trey's father is a famous judge who's donated mad paper to the school, you feel me? The only connection I got is Elbows McCarthy, the junkie on my block that used to

chauffeur Donald Trump's limo in the eighties. I ain't got *shit*,
T. So I'm out."

She looked at him, speechless, and then began to cry. He
put an arm around her, and she collapsed against his shoulder,
devastated. There was so much she wanted to say! What about
his grandma? What about all the dreams they had had when
they were little? Tangie was going to dance on tour with stars
like Ciara, Usher, and Britney, while C.J. would be a famous
artist, showing his work at the Met, the Studio Museum in
Harlem, and all over the world. Even without a family to support and encourage him, he'd already made a name for himself
with his art. And now, he was going to lose everything he'd
worked for. It was so unfair.

"It's okay, T.," he said, reading her mind. "Listen, don't be
upset. I got good news, too."

"Really?" Tangie looked up at him, her nose red and her
eyes dripping.

"I was truly grindin' over the weekend. I hollered at
OutKast's art director, asking her if she knew any reputable art
agents, and she put me on to this dude Chauncey Willis, who
manages some of the dopest young talent out there. I met with
him yesterday afternoon, and he was really feeling me. He's
talking about selling some of my pieces, like, ASAP. And he
renegotiated my deal with OutKast, and yo, I'm getting
fifty-five thousand dollars. *Fifty-five g's!* So what do I even
need Armstrong for? It's like LeBron James—he got drafted to
the NBA outta high school and was making millions, so he
didn't *need* college."

"That's really exciting, C.J. I'm proud of you, I really am. But . . . will you go to school at all?"

"Of course. I'll go to PS 431, around my way. It'll be good, T. You'll see."

Tangie wanted to be happy for him, she really did. But it was all happening too fast. It wasn't the plan.

"Well, I mean, if you're sure you're gonna be okay . . ."

"Come on, baby. I'm C. J. Parker."

She smiled at him weakly. It was a selfish thought, but Tangie felt as if now, with C.J. going to a different school and really pursuing into his art career, they'd *never* have a chance to get together. And she was sick of all the back-and-forth. Tangie knew she loved C.J.—and she knew he felt the same—but when would they ever be at the same place at the same time?

They sat there, shoulder to shoulder, for a couple more moments. The sun had completely set by now and the streets were quiet. Finally, she spoke up.

"What's gonna happen to us?"

C.J. didn't have an answer. So, he leaned over and finally, *finally*, kissed her.